Chasing Cheer

BY

HEATHER SCHNEIDER

CHASING CHEER

This is a work of fiction. All names, characters, and events are the work of the author's imagination. Any resemblance to real people or events is entirely coincidental.

Summary: Holly Claus's magical world is turned upside down when she visits a small town with too much Cheer and befriends local businessman Ash Hayes.

Editor: Red Adept Editing Services

Cover Design: Kylie Sek

ISBN: 979-8-9850507-2-1 (paperback)

ISBN: 979-8-9850507-3-8 (ebook)

Chasing Cheer

BY

HEATHER SCHNEIDER

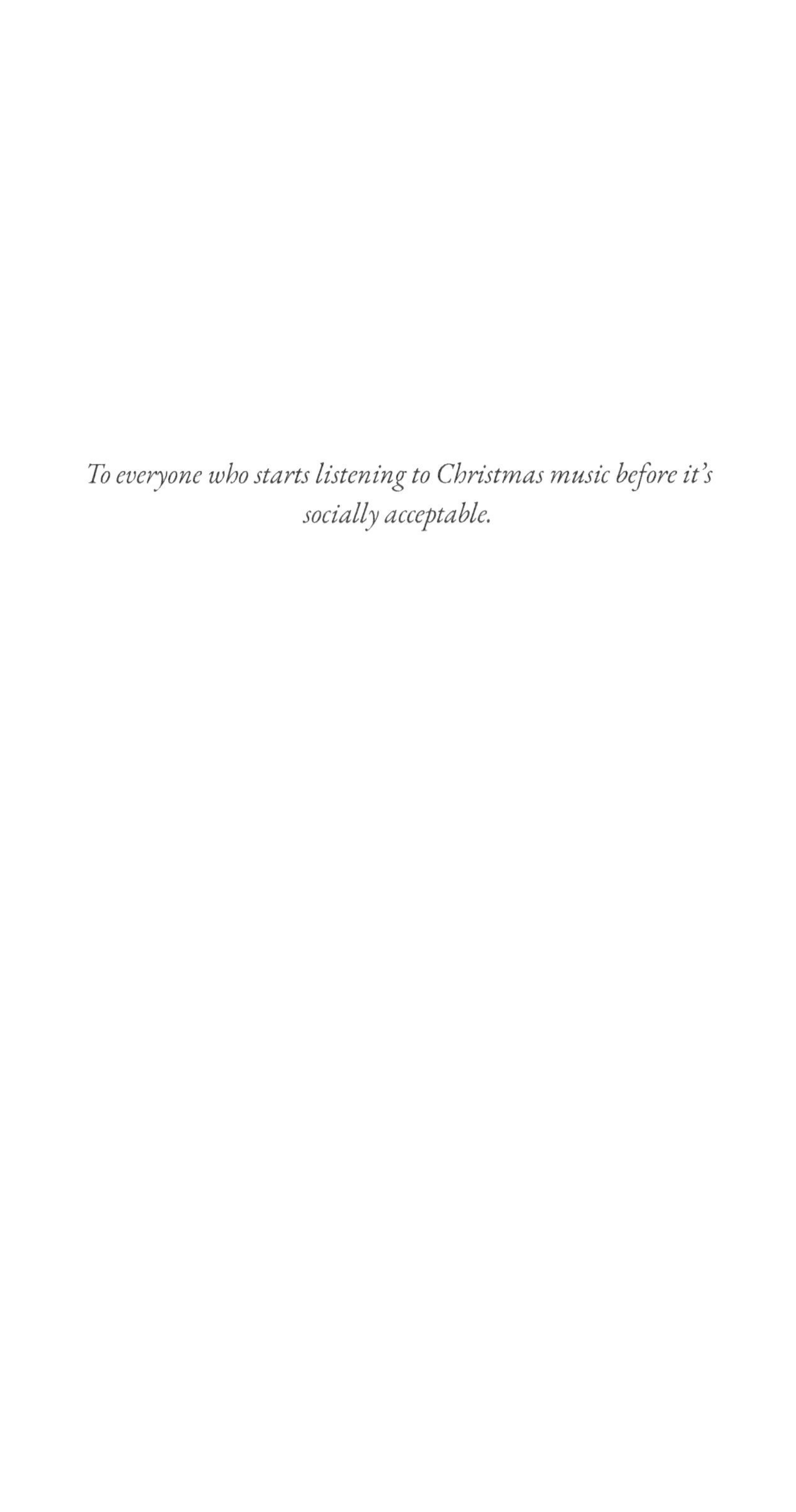

To everyone who starts listening to Christmas music before it's socially acceptable.

Chapter One

Holly Claus made her way down a well-worn path deep in the woods. Her forest-green velvet dress, which was lined with white trim like piping on a sugar cookie, billowed softly on the snow around her. Elves followed her in a line, holding their lanterns aloft.

Slipping through a thicket of trees, Holly entered a clearing. Inside stood two tall evergreens, their branches magically lit with shimmering candles. They illuminated the night as perfect year-round Christmas trees.

The elves formed a semicircle around her and waited. They were all familiar with the yearly routine. Holly's parents, Santa and Sylvie Claus, weren't buried there—they weren't buried at all. They had passed through the spirit portal together when their time at the North Pole had drawn to a close. A small portion of their spirits had remained behind, illuminating the two trees forever.

Holly set down her lantern and approached. She pressed a hand against each trunk, letting the magic of the place surround her.

She didn't cry or even feel sad as she rested her hands on the trees. The cycle that brought Clauses through the North Pole and eventually into the land of everlasting Christmas was filled with joy, not sorrow. If anything, Holly came to her parents with questions. As always, she wanted to know more about the Cheer and the precise way it was powered.

She wanted to know about the magic that ran the North Pole and gave her the ability to speak any language. And cycle after cycle, year after year, Holly hadn't been able to shake the sense that she was doing something wrong. *Why was Cheer so much easier for my father to gather?*

He had been able to spend the majority of the cycle at the North Pole, only needing to venture out to gather Cheer a few days each time. Holly's production strategy was nearly the opposite. And the North Post had always seemed to glow more brightly when her father was around, though Holly had become less certain of that. It had been so many seasons since she'd seen him, and her memory might have been playing tricks on her.

But any explanations her parents had known had gone with them to the land of everlasting Christmas, and Holly had to do her best to discover the answers on her own. Still, she came to the clearing each year on the anniversary of their passing and hoped it would be the year the answers came.

Holly murmured a quick thank-you to the trees then turned back to face the elves, whose glowing faces sent cheer through her that was different from what she captured in her Cheer meter. The elves loved and respected her, as they had loved and respected her parents, and more than anything, they loved Christmas. It was for them and all the people on Earth that Holly must figure out the secret to maximum Cheer.

She began to walk back through the forest, her boots not leaving so much as a mark on the powdery snow, ready to take on a new Cheer cycle.

HOLLY HAD BEEN TO DISNEYLAND MORE THAN MOST humans, with the likely exception of those who worked there. Her magic allowed her to travel there whenever she liked, free of charge, and it was also the reason she needed to frequent the so-called happiest place on Earth. To her, it was just a place in Anaheim, California, USA, that proved an effective way to do her job.

Her magic was perfectly suited to the task she needed to do nearly every day. If she wanted something, she had only to ask. Of course, there were exceptions. She didn't have the power to make people do something they wouldn't normally do. Instead, they thought Holly was one of the nicest people they had ever met and, therefore, someone they should trust.

So when Holly asked the man at the turnstile outside the amusement park to please let her through, he did, no questions asked. Holly brushed through the entrance with the ease of someone who knew where they were going.

She swept past the lines for food—they were minefields of mixed emotions. Queues often brought negative feelings, which could suck power from her Cheer meter, but they could hold anticipation as well, which ranked in the middle of the Cheer scale.

She continued walking, crowds of people in colorful clothes and mouse ears swirling around her. Holly didn't stop to take any of it in. She never did. She was on a mission.

A swath of shiny blue fabric caught her eye.

There, Holly thought.

She got within range of the princess and took a seat on a well-disguised retaining wall to wait for the joy to appear, glancing at her Cheer meter. To humans, the meter looked like a simple gold watch engraved with delicate snowflakes, but it functioned like an advanced machine.

The Cheer meter took in all the emotions around her—sadness, joy, confusion, anxiety, excitement—and sifted through them. It sought the energy source known as Cheer, and the delicate bracelet, in Holly's estimation, was the most important object on Earth.

A little girl in a blue dress and a red wig, which matched the princess's exactly, approached in excitement.

"Hello there," the adult mermaid princess said. Her voice was as sweet as the syrup on Holly's pancakes at the North Pole.

The little girl smiled at her and said hello while her parents snapped pictures. Holly barely watched. She had seen the same scene hundreds of times before. Her watch was vibrating rapidly, the Cheer meter soaking up emotions that were instantly converted to power, and that was what held Holly's attention. She allowed herself a small, satisfied smile.

The next day was the full moon, which meant it was time to return to the North Pole for a few days, and she was sure she would meet her Cheer quota for the month by then. Holly was already looking forward to the approval and admiration that always came from the elves after a particularly good Cheer cycle.

The smile slid off Holly's face as her Cheer meter vibrated again. The vibration was subtly different from the previous one. The ones that fed the meter felt pleasantly warm and jubilant, like atoms were bouncing around in a dance. But the current ones were cold and frantic, as if particles were being dragged into a deep chasm. She looked up in alarm.

A few feet away, a scoop of a child's ice cream cone had fallen off and splatted to the ground. Holly's watch had clocked the emotion before the child even started to cry. His low whine of surprise turned into a wail of devastation. His mother picked him up, but the child was inconsolable.

Holly peered at her watch nervously. The Cheer numbers were

dropping fast. Though the nearby mermaid princess was thrilling the young guests, a strong negative emotion could counteract that rapidly.

Holly stood abruptly. Most people, aside from the mother, ignored the child's despondent wail, but Holly couldn't. She had to get far away from the situation quickly. With one last reluctant look at the mermaid princess, Holly headed toward another sure-fire Cheer magnet.

Minutes later, having easily been escorted to the front of the line, Holly got in a boat, not exactly thrilled to be doing the ride again, packed in with tourists. Still, the colors and music of the boat ride were guaranteed Cheer bringers. And no food was allowed, so a ruined ice cream cone wouldn't be able to threaten her numbers.

She did some quick estimations in her head. The boat ride should be enough to salvage the near disaster caused by the fallen ice cream, so she tried to relax.

As usual, Holly's calculations were correct. After a few minutes, her Cheer numbers had more than recovered from the ice cream incident, and she even sang along to the final, iconic number. It would be stuck in her head for the rest of the day, but it was worth it to meet her Cheer quota.

Holly's shoulders relaxed as the boat glided through the tunnel, the sounds of animatronic voices mixing with those of the humans around her and, against her will, her own.

Chapter Two

A golden sleigh and Holly's fleet of reindeer, which were invisible to humans, picked her up on a grassy knoll near the massive parking lot, ready to whisk her back to the North Pole.

As a teenager, Holly had run different experiments, including changing the amount of magic lichen they consumed, to test whether humans would see the reindeer under various conditions. She'd faithfully recorded the variables and results in her notebook, but nothing other than a null result had ever occurred.

Holly climbed into the sleigh with ease, and they were on their way. Leaning her head back, she closed her eyes as they made the familiar journey. Time passed quickly as she planned her next Cheer-collecting trip.

Holly opened her eyes just as the reindeer glided toward a massive ice cap, slipping through a gap between two glaciers that would be invisible to a human eye. Inhaling deeply, she sensed the magic and spirit that filled the North Pole draw closer. As much as Holly enjoyed the thrill of a successful Cheer cycle, she always looked forward to seeing the elves and having a few precious days of downtime when she returned.

The reindeer landed efficiently, and afterward, Holly gave them each a quick rubdown and an extra treat before handing them off to some Keyblar elves who worked the stables. Then she closed the stable door and embarked down one of the many lighted-arch-covered paths in the North Pole that would lead her to Merriment Square.

Before she could make it to the end of the first path, the elf mayor, Clementine, joined her. Like all Kringle elves, Clementine was quite human in appearance, aside from her golden eyes and her pointed ears, which extended back from her forehead. She stood just over five feet tall.

"Welcome home, Ms. Claus. Good Cheer run this cycle?" The smile on Clementine's face was so expectant that Holly couldn't help but return it.

"And then some," Holly said, tapping her watch.

Clementine nodded, then they walked together toward Merriment Square. Soft but upbeat holiday music played, shifting to different languages, as the North Pole blended the music and Christmas holiday customs from around the world. Holly and Clementine padded softly down the path, their feet leaving no footprints in the perfectly fluffy layer of snow that always adorned the ground.

"How was everything here this cycle?" Holly glanced at Clementine out of the corner of her eye. Clementine wore a perfectly tailored suit, as usual. The suit was velvet and consisted of a white jacket and green pants paired with soft fabric boots that jingled delicately as she walked.

"We've been making great progress. Now that we're deep into the third quarter of the year, operations in Festive mode are wrapping up." Clementine's voice was bright and crisp.

The first two quarters of the year brought Evergreen and Tinsel modes, while the fourth quarter consisted of Advent mode. By Advent time, the countdown to Christmas was on. Advent was by far the busiest time of year at the North Pole, with Festive coming in second.

"Good. Thank you, Clementine," Holly said as they passed under the final ring of lighted arches and emerged into Merriment Square.

With a contented sigh, Holly surveyed the village. Snowcapped buildings with deeply angled roofs that held the various Dream studios surrounded a small-town square. Beyond those was a broad forest glistening with lights from the tree houses where the elves lived. Most of them would be at home at that time of night, with the youngest elves already asleep. During the daytime, elves who had the day off might be found even farther in the distance, beyond the forest, skiing or sledding at the ski park or relaxing in the hot spring pools.

But instead of the forest, Holly's eyes lingered on the lamppost in the center of Merriment Square. The bronze post was taller than everyone at the North Pole, Holly included, and was adorned with green garlands and red bows. Holly headed straight to it, Clementine following closely behind.

Holly rested her watch hand on the post, right near the center, where a hand-sized snowflake was engraved. When her hand made contact, the snowflake glowed and pulsed brightly, causing a warm sensation as the Cheer flowed from her Cheer meter into the post, transferring the magical energy that powered Merriment Square and the entire North Pole.

As the last of the Cheer passed from her to the post, Holly exhaled with relief. The light at the top of the North Post was noticeably brighter than when Holly had approached it moments before. Clementine rang a little bell nearby, signaling the filling of the post.

Holly looked around to see that a number of late-working elves, mostly Keyblers, had emerged from the studios to watch the ritual. At the sound of the bell tolling, a cheer came from the elves in their nearby tree houses.

"Another successful cycle, Ms. Claus." Clementine nodded at Holly approvingly. "When will you head out again?"

"Tomorrow," Holly said firmly, though the adrenaline rush from discharging the Cheer was starting to leave her already.

Clementine nodded solemnly. Though no one knew the precise reason why, everyone at the North Pole understood that Holly needed to be gone much more than her predecessor, Mr. Claus, had in order to power the North Post and sustain the North Pole. As a result, Holly rarely lingered at the North Pole for more than three days in a cycle.

Holly waved to the elves standing in front of the Dream studios and wished them a good night then turned toward her house. Satisfaction was rapidly turning to the weariness that came from deenergizing the watch, and Holly stifled a yawn.

Clementine knew the pattern all too well, and she quickly tapped the forest-green jeweled ring on her finger, signaling Auryn, Holly's current elf assistant. By the time Holly was at the door to her home, a spectacular log cabin lit outside and in with hanging bronze lanterns, Auryn was at her side, opening it for her.

"Welcome home, Ms. Claus," Auryn said breathlessly.

Auryn had only been her assistant for six cycles, and Holly thought he still seemed a bit nervous. Despite her fatigue, Holly studied her young assistant. Like Clementine, Auryn was also a Kringle elf, but while Clementine had light skin and hair and rosy cheeks, Auryn's skin was a soft brown, his hair dark.

Auryn was a teenager by elf standards, and the cap he wore was a new style Holly had never seen before. Instead of the long, thin fabric that curved at the end and usually had a small pom-pom, Auryn's sported a large red pom-pom right in the top center. His eyes widened as Holly studied him then relaxed as she smiled pleasantly and passed through the door he was still holding open.

"We've got dinner ready for you," Auryn said, speaking slightly too quickly. "And the drink bar is fully stocked. Hot cocoa, apple cider, spiced pear, warm milk and honey, turmeric tea..." Auryn continued to rattle off the names of drinks as Holly took off her black boots then slipped her feet into pure-white slippers that could have been made of clouds.

"That all sounds wonderful, Auryn. Thank you. I think I'm going to have a bath then go to bed. Will you tell Clementine thank you for me?" Holly asked kindly.

Auryn nodded, his eyes still wide. Holly reached behind her kitchen counter and pulled out two jingle pops. They were the one food item Holly made herself, a secret Claus recipe passed down from parent to child. Auryn's eyes looked like they were going to pop out of their sockets. "Give one of these to your sister. Have a good night, Auryn."

Auryn took the two pops eagerly, muttered his thanks, then quickly backed out of the room. Moments later, Holly heard the front door close softly. She let out a slow exhalation and stretched her arms above her head.

She might only be able to stay there for two to three nights per cycle, but her place at the North Pole still felt very much like home. Holly had grown up there with her parents.

After walking to the spacious bathroom, she turned on the glistening white fountain that filled her bathtub. The room was Holly's favorite in the house. It had a large fireplace on one wall, and another wall was made entirely of glass. Through it, Holly could watch the northern lights as she lounged in the warm water.

While the bath filled with evergreen-scented mineral water, bubbles forming, Holly went to the drink bar and poured herself a mug of steaming spiced pear cider. She set it on the silver tray table next to the bathtub, which would look like a small pool to most humans. Then she quickly stripped and stepped inside.

Holly thought there must be some healing magic in her bath-water, because she instantly relaxed as the warm liquid flowed over her shoulders. She rested her head on the side of the tub and watched the northern lights, which were always on display there, as if they were a canvas painted just for her. The patterns were never the same for any two nights, and Holly was just as mesmerized by them as she had been as a child.

Those phenomena, like the fireflies she'd seen in the southern United States and Thailand, instantly sparked her imaginative, less scientific side. Of course, there was science in nature, but phenomena like that got into the soul.

Holly's thoughts drifted to the Kringle and Keyblers elves, who were so different in personality and appearance but united in their determination to make the perfect Dreams, all huddled at home with their families and friends. It felt nice to make them proud, to bring home Cheer every cycle and keep things running at the North Pole.

But she was slightly weary from the busy cycle and, in spite of the relaxing bath, began to wonder if she needed a mental break— just a few hours, even, to slow down while still collecting Cheer. She took a sip of her cider and thought suddenly of Lia. *Time for another visit.*

Chapter Three

Ash Hayes sprinkled the last dash of nutmeg onto the hot chocolate mix and sealed the container. He didn't do much of the food prep in the kitchens at the Emerald House anymore, but the recipe was an old, secret family one, so no one else could make it.

He took off his apron and hung it on the hook then opened his phone to listen to a message from a call he'd just missed. Shaking his head, he listened, his heart sinking. Another one of the businesses on Main Street was closing down. The chamber had confirmed it.

He ran a hand through his hair. That was the third one in a year. The cycle was repeating itself lately. An incredible little business popped up, but the town just didn't have enough people shopping locally to keep it afloat for long. The Emerald House was one of the few exceptions, and he'd been working nonstop for years to ensure that it, too, didn't succumb to the plague of so many small towns. But his duty wasn't just to his own business.

He left the kitchen and stopped to say hello to Sofia as she was signing on for her shift. "Hey, Ash. Whoa, what's wrong?"

He plastered on a smile. "Nothing. All good. How was your weekend?"

Sofia stifled a yawn and headed toward the coffeepot. "It was great. My garden is putting out a huge yield this summer, so I was busy making salsa."

Ash was often impressed with his friend's gardening skills. Farm-to-table was an idea he fully supported, and it was on his never-ending list of improvements to make to the place. "Make sure to bring me a jar of the hottest one you've got."

Sofia reached into a tote bag hanging from a peg on the wall and pulled out a mason jar. A red chili pepper had been painted on the side of the glass. She handed it to him. "Done and done."

"I don't deserve you," he said, pretending to inhale the flavors of the salsa through the jar.

"No, you don't," she teased him.

Ash headed through the lobby, where a group of fishermen was gathering before heading out to the river, and down the hall to his small office. He swirled the mouse to warm up the computer and sank into his chair, strumming his hands on the desktop. An idea had been jostling around in his mind for a while. After that message, maybe it was time to act on it. He navigated to Hallmark's website and read the details for entry into the Best Small-Town Christmas Faire contest.

After pulling a bag of chips from a drawer in the desk, he cracked open Sofia's salsa. Emerald Hollow's Christmas faire didn't *technically* meet all the listed requirements, but they were close enough. He filled out the application, embellishing here and there.

He had time. He could get the faire into the shape it needed to be in by December. He didn't expect to win, but even being part of a Hallmark contest was bound to put Emerald Hollow on the map. Besides, people always said the Emerald Hollow Christmas faire was magical. That year, he would make sure to take that magic to a whole new level. Maybe it was his chance to save his town.

He wrote the last sentence, reviewed the application, then clicked Send.

Chapter Four

Holly sat at a café in Finland with Lia, whom she'd met nearly two years ago, and the seventysomething café owner was Holly's only human friend. Holly made it a point to stop in and see her whenever she found herself in Helsinki. The two always met for a fika, the Swedish act of having coffee or tea and a pastry together.

"How are your grandchildren?" Holly asked, relaxing back into the comfortable patio chair.

Lia's face lit up. "Isla and Jesse are splendid and doing well in school. Isla's old enough to start helping with the baking, and she absolutely loves it. It warms my heart."

"Well, she's learning from the best. Your pastries are the finest in the country. Trust me. I've tried them all." Holly bit into the warm one Lia had provided.

Lia flushed happily at the compliment then steadied her gaze on Holly, a question behind her eyes. Holly tensed. Lia worried about her, her lack of family, and what Lia viewed as a normal life. As far as Lia knew, Holly was an ambitious corporate woman in her mid-to-late twenties who traveled around the world doing market research. Holly was a bit older than that, but Clauses aged differently than humans. In Lia's view, Holly's life didn't look very rich, at least not in the ways that counted to Lia.

Holly couldn't tell her about her friendship with the elves, the billions of people she delivered Dreams to every December, or the fact that Holly's Cheer numbers were always solid, and she was successfully gathering data during each Cheer cycle that helped her refine her practices. But any worry Lia felt didn't register on Holly's Cheer meter. The woman's emotions always remained remarkably stable. Lia was easy to be around, and Finland certainly had its perks.

In recent years, Finland had gotten a lot of hype as one of the happiest countries on Earth, and not without reason, Holly had found. While it didn't have as many large, drastic peaks of Cheer as Holly had experienced in places like Disneyland, there was a steady drumbeat of contentedness, which scored fairly well in the Cheer metrics. There were also fewer negative emotions to crash her numbers.

Finland was a good place to go after Holly had collected a large cache of Cheer and wanted a little vacation. She didn't have to constantly chase the Cheer, and her Cheer meter would hold steady for at least a few minutes or sometimes hours, if she was lucky. Holly wondered if it wasn't a coincidence that the Finnish claimed one of their villages was Santa's original home.

"I'm not sure where you're off to next, but make sure to check on the bulletin board for events. There are some big ones coming up that might be good for your research." Lia took a sip of her cappuccino. The air was still pleasant in late summer, though it was starting to cool, and she was wearing an apron over her short-sleeve shirt. Holly wore a long-sleeve shirt with a plaid skirt and leggings.

As a function of Holly's magic, she always dressed appropriately for the weather of the time of year in the city she was visiting. The temperature didn't affect her like it did most people. She could get a slight chill or feel a little warm, but she was never really threatened with being too hot or cold like humans were.

She nodded. "Thanks. I will."

"You sure do have an exciting life. Most people will never see half the things and places you do." A soft smile played on Lia's lips.

"Well, I enjoy my job, and I take it very seriously. So it all works out." Holly was suddenly distracted by the vibration coming from her watch. It was picking up some nearby negative emotions. Holly sighed reluctantly. She would have to end the pleasant afternoon fika.

"I'm sorry, Lia. I'm going to have to get going." She tried to savor the last few sips of her drink.

"I thought you might. One notification on that watch of yours, and you're on your way." Lia sighed, focusing on Holly again.

Holly tensed at Lia's words. Lia never pried—not outright—and Holly appreciated it. It was another reason to maintain their acquaintance. *Is that going to change today?*

"I'll come see you again as soon as I can," Holly said, knowing that could be months away. The thought saddened her, but the quality of her research depended on getting as many different samples and experiences as possible.

"Don't worry about me, dear. I've got plenty of people to keep me company." Lia placed her hand gently on top of Holly's. "I just wonder, well, don't you ever get lonely?"

Holly pulled her hand away, surprised at her reaction to the words. By most human standards, Holly did live a somewhat lonely life, traveling around on her own for most of each cycle. But

Holly wasn't human. She was a Claus, and her priorities were different.

"I have plenty of friends back home, Lia. Remember? I see them every time I go back to headquarters." Holly tried to keep a defensive tone out of her voice.

"So your friends... They are coworkers?" Lia asked.

Holly frowned again at the expression on her face. Her watch was vibrating rapidly, but she ignored it.

"No, not exactly. It's hard to explain. But they're friends I grew up with, and we all care for one another. It's kind of like..." Holly racked her brain, trying to think of some of the human history books she had read as part of her childhood education. "Kind of like a company town. We live and work in a tight-knit community. We look out for one another. So don't worry, Lia. I'm not lonely. Not at all."

The sincerity in her voice seemed to placate Lia. "All right then, dear. I'll take your word for it. And you come back whenever is right for you."

Holly's watch was vibrating coldly. She looked up and saw a young couple arguing across the street. She needed to go.

"Thank you, Lia. I'll see you in a while." Holly put on a bright smile.

"Please do. You know how I love all the stories of my favorite nomad. It gives me something to tell all the other grandmothers at our luncheons. They think I'm most interesting."

Lia winked, and Holly laughed. It might be months or longer before she returned to Finland, but Holly knew Lia would open the doors for her when she did, a perfect pastry in hand.

They said their goodbyes, and Holly remembered at the last moment to pop into the café and look at the bulletin board. She mostly did it to satisfy Lia, since the woman knew events were part of Holly's travel and research, and attending something nearby gave Holly an excuse to come back.

The board was situated in a narrow hallway just inside the door that led to the café's counter. The rectangular piece of cork was fairly full, cluttered with flyers advertising events in Helsinki and other areas of Finland. Some of the flyers were for annual events that Holly had attended in previous years.

Holly quickly scrolled through her mental calendar of holidays and events around the world that would be coming up soon. One good festival could sometimes max out her Cheer quota for a whole cycle, but that was rare.

Suddenly, a poster in English caught her eye. It advertised a fall festival in Oregon, in the United States, at the end of October. Curious, Holly studied it. *What is a flyer for a small-town festival taking place across the world doing here, in a little café in Finland?*

She thought she heard the tinkle of the bell that signaled the door opening behind her, but when she looked back, no one was there. Holly gently tugged off one of the little strips with the details of the festival, folded it, and tucked it into her pocket.

Chapter Five

The Keybler elves who worked the stables had readied four reindeer—Dasher, Gale, Ivy, and Clove—for the trip. Ivy and Clove had seemed eager to take their first turn pulling Ms. Claus and the famous golden sleigh. Dasher and Gale, two of the most seasoned reindeer, had been more stoic. Holly could tell that they took their role of supervising the two young reindeer's maiden voyages seriously.

When they landed perfectly in a large forest in the United States Pacific Northwest, Holly gave them each a salted apple, and Ivy and Clove scampered around in excitement. Dasher and Gale eyed them with reproach but happily accepted their treats.

The flyer about the fall festival had occupied Holly's mind since she'd left Lia's café. Something about it called to her, and she thought it might be her subconscious working on a new theory. Perhaps it was time to test the hypothesis that small towns could be just as fruitful sources of Cheer as massive events. Maybe that was what she had been missing, jumping around from concerts to festivals to sporting events with thousands of people.

The flyer also reminded Holly of her latest conversation with

Lia, and she kept trying to push the memory away. After visiting Lia, Holly had spent several weeks in Spain, Germany, and Brazil. The trips had been highly productive, but Lia's words had been bugging her. *Why is Lia so concerned that I'm lonely? How could I be lonely when I have a village full of elves who adore me, and I get to travel the world for most of every cycle?*

Sure, occasionally, Holly wondered if it would be nice to have someone to sit with on the back porch and watch the sunrise or the northern lights, as her parents had done together for so many years. But she always shook the thought away quickly. She had work to do, and the Cheer always came first.

The reindeer landed in a large clearing in the woods near the edge of town. Holly walked around for a bit to get the lay of the land and came to a bus stop just inside the small town's limits. A wooden sign nearly the size of her sleigh read Welcome to Emerald Hollow. Holly couldn't help but smile at the name. Her mom had always told her that her eyes were the color of emeralds.

Holly glanced at her Cheer meter, which was still very low so early in the cycle. If things didn't start well in Emerald Hollow, she would hit up an old staple like the nearby California beaches and amusement parks or maybe head east toward a national park.

She followed the signs through town as if she were a tourist. There was a local chamber of commerce, a bustling restaurant, and signs advertising hay rides to the fall festival that weekend. Her Cheer meter started to buzz mildly as she approached a large dark-wood building that appeared to be a central point of the town. She could smell food cooking inside.

After passing the sign reading The Emerald House, Holly stepped inside and looked around. She quickly realized it was more than just a restaurant. Straight ahead was a front desk for guests to check in for a hotel stay, to the right was a coffee shop brimming with books, and delightful scents came from the restaurant to the left.

The whole place was tastefully decorated for the fall and was crammed full of individuals in colorful sweaters, scarves, and caps. Holly paused at a sharp buzzing from her Cheer meter. She couldn't get a reading on any specific emotions, but her meter was registering a lot of Cheer in the area.

Holly took a left and passed into the restaurant, where she asked for a booth and was told to take any open spot. Holly slid her small, sleek black travel backpack—appropriate for a business-woman taking a little side trip—into the booth nearest the front of the restaurant. From there, she had a view of the lobby and the coffee shop. Her watch was still buzzing much more rapidly than normal. Holly glanced around, trying to pinpoint the source of all the Cheer.

Most of the booths in the restaurant were full, and a few people were sitting at the large wooden counter that faced the kitchen. Holly experienced an odd sensation as she looked around. Something about the place reminded her of the North Pole, and that was quite unusual.

In spite of her growing confusion, Holly put on a charming smile when a female server approached her to take her drink order.

"Do you have any hot chocolate?" Holly asked.

The woman nodded and jotted it down. "You're in for a treat." Then she turned back toward the kitchen.

Of course, Holly knew that no hot chocolate compared to that of the North Pole, but it didn't stop her from trying it whenever she went somewhere that served it. She still held out a tiny bit of hope that one day, she wouldn't be disappointed.

Soon, the server returned with the large glass mug of steaming cocoa topped with cream and peppermint shavings. Holly took a sip, and she nearly gasped in surprise.

"Good, right?" The server, whose name tag read Sofia, grinned and put a hand on her hip. "We're kind of famous for it. Would you like to order food? We're known for our omelets too."

Holly barely processed the woman's question. She was still stunned by the hot cocoa. It tasted exactly like it did at the North Pole.

Holly nodded, trying to gather her thoughts. "Sure, yes. I'll take an omelet. Whichever is your favorite."

Sofia smiled and turned away again.

Holly stared at her hot cocoa, eyeing it with both awe and suspicion. The whipped cream must be homemade, and the peppermint crumbles perfectly complemented the rich cocoa. She took another sip then another, only pausing to look up when a shadow passed over her drink. A white man with lightly tanned skin and warm brown hair was leaning casually on the other side of her booth. A dishrag was slung over his shoulder, and an apron was tied around his waist.

"Enjoying our famous cocoa?" the man asked as Holly met his eyes. They were a deep rich brown, reminding Holly of the bark on the trees at the North Pole. As he smiled at her, Holly's watch continued to buzz insistently, like it did whenever she'd struck a Cheer gold mine, which wasn't often. *This is so odd.* She forced herself not to glance down and instead focused on meeting the man's searching gaze.

"What? Oh, yes, the hot cocoa is delicious." Holly gathered her composure as she continued to study the man. He didn't have the feverish joy of a sports fan right after their team had won or the wide-eyed wonder of a child who had just met their favorite action hero at a theme park. He looked like any other man going about his day, although he seemed more self-assured than most. But according to the activity in her meter, something about the people in the area was registering more Cheer than any single event she'd ever witnessed. She crossed her legs nervously underneath the table. She needed to know more.

"Are you here for the fall festival?" the man asked.

She searched for a name tag like the one she'd seen on Sofia, but he wasn't wearing one. "Yes, I heard Emerald Hollow hosts a big one. I wanted to see what all the excitement was about." Holly removed her hands from around the mug of cocoa and placed them on her lap under the table. The vibrations of her watch refused to cease, and Holly didn't want to risk glancing at the meter in the middle of the conversation.

"Well, you've come to the right place. Are you staying here at the house? I'm Ash, by the way."

As they locked eyes, she couldn't help but notice how handsome he was, with his easy smile. There was something else too. He knew where he belonged, and that was rare.

"This is my place." Ash said it casually but with a subtle pride in his voice. He quickly looked around the restaurant, and one or two patrons waved at him. He returned the greeting then focused on Holly again.

"You own the Emerald House?" Studies had shown that small-business owners were disproportionately happy people. *Could that be the secret to whatever is going on in this building? Or do the people here spend a lot of time outdoors?* The place was surrounded by forest. Studies also showed that time in nature was good for happiness.

Suddenly, Holly was intensely, scientifically curious about the town of Emerald Hollow. Maybe her theory about small towns was going to pan out, though even she had to admit that whatever was happening was beyond her wildest expectations.

Ash rested his hand on the dishcloth hanging over his shoulder as if he were about to pull it down and start cleaning the table. "Sure do. For about the last five years. Took it over from my dad and expanded the place. Don't worry. I won't be offended if you're staying in a local motel or even a vacation rental," he teased.

Holly didn't usually have conversations with strangers. Aside from Lia, she made it a habit to focus on the mission of gathering Cheer. For the most part, that didn't require interacting on a personal level with humans, and most humans didn't go out of their way to talk to strangers either. But Ash was different. He appeared to be an open book.

Holly struggled to keep her face pleasantly neutral as she listened to him. Her watch vibrated furiously, and she clasped her hands together under the table. When she realized that Ash had stopped talking, she blinked, trying to focus on what he had been saying. His gaze still rested on her expectantly, a small smile pulling at the corners of his lips.

Pull yourself together, Holly. She straightened in her seat, flipping her hand over so that the watch face was buried in her thigh. "Oh, I haven't decided where I'm staying yet. I thought I'd get a feel for the town first." Holly tried to stick as close to the truth as possible, as was her habit.

He leaned in and spoke a little more quietly. "Well, the first night's on the house, if you want to stay here at the Emerald House. But don't advertise that. It's not my standard practice." His easy confidence slipped for a moment, and his shoulders briefly tensed, as he seemed confused by what he'd just offered. In that, at least, Holly could see that the people of the town were normal. Her magic, apparently, wanted her to stay at the Emerald House for the night, and Ash, naturally, had complied.

"You know, I think I'll take you up on that." Holly was still trying to get a sense of the room and what was going on in it. *Why is the meter reacting this way?* Staying in Emerald Hollow, near all that Cheer, didn't seem like a bad idea at all. She wondered whether it was just the hotel giving off so much Cheer or if the whole town was a gold mine. She had to find out.

"Great!" Ash exclaimed, and his voice sounded full of warmth. Holly wasn't sure if that was the magic or his typical personality. "When you're done eating, just head over to the registration desk there, and Tamara will get you checked in."

Just then, Sofia returned with Holly's omelet. She smiled at Ash as she set the plate in front of Holly.

"This meal's on the house, Sof," Ash said to the server, who raised her eyebrows but nodded. "Nice meeting you... Sorry, I didn't catch your name," Ash said, leaning in slightly to allow a guest to slip past him out to the lobby. The guest gave Ash a quick fist bump. Ash's gaze returned to Holly again. Little flecks of amber in his brown eyes glimmered.

She paused a moment too long before replying. "Holly. Nice to meet you too." She wrapped her hands around the mug of hot cocoa, having completely forgotten about the taste.

Ash nodded. "Enjoy your meal, Holly. I'm sure I'll be seeing you around."

"Certainly," Holly replied politely.

Ash smiled one more time, nodded, and walked away.

ASH MOVED IN THE DIRECTION OF THE CAFÉ, UNSURE where he was going. A strange feeling had taken over him when talking to the new visitor. He had felt a strong pull to stay longer, to chat with her more, but hadn't been able to think of any more excuses to keep the conversation going.

The woman, who was seated in his favorite booth, had the brightest complexion he had ever seen. Her face was a stunning combination of glow and dew that he figured must have required some expensive makeup, though it looked natural. Her eyes were a green as deep as the needles on the evergreen trees in the forest. Those two factors, paired with the soft and sleek red jacket she was wearing, sent his mind straight to thoughts of Christmas.

If Christmas were a person—a stunning person—that woman would be it.

Ash chanced one last look at her as he left the restaurant. She was staring at her hot chocolate as if it were the strangest thing she had ever seen. Still, her face radiated warmth, and her dark-brown hair framed her face like a halo.

Of course her name is Holly, he thought. *How fitting. She's Christmas personified. How could her name not be something like Holly?*

He shook his head, trying to get rid of the feeling that there was something about her he had never encountered before. *Who on Earth just booked a stay in the Emerald House?*

Chapter Six

Holly sped through her meal, hardly noticing the omelet's rich flavors. Her brief encounter with Ash and the strange way her watch had reacted to her time in the diner had thrown her off-kilter. *And why is the hot chocolate here perfect?* She'd been surprised twice within in the space of a few minutes.

Usually, she could predict what was going to happen when she went somewhere or at least anticipate things a few seconds in advance and plan her response, but Emerald Hollow was unlike anywhere she had ever been before. For once in her life, Holly felt as if she had no idea what would happen next.

Holly checked in with Tamara at the front desk, as Ash had directed, then passed down a hallway lined with wood-paneled wainscoting to get to her assigned room. After opening the door with an old-fashioned room key, she let her eyes rove over the room. The place felt homey.

She'd been given a charming suite with a queen bed draped in a lace-print quilt. A faint smell of fresh greenery filled the air. Holly stepped toward the window and drew the subtly floral-printed curtains aside to see a breathtaking view of the pine forest that fanned out from behind the Emerald House. Maybe that was what had reminded her of the North Pole. She could almost imagine the elves' homes were somewhere in those woods.

Holly set her backpack on the round wooden end table and flopped down into a plush chair near an old-fashioned wood desk. When she checked her watch, her pulse spiked. She closed her eyes and reopened them. Finally, she shook her head, astonished. Her Cheer meter was nearly full.

That can't be right. It's the first day of the cycle.

She tapped the screen, trying to see if the magic needed to refresh. It typically took her close to a full Cheer cycle to meet her quota, twenty-five days at least. *How could I be nearing that volume in one afternoon?*

Despite that Holly should be overjoyed by such a sudden windfall of Cheer, a strange sensation prickled up her spine. She was used to being in control or at least to being able to read situations and react accordingly. Sure, she'd been a little nervous a few times when the cycle was close to ending, and she hadn't quite met her quota, but those nerves just helped her get creative. As a result, she'd always gathered the required amount of Cheer, even if just barely.

Holly slouched in the chair, knitting her brow in consternation. She took one last look at her watch, triple-checking that she was reading the meter correctly. There was no mistake. *What in the stars is going on in Emerald Hollow?*

HOLLY SLIPPED OUT LATER THAT EVENING TO CHECK ON the reindeer. The Emerald House had multiple paths that led toward the woods, and she took the one that led in the direction of the clearing where she and the reindeer had landed earlier that day.

The four animals found her easily when she entered the clearing. Dasher and Gale strode up to greet her, while Ivy and Clove rolled in a pile of leaves. When Dasher twitched his ears at them in Holly's direction, they jumped up at the sight of her.

They had been trained to be self-sufficient while she was on Cheer-collecting missions, scavenging for food and going out for quick flights to stretch their legs as needed. She glanced over to see the golden sleigh glistening in the early-night moonlight.

The sleigh was invisible to humans, of course, but it was also Holly's connection to the North Pole, and she kept a close eye on it when she could. She gave each of the reindeer a handful of magic lichen and a quick pat good night then retraced her steps to the Emerald House.

The place had slowed down a little for the evening, with the café closed and the restaurant getting ready to shut down for the night. Holly passed through the lobby and the hallway that led toward her room, which were lit with electric bronze lanterns. The place was tastefully decorated for fall, and Holly imagined it looked festive and beautiful at Christmastime too.

For a moment, she thought it might be nice to see the Emerald House then, in a few months, but she let the idea pass. With her nomadic lifestyle, it was unlikely she would be back there in less than a year, if ever. Once she figured out what was fueling the spike in her Cheer, she would be able to return to the North Pole, update her research, and improve her efficiency for good. It could be a breakthrough, but it was still one of many temporary stops for Holly.

"Hey there," someone with a kind, deep voice said, and Holly paused in the hallway before turning around. She recognized the warm voice instantly.

Holly turned. "Hello." She was normally good at small talk, part of her magic, but she was so distracted by her watch that she had a hard time thinking of anything beyond a simple greeting.

But Ash filled the silence without missing a beat. "Sorry. You were probably heading to your room for the night. My apartment is around the corner, but I wanted to take Comet for a walk before we turn in."

Holly suddenly noticed the sleek black dog with a streak of white going down its back sitting patiently at Ash's feet. He didn't have a leash on, but he was sporting a brilliant red collar with a small gold metal tag in the shape of a dog bone.

"Your dog's name is Comet?" Holly asked, surprised. "Like the reindeer?" She was familiar with most of the commercial Christmas myths and reindeer names. They'd actually named some of their reindeer after those characters, like Dasher, because her dad thought it would be funny and ironic.

Ash laughed and shook his head. "Like the cosmic snowball. Named after the streak on his back. But sure, like the reindeer too."

Holly had been around dogs before, of course. They brought their owners astonishingly high levels of joy, and dog parks were good places to soak up Cheer. But there were no dogs at the North Pole, only reindeer, penguins, and other forest creatures, and Holly wasn't sure what to do. *Should I greet the dog, like I would the reindeer?*

"Hello, Comet," Holly said, deciding to give the dog a soft pat on the head, imitating what her reindeer liked.

Comet seemed to approve, because he nuzzled his face against her palm. Ash watched the encounter, his eyes lighting up.

"Would you like to come with us?" Ash asked, and Holly slowly lifted her gaze. "On our walk? It's really nice out this time of night."

Holly paused for only a moment, her watch vibrating insistently.

Why not? she thought. She was there to do research, and that would qualify.

"That sounds nice."

She followed Ash and Comet out into the starry night.

Chapter Seven

"So, where are you from, Holly?" Ash asked.

They were strolling through the little gardens behind the Emerald House. Most of the garden's plant occupants had started to change colors for the fall, and some had already dropped their leaves.

For a moment, Ash wished Holly could see it in the spring, when the gardens were at their most vibrant. Fall had a beauty of its own, though, and Ash's gaze landed on his favorite tree, which was a brilliant fire-engine red. Holly's eyes seemed to follow his, and he noticed her appreciate the color too.

"Canada," Holly replied.

Ash was surprised by this answer. He hadn't picked up a trace of anything besides a typical Pacific Northwestern accent. He focused on the path in front of him rather than analyzing her face. She was again wearing that shade of bright red that set off the bit of color in her cheeks and lips.

"Canada? Really? So what brings you to Emerald Hollow? Is our fall festival really advertised so far up north?" He laughed, trying not to convey how curious he was.

"I travel a lot for work." Holly paused, seeming to consider something. When she spoke again, her tone had a note in it he couldn't quite place. *Confusion?* "I actually saw the flyer for the fall festival while I was on a business trip… in Finland."

His eyebrows shot up at that. "In Finland? I wish I could take credit, but I definitely don't have any part in advertising all the way over there." *Finland? Really?*

"I still have the poster strip in my pocket, actually." Holly slipped a folded-up rectangular piece of paper from her pocket. She carefully opened it and offered it to him.

It was from one of the posters they tacked up in businesses around town and in nearby counties.

"Wow. This is one of ours, but I'm just as confused as you are as to what it was doing in Finland. Where exactly did you come across it?"

Holly seemed troubled, and Ash wondered what was distressing her. "In a little café there. One that belongs to a friend. They post flyers for lots of events throughout Europe, but I was pretty surprised to see one for a small town in Oregon."

Ash handed the little piece of paper back to Holly, and she tucked it into her sweater pocket. "So I stored it away and figured if I could squeeze in a trip for the festival while I'm on the West Coast anyway for business, why not?"

Ash decided not to press any further, though he still couldn't imagine what one of his flyers was doing in Finland. He would have to ask Sofia if she'd emailed them to any of her connections overseas. "Well, however it got there, I'm glad it did. We're always happy to have new people stumble across our events. Are you here by yourself, then?"

Ash guided Comet around a corner to a small courtyard where a white gazebo was decorated with lights and garlands made of fabric leaves and pumpkins. Comet trotted over to it happily, sniffing the large pumpkins on the ground near the steps. Holly smiled at the scene, and her pleasure at his creation caused him to smile as well.

"Oh yes, I always travel by myself," Holly said, following Comet as the dog continued to walk and sniff.

"Do you have family at home in Canada?" Ash sensed she was holding something back, and he didn't want to push too hard. If she shut him down on that question, he would take the hint and try less personal topics. He whistled to Comet, who returned to his side immediately. They strolled past the gazebo and toward a trail leading to the edge of the forest.

"No, not exactly. I don't have any family, but I have good friends back home." Her voice sounded almost melodious, the cadence somehow measured yet perfectly normal. Her eyes roamed over the forest as she spoke.

"That's good. I don't know where I'd be without my best friend, Sofia. You met her in the restaurant. She was your server," Ash said, pausing as Comet sniffed a tree.

He loved being out in the forest, engulfed in the scent of pine, hearing the rustle of leaves in the breeze, and having no one around but Comet. He almost always took their evening walks alone because he was around people all day, every day, helping and entertaining. While he thrived on that, the evenings of solitude with his dog were restorative. But he was glad to have Holly with him. She seemed just as at home in the woods as he did.

"This is a beautiful forest you have here," Holly said, almost as if she were reading his thoughts.

Ash watched as her gaze moved over the rows of trees stretching beyond the Emerald House as far as the eye could see. The forest sloped upward slightly as it stretched away from the town. Ash smiled, struck by how she had worded her compliment. No one had ever said that to him before. Usually, people commented on his business or his work around town, but few stopped to recognize the forest his family had had the responsibility of stewarding for decades. He took a look around them and up at the stars, which were visible through the treetops.

"You're right. We're very lucky to have this. There's a clearing not too far from here where a lot of the fall festival activities are held. I guess you'll see it tomorrow."

He wanted to know more about what she'd said about her family, but it felt like she didn't want to share. Sometimes, family matters were complicated. He knew that better than most. So Ash stayed silent and continued to stroll down the forest path, the Emerald House visible just on the other side of the trees.

Holly matched his pace easily. She turned her head suddenly at the snap of a branch, and her eyes narrowed. Ash heard a rustling noise but didn't see anything by the time he followed her gaze.

"Don't worry. The bigger wildlife doesn't usually come this close to the house. I've never seen anything more than birds or squirrels on this trail, day or night."

It almost sounded like Holly stifled a laugh, and he looked at her in surprise. She simply shook her head and kept walking.

"How long have you lived here?"

Surprised that she'd initiated some conversation, he picked up a stick to throw for Comet. The dog immediately sprinted ahead of them to retrieve it.

"My whole life," he said proudly. "Well, almost. I moved away for college to get my business degree but then came right back to help my dad with the place. He retired a couple of years ago, and I took it over full-time."

"That's nice. I took over the family business too," Holly said then inhaled sharply.

Ash glanced at her out of the corner of his eye and saw that her lips were clamped firmly together.

Does she regret offering that piece of information? Why? "Oh really? What kind of business is it?"

Holly adjusted her sweater, and when she spoke, her voice was calm, as if Ash had imagined her hesitation. "We do market research. That's why I need to travel so much. The markets are different all over the world, and they're constantly changing. There's a lot to keep up with."

"I can imagine. What kind of market do you do research for?" Ash asked as they emerged from the thicket of trees.

"All kinds of things. But consumer goods, especially those related to sleep products."

That caught Ash's attention, though every word she said made him want to know more. He was normally so good at reading people, which came in handy as a business owner. But with Holly, he felt he was only glimpsing the tip of an iceberg, the shape of which he couldn't even begin to guess.

"Interesting. I took a few market-research classes in business school, though there was too much statistics involved for my liking."

Holly laughed, and the sound sent a little trill through him.

"I love statistics. It's something I can wrap my brain around. And I'm constantly trying to improve my process. There are so many variables to—" Her face flushed. "Sorry. I'm probably boring you."

"Not at all. As long as I don't have to do any calculations, I could listen to you talk about variables all night," he teased her, and the sight of Holly's smile warmed him all the way through.

Chapter Eight

The first thing Holly did when she woke up the next morning was study her watch. A niggling feeling still warned her that the thing must be broken. After her walk the previous night with Ash, the Cheer meter had signaled that she'd met her quota for the cycle, stunning Holly. She still had weeks before the next full moon.

While she could capture some Cheer over her quota, the reserve storage wasn't infinite. Maybe she could actually return to the North Pole early, spend some more time in the studios, or record her latest findings on Cheer. The cycle must be an outlier. Either that, or there was some source of Cheer in Emerald Hollow that exceeded all others Holly had encountered.

The outlier theory seemed more likely. She'd gotten lucky. If she returned to Emerald Hollow next cycle, she would probably only be able to store a normal amount of Cheer proportional to the amount of time spent there. Still, that did give some credence to her idea of exploring small towns. She would have to visit a few others to see if they yielded similar results. She had so many lines of research to focus on that it was difficult to know where to start.

Holly jotted down a few thoughts in her gingerbread-house notebook.

Her other question was why her Cheer wasn't going down anymore. She'd been on the lookout for negative emotions all evening after she returned to the hotel, but there were none. That was impossible.

Negative emotions were common even in happy places—nervousness, fear, jealousy, frustration, or restlessness. There had to be at least some of them occurring in the Emerald House. The only explanation she could come up with so far was that whatever had caused her Cheer to spike was also somehow blocking out the negative emotions. That idea was fascinating and one Holly intended to chase down.

Finally, she got dressed to go to the restaurant for breakfast. As she pulled on her red sweater from the night before, her mind stuck on all the near catastrophes that had occurred during her conversation with Ash on their walk in the woods. She groaned. He had asked so many questions, and her answers were woefully inadequate.

And Holly had also spotted Ivy watching in the woods. Though she knew Ash wouldn't be able to see the reindeer, that Ivy had shown up out of nowhere, while Holly was floundering through their conversation, hadn't helped her spirits. Ash probably thought she was standoffish, but her mind had been occupied with too many things she couldn't make sense of.

She had tried to stay as close to the facts as possible, as was always her practice. She *did* travel frequently, and she *had* heard about the fall festival and decided to investigate it. To the best of her ability, she had told Ash the truth. She had thrown in the part about having lots of friends in Canada based on her experience with Lia. If she simply said no, she didn't have any family waiting at home, Ash might think her strange.

And she'd nearly slipped when he asked about her work. *Why did I spill that I took over the family business?* She normally just told people she worked in marketing, though it rarely came up at all. Her interactions with people were too brief. Even Lia didn't know much more than that about her work. *What is going on with me?* She blamed it on the incessant vibration and heat on her wrist. Emerald Hollow was not normal. She just had to find out why.

AT THE RESTAURANT COUNTER, HOLLY REQUESTED A few pastries to go and said she would be back soon for a table. The server had merely nodded politely and handed her a white paper bag with the Emerald House logo on it—the letters *E* and *H* over a few pine trees.

Holly went outside with the bag of pastries, ready to surprise her reindeer. Though they were probably full from having access to a whole forest the previous night, she felt like spoiling them. As she crossed the front lawn, Ash emerged from the parking lot and waved at her.

"Holly, hey!" he called warmly.

"Hi, Ash," she said, keeping her tone polite, though she did feel unusually glad to see him. Despite the disaster that had been their conversation the previous night, Ash was easy to be around.

"Got any plans today?" he asked, striding toward her and shoving his hands into the pockets of his light jacket. His short brown hair rustled slightly in the autumn breeze.

"Oh, I'm not sure yet." She couldn't very well tell him that she planned to explore every inch of the town to figure out what was causing her Cheer meter to go haywire. Her watch was currently vibrating and putting off as much heat as ever against her wrist. "I thought I'd do some sightseeing."

Ash scratched his cheek, where a bit of dark stubble was beginning to appear. "Nice. Well, if you need any suggestions, just come find me. I'm working until two, but after that, I'd be happy to show you around. Unless you prefer exploring on your own. That's fine too." He added the last sentence in a rush and cast his eyes off toward the forest.

Holly wasn't sure how to respond. She wanted to do some serious sleuthing around town, testing her Cheer meter on some of the other locals. Still, with a strange tightness in her chest, she couldn't deny wanting to spend more time with Ash. She chalked it up to her extreme curiosity.

"Thanks. I'll let you know." She smiled at him.

They held each other's gazes for a moment before Ash cleared his throat.

"Sounds good. See you later." He turned and walked toward the door of the Emerald House, pausing only to hold it open for a couple walking out. Holly continued down the drive and around the corner to the clearing where her reindeer were waiting.

"I hope you all found some comfy twigs to sleep on last night." She gave Gale a pat on the head and the first of the four pastries. Ivy and Clove gathered around her excitedly, but Dasher stood steady and upright, like the well-trained reindeer he was, waiting politely for her to come to him. Clementine would want Holly to lecture Ivy and Clove on their manners, which they had been trained on for months, but they were just too cute.

Holly gave them their warm pastries immediately, and they rubbed their antlers happily against her hips. She pressed past them and gave Dasher his pastry, whispering, "Good boy," as she rubbed the side of his head. He looked pleased by the compliment, which the two younger reindeer hadn't received, and took the pastry gracefully from her hand.

"I'm off to do some investigating here in Emerald Hollow. Is that okay with everyone?" The reindeer all stomped their hooves in agreement, and Holly gave them each a few more grateful pets.

She remained with them in the clearing for several minutes longer, enjoying the feel of the sun on her skin as it crept through the trees, ready to start the day. Mystery seemed to fill the air, a variable to unmask, a thread to tug. And Holly was the one to pull it.

When Holly returned to the Emerald House for her breakfast, the server she had met the previous day, the one Ash had referred to as his best friend, was working again. Without looking at her tag, Holly remembered that her name was Sofia. She gave her a warm smile.

"Can I get you started with some coffee this morning?" Sofia asked, paper pad in hand and pen tucked behind her ear. She had light-brown skin and curly brown hair with golden highlights. It was pulled back into a loose, chic bun. A few delicate curls sprang from it, and some spirals framed her face as well. A smattering of freckles was scattered across her nose. She was at least a few inches shorter than Holly, but energy radiated from her small frame. Guitar-shaped earrings dangled from her ears.

Holly shook her head. "I'll take another one of those hot chocolates, if you make them this early."

"Of course. I'll bring that right out for you. I'm Sofia, by the way." She pulled the pen from behind her ear and pointed it lazily toward her name tag.

"I'm Holly. I'd like to check out a few more small businesses in town today. Is there any place you'd recommend?"

Sofia's eyes lit up. "Oh yes. Just go down to Main Street. There's a cute little bookstore, a souvenir store, and a local art and jewelry gallery. And some evenings, we have live music here in the café." She hesitated then arched an eyebrow. "There's actually a show on tonight. I'm not working this evening, and I was thinking about coming back for it. This week's group is one of my favorites. Would you like to join me?" Her round brown eyes studied Holly from behind thick, dark lashes.

"Absolutely," Holly replied, not needing to think about her answer. Concerts were always good for Cheer levels. Even though her Cheer meter was still full, and nothing was causing it to go down, it would be a good opportunity to run some tests with a few more locals if she didn't have any luck during the day. "What time is the show?"

"It starts at seven." Sofia's face brightened, and her warmth radiated from the inside out.

"Okay. I'll meet you in the lobby?"

"You got it, girl." Sofia gave one last smile then turned on her heel and disappeared into the kitchen.

Holly was surprised by the anticipation she felt for the evening. She'd been to concerts many times but never via invitation. Sofia, as far as Holly knew, had no other agenda for the evening than enjoying some music with friends.

Holly was still thinking about the concert when Sofia slid her hot chocolate across the table. "Enjoy." Sofia gave her a quick smile then walked over to seat a couple who had just entered the restaurant. Holly inhaled deeply before taking a sip. The cocoa was just as good as it had been the day before, the whipped cream and peppermint topping a perfect pairing. She was beginning to suspect that Emerald Hollow had some kind of magic of its own.

Chapter Nine

Holly took Sofia's suggestion and visited Main Street. Her Cheer meter held steady as she browsed the shops, playing the role of a tourist in town for the fall festival. Though she was wearing the red sweater from the previous day, she had paired it with a plaid skirt and gray leggings instead of jeans, and she thought she fit in well.

She studied the downtown of Emerald Hollow with practiced care. Some small, incredibly charming shops were obviously doing well, but every few buildings was an empty shop with a For Rent sign in the window. Despite the constant comings and goings of guests at the Emerald House, it seemed that the town might not be doing so well economically.

She kept a close watch on her meter as she chatted with the various small-business owners, but none of the shops or their shopkeepers seemed to cause the incessant heat on her wrist that she'd experienced multiple times at the Emerald House.

After going into five different shops, Holly continued to mill around Main Street, unsure for once what her next step should be. She'd tested her watch on multiple subjects, and she hadn't come away with any answers for why her Cheer meter wasn't declining. It seemed as if the detector for negative emotions was broken. *How else can I study whatever is going on?*

The only path forward that she could think of was to continue to spend time in the town and hope that a revelation would come to her at some point. The idea made her feel antsy. She didn't know how to stay in one place for very long, especially without the constant stimulation of emotions flying at her from every direction.

When she turned a corner, she spotted an old movie theatre. The name was borne on what appeared to be the original white marquee with red letters jutting out from an old brick building. A sign on the door read "Showing your classic favorites."

Holly generally avoided movies. Even the happy ones tended to have tense moments that caused a spike in anxiety, sadness, or fear in the viewers. Comedies were a safer bet, but she didn't always understand the humor, and they sometimes sparked embarrass-ment in certain viewers, which sent her Cheer levels crashing.

In fact, she could probably count on two hands the number of movies she'd seen, and she'd been able to sit all the way through less than half of them without getting up to escape an onslaught of Cheer-tanking emotions.

But since she didn't have emotions to chase her away from a movie, she pulled open the glass door and went inside, staring up at the list of showtimes as she approached the counter. A movie was starting in ten minutes.

"I'll see that one." Holly pointed at the poster that was taped to the glass display counter. The theater attendant nodded and printed her a ticket.

"That's one of my all-time favorites. My mom watched it a lot when I was growing up." The girl, who appeared to be a teenager, handed Holly her ticket. "Theater number three." Holly hadn't paid much attention to which movie she was selecting, but she smiled at the girl before passing into the theater.

The seats were red and cushioned, obviously not one of the original components of the theater. So far, the only other attendees were two elderly women who sat together, and Holly took a seat a few rows behind them, settling in toward the center of the large room.

It quickly became apparent that the movie Holly had selected was what humans would call a romantic comedy. A big-city woman returned home to her small town and eventually fell for her first love again. Holly sat in her plush red seat as the story played out, perplexed. The woman had it all. She was accomplishing everything she wanted to in her career, and she was on track for a big promotion, achieving a dream. *Why would she leave all that behind? Did she receive a new Dream?*

Holly thought about the Dreams she delivered to humans on Christmas Eve. The commercial stories of Santa Claus delivering toys were always good for a laugh at the North Pole because the Clauses and elves knew that the Dreams they crafted and delivered were so much more important than any toy. Everyone received a Dream, no matter their age. For children, the Dreams tended to burn brightly all year round, though the exact focus of them might change from day to day.

Adult Dreams were more challenging. Many adults forgot their gifted Dream by the time they woke up on Christmas morning. Some thought they were undeserving and squashed the Dream immediately. Others turned the Dream into New Year's resolutions, which were typically either pursued fervently for a short time then cast aside, or occasionally, a human chipped away at the Dream with the small, day-to-day actions that seemed insignificant but were most likely to lead to success. Those led to a Dream fulfilled, and that was what Holly and the elves lived for.

Maybe the woman in the movie had once dreamed of career success but had moved on to a different kind of happily ever after. Holly thought for the first time in a long time about her parents' love story. As a child, she'd asked about how they'd met, and they always told her that their hearts had sought each other out, her dad from the North Pole and her mom from the human world. They'd been together ever since. It seemed so easy, with none of the soul-twisting angst that humans used to portray love.

She shook her head but continued to watch the love scene on the screen with interest. The protagonist and the love interest shared a passionate kiss on the beach. Lightning flashed in the background, and Holly's thoughts turned to Ash and walking close to him in the forest. But she tried to stay focused on the fictional characters, not her real-life issues. Both were confusing, but one she wouldn't have to think about after she left the theater.

When the movie ended, Holly quickly got out of her seat, passed down the few rows behind her, and walked back into the lobby. The bright light greeted her harshly, but her eyes adjusted instantly.

"What did you think?" the teenage attendant asked as Holly walked by. "I got the feeling you hadn't seen it before."

Holly nodded. The young woman was observant.

"The cinematography was lovely," Holly said. The word *cinematography* had jumped into her mind inexplicably. It was probably her magic feeding her a vocabulary word she'd never needed to use before.

The girl's mouth twitched at the corner, and she looked puzzled, but she wished Holly a good evening.

Holly continued to think about what she had watched as she exited the theater and carried on down the sidewalk. She'd noticed one of the elderly women wiping away a tear at one point, and she wasn't sure whether it was out of happiness or some other complex emotion. Normally, anywhere other than in Emerald Hollow, her Cheer meter tipped her off to that. She snuck another look at her watch, which was still stuck stubbornly at full.

A few other people were out and about, but the street was fairly empty on a weekday afternoon. She glanced at the time and turned toward the street that would take her back to the Emerald House.

As she turned the corner, she ran smack into Ash.

Chapter Ten

Holly nearly tripped out of surprise. Similar to how people never walked into the reindeer, even though they were invisible, there seemed to be some kind of magnetic field that stopped people from touching her while she was working.

Ash reached out quickly and steadied her, and his hands rested on her arms for a few moments as they stared at each other. Her heart stuttered like a penguin skating across the ice for the first time. *Why did he appear here just now, when I've been trying to tuck away any uncertain thoughts about relationships?*

"Hey, Holly. Sorry about that. You good?" Ash asked, his molten brown eyes still studying her with concern.

"I'm fine. Thank you. I guess I should watch where I'm walking." Her meter was going wild, a rapid vibration making heat spread across her wrist. She ignored it and put on a bright smile as she gently extricated herself from him. It was impossible *not* to smile around him, as he seemed to carry the charisma of the entire town on his shoulders.

"Me too," Ash said, holding up his phone guiltily. As he

slipped it into his pocket, it buzzed. "How did your sightseeing go?"

"It was nice. The shops here are lovely." Holly was struck once again by the flecks in his warm brown eyes.

"But you're still on the hunt?" he asked, looking at Holly's empty arms.

"I guess you could say that. All the shops were great, they just... didn't have what I was looking for." She shrugged, wishing she had thought to purchase something to maintain her cover.

"And what are you looking for?"

His tone was so sincere that Holly nearly answered honestly. The words were out of her mouth before she could fully process them. "Do you know if there's anything... unique about this town?" Something was causing all the Cheer there—something very out of the ordinary. Maybe there was no one better to point her in the direction of its origin than a local.

Ash tilted his head, looking at her strangely. "Unique... how? Good? Bad? Downright ugly?" A smile tugged at the corners of his mouth, and she bit her lip to suppress a grin.

"I can't really explain it. I just get the feeling that there's something... different about Emerald Hollow. Something in the air, maybe?" She tried not to groan after she said the words. He would think she was a mystic or something. She wasn't *mystical* so much as *mythical*.

"We do have the fountain of youth tucked away in the woods," he said smoothly.

Holly's eyes widened with surprise, then she saw the tug at the corner of his mouth again.

"Okay, I deserved that. Never mind. It was a weird question."

But Ash was looking at her strangely again, almost as if he could sense that the question she'd asked wasn't exactly what she wanted to know.

"The closest thing this town gets to magic is our Christmas faire."

Holly's heart rate picked up. Maybe Ash was giving her the answer she'd been searching for after all. "Christmas faire?"

"Oh yeah. We're almost as famous for that as we are for the fall festival. Actually, this year, we've put in for a national contest called the Best Small-Town Christmas Faire. We're in the running to be sponsored by Hallmark next year. The company is sending out a rep and everything. I have a ton of work to do for it, but I've got big plans."

Holly thought Ash was trying to play it cool, but his chin had risen slightly at the announcement. She didn't usually think too long about what people's emotions were and why, only about their effect on her Cheer meter, but for a moment, she wished she had that capability again. Her watch was still buzzing intensely but giving no other indication about the types of emotions in the area. Ash's seemed like they would be fun to experience.

"I should have known," Holly murmured, trying to suppress a smile.

"Should have known...?"

Ash's eyes were glowing, and Holly couldn't help looking at them more closely, studying the warm brown flecks, the dark eyelashes, and the way they creased at the corners when he smiled. Her stomach gave a little flutter, a feeling she'd never experienced before. She took a half step back and refocused on their conversation.

"Oh, just that you have holiday cheer written all over you. Organizing the Christmas faire seems like it would be right in your skill set."

"I'd pretend to be offended if you weren't so spot on." Ash laughed. "The house helped with the fall festival and the

Christmas faire for a while when I was a kid, so I restarted the tradition when I took over."

A Christmas faire in Emerald Hollow, the place currently throwing everything I know about Cheer into question. It seemed like too good of a research opportunity to pass up. Maybe the two were connected somehow. Christmas villages were typically excellent sources of Cheer, and she visited a few every December. She actually got a little kick out of seeing what humans got right about the North Pole and what they got utterly wrong. The elves loved hearing stories about it after the Advent season ended and things slowed down a little. "That sounds like something I'd like to see," Holly murmured.

"Really?" Ash's face brightened. "You won't be doing research in Egypt or India or somewhere in December?"

Surprised, Holly didn't realize she had spoken out loud. "Well, I might be. But maybe I can move some things around." Holly's wheels were turning. Yes, that would all work out well. She could finish her observations in Emerald Hollow, return to the North Pole to discharge her watch, spend the November cycle with some of her surefire Cheer hot spots, then return to Emerald Hollow in late December to see if their Christmas faire had the same effect on the Cheer meter as the fall season. If so, maybe she could find some answers about the source of the Cheer.

"Awesome. You're welcome to stay at the Emerald House again, free of charge. But you'd better book now. We always sell out for the Christmas faire." Ash's phone buzzed in his pocket again, and Holly wondered if it kept him as distracted by work obligations as her Cheer meter did to her.

"Thanks for the tip." Holly felt surprised that her heart was no longer racing. Instead, it had calmed at the idea of the new lead. She'd been struggling around in the dark, but she suddenly had a direction to go in and a plan for when and how to pursue the lead.

"I'd offer you a ride back to the Emerald House, but I have a few more errands to take care of here for the fall festival. Will you be all right getting back?"

Holly was startled by the question. Clauses took care of themselves, and Holly had made so few close relationships with humans that she rarely had one know her well enough to want to look out for her. It was probably just an offhand comment by a man used to providing customer service, but it still warmed her.

"Of course. It was a nice walk down here. I'm sure I'll see you back there later."

He agreed and gave her a bright smile then passed close by her to enter the building she'd barely noticed they were standing in front of. She caught a hint of tree scents, maybe pine, as he passed her, like he was carrying a piece of the forest around with him.

She had barely turned away from him when she checked her watch and narrowed her eyes. It had been vibrating nonstop during their conversation, and a warm patch radiated around her wrist. "What is going on with you?" she whispered to it then picked up her pace as she walked down Main Street, away from Ash. Still, in spite of her intense confusion and curiosity, she had a smile on her face.

Ash tried to avoid grinning in public as he watched her go, her hair sparkling in the bright autumn light. She had looked adorable in her plaid skirt and tights, her red sweater complementing the constant blush in her cheeks, and he again had the strange sensation that she carried an aura of Christmas. She'd even smelled like Christmas—like cinnamon or clove maybe—when she tumbled into him.

He shook his head and scrubbed a hand over his mouth. *I prob-*

ably need to get more sleep. He opened the glass door to his right and walked into the office of his accountant.

"Hey, Ash," the accountant, Luis, greeted him. "How's everything coming along for the fall festival?"

"It's getting there. Still some things to do, but it'll get done." Ash slipped into the seat in front of Luis's desk. He pulled out his phone and quickly responded to a message from his front-desk manager.

Luis nodded. "What can I do for you today?" He leaned back in his chair and steepled his fingers below his chin.

He and Ash were old friends, and when Ash had asked him to be the accountant for the Emerald House a few years ago, he'd gladly accepted. The walls of the small office were covered in framed newspaper clippings of local sporting events. Luis coached soccer and baseball for the town's high school.

"How is all the paperwork looking for the vineyard deal?" Ash asked.

Luis nodded again, scooting his chair closer to where a computer monitor was perched on his desk.

"We're making progress, but I'll be honest, it feels like they're dragging their feet a bit."

"Is there anything we can do to get things moving along? I was hoping to have it closed by Christmas." Ash strummed his fingers on Luis's desk.

"Could you give them a little taste of what they'd get from working with you?"

"That's a good idea. With the fall festival coming up this weekend, maybe I could sell some of their wines at our booth there. We could create a special sangria with their fruits too. If we turn a good profit, it'll show them the potential there is in partnering with us." Ash's mind was already jumping ahead to the logistics.

He would have to work on it as soon as he got back to the

Emerald House. The fall festival and the Christmas faire both needed to be successful. He had to take more risks and push harder in his endeavors in order to recreate the vibrant town his dad had experienced growing up.

"Brilliant. I think that could work. Hey, who was that woman you were talking to outside a few minutes ago? I don't think I've seen her around here before."

"Her name's Holly. She's here for the fall festival and staying at the house."

"Seemed like there might have been a little spark between you two or something, but maybe I'm overstepping." Luis gave a boyish grin, and for a second, Ash pictured his friend in high school, teasing him over a crush.

"As far as I know, she's just passing through, Lu," Ash said, a little disappointed at the thought. Her forest-green eyes popped into his mind unexpectedly. They always seemed to be searching for something he couldn't see. *What is she looking for here in Emerald Hollow?* His phone buzzed again.

"Got it. Well, thanks for stopping by. Let me know if there's anything I can do to help this weekend."

"You still up for overseeing the potato-sack race?"

"Sure."

"Then that's already a huge help. See you later."

They slapped hands in a casual shake, and Ash left the building, his thoughts suddenly focused less on the vineyard deal than on Luis's comments about Holly.

He didn't want to admit it, but he'd felt the spark Luis was talking about and not just when they'd bumped into each other. Since the moment they'd met, there'd been an insistent tug of an unseen string linking them, though he was sure he was the only one who felt it.

Ash had never met anyone like Holly, and he was startled by his reaction to her. His ease with words, which never seemed to fail him, were doing just that since she'd arrived. He was tongue-tied when she was around. But as much as he was drawn to her, he couldn't afford a distraction from someone who was just passing through.

He had worked long and hard to build up his business and the town, and he was on the edge of taking things to the next level. The town would become one where people wanted to stay forever, not the type of place young people dreamed of escaping from.

Shaking his head, he tried to refocus on the reason he had visited Luis in the first place. He had work to do.

Chapter Eleven

"Oh yeah, I've known Asher Hayes since we were in elementary school. We go way back," Sofia said, settling onto a barstool.

She and Holly had met in the lobby promptly at seven, and many townspeople and guests of the Emerald House had already filled the small café. A local bluegrass band was warming up on a small stage, and Sofia had guided Holly to seats in the window.

When Holly had asked about Ash, Sofia seemed eager to share. She wasn't sure whether that was Sofia's natural inclination, or her magic was at work, helping her discover the mysterious source of Cheer at play in Emerald Hollow.

Holly took a seat on the barstool next to Sofia. "It seems like he's very involved in town."

"Ash practically runs the place." Sofia leaned in a little closer. Her guitar earrings, which appeared to be hand-painted, jangled as she moved. "His mom took off when we were kids, and since then, Ash's been a bit of a people pleaser. Well, more than a bit." Sofia laughed, rolling her eyes.

"Do you think he believes that if he pleases people, they won't leave him?" Holly asked.

Sofia seemed surprised by Holly's directness, but her face quickly relaxed. "Well, yes. I think that's probably right. That's what a psychologist would say, I guess. What did you say you did for a living?"

"I'm in market research. It's part of my job to read trends."

"Well, I think you've read Ash right. But it seems like he enjoys himself too. I've never seen a more born extrovert. Well, besides me. Maybe that's why we get along so well."

The band began to play a jaunty tune, contributing to the cozy atmosphere in the café. A couple sitting near Holly and Sofia stood up and began to dance. Holly's watch vibrated.

"Speak of the devil," Sofia said.

Following her gaze, Holly spotted Ash walking in, a full box in his arms. It must not have been very heavy, because he didn't seem to strain under the weight. He passed the café and reception desk, heading down the hall.

"He must be taking those to the storage room. I should see if he needs help," Sofia said, though she was tapping her hand on her knee to the music.

"I'll go," Holly said before she could think about it.

"You're an angel. Come grab me if the two of you need another hand."

Holly rose from her barstool. "Thanks for inviting me tonight, Sofia. You're right. This band is great."

"Of course. It's nice to have someone to get out of the house with. Ash is always too busy for stuff like this."

Holly brushed lightly past the other people in the crowded café until she entered the quiet hallway. *Which way did Ash go from here?* Her watch was continuing to vibrate and give off heat, and Holly took a guess that might have been aided by magic and turned left. At the end of the hall, she found a door labeled Storage. She stepped up to it and knocked.

AT THE SOUND OF A SOFT KNOCK, ASH PULLED OPEN THE door to find Holly. Seeing her there with her bright smile threw him slightly off-balance, and he quickly set down the box he was holding. Behind him, other boxes were stacked high, many of which overflowed with orange-and-yellow decorations.

"Holly!" He opened the door wider to welcome her in. "Is everything okay with your suite? Do you need anything?" He quickly slid a box out of the way with his foot to make room for her.

"I was actually at the concert with Sofia, and we saw you walk through with a big box. Sofia thought you might need some help."

If he were anyone else, seeing the beautiful woman standing there in a deep-green sweater dress, looking as radiant as the sun and offering help, might have rendered him speechless. But he was Asher Hayes, and he could pull words out from somewhere, even if they were often a jumbled mess around Holly.

"Thanks. That's really nice of you. But are you sure you want to help now that you've seen this place? Some of these boxes are kind of dusty, and you're... dressed so nice." He waved a hand in the direction of her dress, but Holly just smiled. *Dressed so nice.* He cringed internally.

"I don't mind at all. The dust won't bother me."

He wasn't sure why, but he believed her.

"What are we doing with these?"

"The one I just brought in is some signage and paperwork that I'll need to set up here at the Emerald House after the concert tonight. That pile over there"—he gestured to a few stacks of boxes, each about four high—"needs to get loaded into my truck." He looked at her small frame and sweater dress again, frowning. "Seriously, though, I can handle it."

"Just point me to the lightest ones," Holly said adamantly.

Ash shrugged. If she wanted to help, he would let her. He realized he liked the excuse to have her around again. After walking over to the stack, he did some rearranging.

"There. Those should be easier to carry. They're mostly lightweight decorations." He squatted and scooped up one of the heavier boxes. "Follow me."

After Holly picked up the nearest box, he led her back down the hallway and out through a side door. He propped it open with a rock then pointed at his truck. "There she is. We can just put these in the bed and keep going back and forth."

"This is your truck, huh?" Her hair fluttered in the slight breeze.

He really hoped the boxes weren't too heavy and hurried to lower the tailgate. "Yep. Kind of a necessity with the business. I haul things around a lot." He slid his box toward the back of the truck then took the box Holly was holding and set it in front of the first box.

"Are you going to wake up early to set all this up for the fall festival?" Holly followed him back into the building and down the hall again.

"I'm actually planning to take these down to the clearing tonight and get at least the basic things set up. A few volunteers will go out in the morning and put the finishing touches on everything."

They each picked up a second box and set out down the hall again. As they reached the truck and loaded the second set of boxes, Ash's phone buzzed. He pulled it out of his back pocket and read the message, his heart sinking.

He tried not to let the disappointment show on his face, but he obviously wasn't successful because Holly asked, "What's wrong?"

"I guess I lied. I usually have a whole family who comes out to do the decorating in the morning, but they just texted to tell me they're all sick." Ash ran a hand through his hair, trying to come up with a solution. It would be difficult to find a small team of volunteers on such short notice. He glanced over at Holly and saw that her brow was furrowed.

"Don't worry. I'll figure it out. I can just stay out there a little later tonight and get it done. It won't be nearly as fancy as when the Weigners do it, but it'll work." He took a deep breath and led the way down the hall for another load of boxes.

"I can do it. I'm a really good decorator."

Ash froze, not sure he had heard right. His mind was still running through scenarios.

"I'm serious," she said.

"Really? I would think a corporate woman wouldn't have a lot of time for things like that." He tilted his head, studying her face. Her expression was relaxed. She seemed calm, the opposite of how he was feeling.

"We don't. Call it a genetic talent." She scooped up another box as if it weighed nothing and flashed an easy smile. "Just do what you normally do in the clearing tonight, and I'll go out there first thing in the morning and finish. What time does the festival start?"

"Not until ten, officially, but sometimes people get out to the clearing a little earlier for photo ops. The hayride and kids train operators will be out there early, getting set up, and some of the food vendors will too. I think the Weigners usually get there around eight, but there are six of them." He narrowed his eyes slightly, feeling that the task would be overburdening for anyone, let alone a woman completely new to town.

"Don't worry about it. Like I said, I have a gift." Holly waved a hand.

She sounded so self-assured that Ash decided to trust her. *What other choice do I have?* A little bit of decorating done by one confident person was better than nothing.

"Okay, then. Thank you. You're really saving me here. I have to be at the restaurant most of the morning. We're usually packed with people before the fall festival. But I'll try to get down there a little before ten to see if you need help with anything." He took the box that Holly was holding, which was heavier than he'd expected, and loaded it into the truck, which was nearly full.

"You know, I never asked you—do you have a car here? The clearing is in walking distance if you're not hauling boxes, but if you want to drive over in the morning, you can take my truck." He closed the tailgate and rested an arm on top of it.

Though he hauled things often, the bit of exertion coupled with the anxiety sparked by the cancellation text had him on the verge of sweating. Holly didn't appear to be fazed by the exercise, though the healthy pink glow that was usually in her cheeks was still present.

Around them, night was rapidly falling, the sunset shimmering brilliantly beyond the woods. The golden-hour light reflected across Holly, and for a moment, they simply looked at each other. Ash waited as Holly seemed to contemplate something, his usual impulse to fill in gaps of silence dampened.

Holly looked down at her watch, studied it briefly, then quickly thrust it behind her back, clearly flustered. He wondered what had caused that reaction. *Did she just receive a text? Does she have to leave? Was it from a significant other?* He kicked the wheel of his truck then wondered why he'd done so.

Holly quickly smiled at him, and her expression was so serene that he almost questioned whether the moment had even happened. "I'll walk over."

Ash nodded. "Okay. Well, thanks again. This means more than you know. And while you'll be the only one on decorations, there will be a small army over there, setting up games and booths. If you need help, you can ask pretty much anyone there, and I'm sure they'll give you a hand." He removed his grip from the tailgate one last time and stepped back toward the side door of the Emerald House.

"Got it," Holly said.

He held the door open for her.

"See you tomorrow."

Ash watched her as she walked back down the hallway toward the café. The lively sound of bluegrass floated to his ears. Once she disappeared around the corner, he removed the rock from beside the door, checked that the door was locked, and returned to his truck, ready to take the boxes to the clearing. He was looking forward to unloading them there alone, where he hoped the cool evening air would clear his head. Holly had left behind a faint scent of cinnamon, and while he had smelled the spice a million times before, it was suddenly making him crazy.

Chapter Twelve

Holly woke up early, ordered hot cocoa and pastries to go from the restaurant, then went outside to see her reindeer, as was becoming her routine. As she went down the trail to the forest, she admired the trees in the back courtyard. A few of them boasted brilliant shades of red or orange, and one in particular held her attention. She had noticed it when walking with Ash to the forest.

As much as Holly had dedicated her life to collecting and studying Cheer, she couldn't help but be amazed by Earth's magic sometimes too. That tree had likely turned from dark green to pale honey yellow then maybe to soft orange before settling on that brilliant shade of red. Then the leaves would drop in winter, and the process would start again in the spring. If that wasn't magic, she didn't know what was.

Dasher and Gale stood regally, ready to greet her, while Ivy and Clove rushed over to sniff her bag of pastries and magic lichen, their short white tails wagging excitedly.

"All right, friends. We came here for the fall festival, and that's finally happening today. My data collecting hasn't been very successful, so I think it may be time to regroup at the North Pole this evening. I have a lot of Cheer to discharge." She pulled the pastries from the white paper bag and gave one to each of the reindeer. "Clementine will be surprised to see us back so early. She's going to have a million questions. I just wish I had some answers."

Holly waited as the reindeer finished their pastries, staring out into the woods at nothing in particular, then she bade them goodbye and walked down the forest path to the clearing. The sun was just starting to rise as she surveyed her canvas.

Holly had never decorated for a fall festival before, but she figured it couldn't be that much different from decorating for Christmas. While the North Pole was beautifully adorned all year round, the Clauses and the elves still went all out during Advent. Holly could hang a garland with the touch of a finger.

Throughout the clearing, a few men were setting up what looked like large machinery. They gave her a wave when they saw her approach the stack of boxes Ash had left the night before. One peek confirmed her suspicions that the cardboard containers were brimming with garlands, scarecrows, fabric pumpkins, baskets, and barrels of all sizes. One box contained a variety of tools.

Holly did a quick sweep of the clearing. The space was fairly large, surrounded by tall evergreen trees. She examined the boxes again, formulating a game plan. The men working near the edge of the clearing didn't seem to be paying any attention to her. Holly smiled and got to work.

TWO HOURS LATER, ASH MADE HIS WAY INTO THE clearing, Comet at his side. The dog wagged his tail rapidly, seeming to anticipate an exciting day.

As Ash approached the clearing, he walked through a massive

arch fashioned out of burlap, fabric leaves, and glittering gems in fall colors. He paused there in surprise. He'd never seen anyone use those materials in that way. Just the arch alone must have taken hours for Holly to put together and most of their supplies. There were pieces threaded into it that he didn't remember seeing before. It would be a showstopper for the festival guests. If Holly had spent all her time and energy there, and it appeared she had, it would make for a great photo op.

Then Ash passed through the arch and into the clearing and nearly fell over. Long strands of dangling lights had been stretched across the clearing from tree to tree, lighting up the morning with a magical glow. Every booth had been decked out from top to bottom in red, orange, and yellow decorations. The clearing looked like it had been made over by a Hollywood film crew, not a single woman. It was impossible.

Just as Ash had that thought, Holly stepped out from behind a tree and beamed at him. *How does the sunlight always manage to catch her hair so perfectly?* She was wearing a long-sleeved oversize white sweater with black leggings and brown boots. Her hair was pulled back in a thick, wavy ponytail, with two tendrils hanging down to frame her face. Ash shook his head, grinning, still awestruck.

"Holly, how?" he asked, at a loss for words.

She was beaming, excitement radiating from her body as she seemed to dance delicately on the balls of her feet. She twirled around, waving her hand. "You like it?"

"This is the best-decorated fall festival I've ever seen. But how did you do it? Did you come out here and work after I dropped off the boxes last night?"

Holly let out a short laugh. He noticed her hand go to her wristwatch, then both hands disappeared into the kangaroo pocket of her sweater.

"It was fun," Holly said simply, looking around the clearing.

Ash shook his head and scratched the back of his neck, perplexed, but couldn't help being thrilled with the outcome. He let out a deep breath, releasing a load he'd unconsciously been carrying since receiving the cancellation text. Holly had really come through, and he didn't know how to repay her.

"The whole town is gonna love it. If I start telling people you decorated it, they're never going to let you leave."

A strange look played on Holly's face at his comment, but it quickly disappeared, and she beamed at the clearing again.

"So, what happens now?"

The clearing was starting to fill up around them. Visitors were walking into the space, pointing, their eyes wide. The locals waved at or fist-bumped Ash on their way in.

"Now, you enjoy yourself. Oh, and I was actually going to ask you to be my partner for the potato-sack race. I was going to race with Sofia, but she said she drank too much wine last night, and now she has a headache." He laughed. His eyes met Holly's emerald-green ones and settled on them for a moment. "She also said she had a really fun time with you at the concert."

Holly seemed to process everything he had said. "You want me to be your partner for the potato-sack race?" Her expression was full of confusion.

"I mean, if you want to. It's pretty fun. There are different age categories for the kids, then there's the adults-only heat. It gets pretty competitive." He was suddenly eager for her to be his partner, to join in another Emerald Hollow tradition.

She seemed to perk up at the word competitive, her posture straightening. "Okay," she said slowly, looking toward the dying grass that covered the clearing and nodding resolutely.

"Okay? You'll race with me?"

"Sure, but do we get to practice first?"

Ash laughed as they turned and walked toward the booth labeled Emerald House Hotcakes.

Chapter Thirteen

Twenty pairings entered the potato-sack race, and Holly studied the others with the eyes of an eagle—or of an elf when someone had stolen their hot cocoa. They all gathered at the starting line, and she glanced toward the sidelines, where Sofia gave her a little wave. Ash jogged over to her.

For the last few hours, he had been busy flitting from booth to booth, checking on vendors and occasionally speaking into a microphone as he acted as the MC for various activities. The potato-sack race was the first event he was actually going to participate in, and Holly felt honored to be his partner.

She realized more and more that Sofia hadn't been exaggerating when she'd said Asher Hayes was a big deal around Emerald Hollow. And she had to admit the competition aspect intrigued her. Holly had never thought of herself as competitive, at least not with humans. She had no one to compete against. But each Cheer cycle, she constantly competed against her last best time and Cheer level. She thrived on a challenge. *Why not see if that same spirit applies here?*

"Are you ready for this?" Ash appeared at her side, grabbed a burlap potato sack from a nearby stack, and offered it to Holly. "Would you like to put your leg in first?"

Holly took the sack and stepped in with her right leg.

"At least some of the teams are more mismatched in height than us. That should help." Ash nodded toward a couple in which the man appeared to be almost a whole foot taller than the woman.

"Those two women over there are almost exactly the same size," Holly said, indicating competitors at the end of the row. "They might present a challenge."

Ash put his left leg into the sack. Holly's watch buzzed erratically as his arm brushed hers. Her brain flashed to the moment on the sidewalk when she'd tripped into him, and her stomach did a little flip that might not have been entirely related to the impending race.

"Don't worry about them. We just need to focus on that tree. Whoever gets to it first wins the harvest potato." When Holly looked at him quizzically, he grinned. "It's a potato stuffed animal made by a local knitting group. It's quite the honor, but I've never won one before."

"Maybe this will be the year," Holly said, locking her eyes on the tree.

A man dressed in dark jeans and a bright-orange pumpkin shirt stood to the side of the large field in the clearing and raised a silver whistle above his head. Ash had told her his name was Luis.

"Potatoes, take your marks!" he shouted, and the crowd cheered.

Ash slipped his arm around Holly's waist, and that time, Holly ignored any sensations in her stomach. She put her arm around his waist, as well, gripping him securely. With no time to think about her watch in that moment, she was solely focused on their destination.

Luis blew the whistle, and suddenly, they were off.

The first few steps were a little awkward, but Holly paid close attention to Ash's rhythm, and soon, they were in sync. She ignored everything else around her, focused only on the tree ahead, which was beautiful, one she had adorned with festive harvest ornaments, like a Christmas tree but dressed for fall.

She pushed away the intense vibrating coming from her watch as she strode, step by unsteady step, to the tree, still gripping Ash tightly. They reached the tree, and Holly tagged it with her hand for good measure then realized Ash had fallen over when she released him. She scanned him anxiously but smiled when she saw him laughing.

"Was that really your first time potato-sack racing?" He laughed, agilely getting back to his feet. "You're a natural."

"Did we win?" Holly looked around. The other couples had reached the tree, but Luis was shouting again.

"And this year's winners of the harvest potato are our own Asher Hayes and his partner, Holly!"

"Sorry," Ash whispered as the announcer strode toward them, holding a knitted potato man. "I realized as I was signing us up that I don't know your last name."

He lent Holly his hand as she stepped out of the potato sack, and her watch heated up again. Together, they took the trophy from the announcer as the crowd clapped, and the other participants gathered their potato sacks to return to the pile for next year's festival. Comet dashed excitedly in circles around them.

"Well done," Sofia said, coming up beside them. "I told you she'd make a better partner than me."

Ash shook his head ruefully. "Who knew Holly was a potato-sack master?"

Holly handed him the harvest potato. "Here. Display it in the Emerald House with pride."

"Are you sure? If you want it—"

"Are we gonna have to work out some kind of joint custody arrangement?" Sofia asked. "Just take the potato, Ash. It'll look nice up there on the counter when people check in. You'll have bragging rights until next year." She elbowed Ash in the side.

"Maybe you'll win next year too," Holly offered.

"Only if you're my partner," Ash said with a wink, and a loaded pause followed as he and Holly stared at each other.

"Aaall righty, then," Sofia said, taking a large step backward. "I'm gonna go get some kettle corn."

"So, what's next? Do you want to join us for midnight apple picking tonight?" Ash asked, still riding the high of their unexpected win, as he and Holly sat down at a picnic table in the clearing for dinner with Sofia. They had just finished checking on the wine booth, and Ash had been assured that the sangria was selling well.

A band called The Tempting Pumpkins had set up at the far side of the clearing, and families were spreading blankets on the ground in front of them. The air was beginning to cool, and parents put hats onto their children's heads.

"Oh, well, actually..." Holly cleared her throat and looked at a place just past Ash's right shoulder. "I have to be getting home tonight. There are some things I need to take care of."

Ash's stomach dropped. "You have a flight out tonight? Are you driving back to Medford? It's already starting to get dark." He glanced up at the sky, where the sun was beginning to set dazzlingly behind the evergreen trees. The Tempting Pumpkins began playing, a lively violin quickly joined by the other instruments. He shouldn't have been surprised she was leaving so soon, but he was unexpectedly disappointed.

Holly pursed her lips. "Um, yes. I have a flight tonight. But I have transportation all arranged."

Ash frowned, wondering if she had made the flight plans suddenly, but Sofia spoke before he could say anything.

"Holly, I know this was just a detour while you were in Oregon for business, but I've really enjoyed spending time with you these past few days. Is there a chance you'll be coming back to this part of the world any time soon?" Sofia's caramel-streaked curls were blowing around her face in the breeze.

Ash had nearly forgotten Sofia was there, and he wondered if Sofia had been making herself scarce intentionally. "You were thinking about attending the Christmas faire, right? We're going all out for Hallmark. We could use a new perspective with the decorating from someone who knows what they're doing. People have been coming up to me all day, asking who decked out the clearing. You're starting to get a reputation around here." The words spewed out of Ash, and he barely had time to question his motivations. *Am I asking because I genuinely need help with the festival or because the thought of not seeing her again is creating an odd sensation in my chest?*

Unlike Ash, the words didn't flow out of Holly immediately. She seemed to contemplate something, and when she finally spoke, her gaze met Ash's again. "Well, I can't let that reputation go to waste."

Sofia's face lit up, and warmth that had nothing to do with Hallmark filled Ash's chest. Maybe by Christmas, he could turn the town into a place someone like Holly would want to stay.

Chapter Fourteen

The trip to the North Pole went by quickly as Holly reflected on her time in Emerald Hollow. Decorating the clearing had been surprisingly enjoyable. She was accustomed to spending each cycle traveling around, trying to find as much Cheer as she could, and dodging negative emotions like the plague. It felt strange to be able to stay in one place for a time, not obsessing about her Cheer quota.

Spending an entire morning focusing on beautifying the clearing was what Holly imagined taking a relaxing vacation would feel like or maybe learning a new hobby. She had been given the opportunity to flex an underused muscle, and it felt good.

But at the same time, Holly had never stayed anywhere for more than a few days. She wondered if she had spent too long in Emerald Hollow. Though she could easily blend in for a multiday cultural festival with thousands of people, in Emerald Hollow, Holly had been starting to make connections. Ash and Sofia, obviously, but even the men in the clearing and those who had joined them later to set up their booths had stopped to chat with Holly about the fall festival.

She felt like she fit in there, which unsettled her. By gathering Cheer and avoiding things that took a toll on its levels, Holly was an outsider to the human experience. She had started to get comfortable in Emerald Hollow, and she wasn't sure what that meant.

When they touched down in the North Pole, Ivy and Clove excitedly trotted over to the other young reindeer, ready to show off after their successful first Cheer cycle outing. Holly gave Dasher and Gale an extra-long brushing, thanking them for supervising the trainees. By the time Holly finished in the stables, Clementine was waiting for her at the start of the path to Merriment Square.

"You're back early. Is everything all right?" She pulled at the bottom of her crisply tailored suit jacket. Night was just beginning to fall, and the northern lights glittered beyond the village like bioluminescent algae.

"Clem, you're never going to believe this," Holly said breathlessly as they began their trek under the arched lights, moving away from the stables. "My Cheer quota is filled already!"

Clementine's ears pitched upward, the elf equivalent of arching an eyebrow.

"I went to this small town for a fall festival to test a new theory." Since Clementine was walking quickly down the path, Holly had to pick up the pace. "Anyway, it was nearly filled on the first evening, before the festival even started. I thought I'd pick up on some negative emotions that would bring it down, like always, but this Cheer was resilient. It was like nothing could affect it! I still don't know what caused it. So I decided I needed to come back here and discharge it in case it turned out to be some outlier."

Clementine's eyes had followed Holly as she spoke. "That is all very strange. Let's take it to the North Post and see if it charges up like normal Cheer."

They emerged into Merriment Square.

"Exactly. I was wondering the same," Holly said excitedly as she strode to the lamppost in the center of the square. A few elves came out of the studios to watch, though it was a smaller group than normal. No one had been expecting her.

A nervous tingle went up Holly's spine. She took a deep breath and pressed her palm to the post, right on top of the snowflake engraving. The warm sensation filled her palm as usual, and she breathed a sigh of relief.

When the elves let out a collective gasp, Holly looked up at a flash of bright light. She took a step back then froze. The North Pole had gone silent. Holly blinked then stared in disbelief.

The North Post was glowing more brightly than it had in many seasons. The last time she had seen it putting out that much light, her parents hadn't yet moved to the other side of the spirit portal. For once in her life, Holly was truly and utterly shocked. As she and all the elves stood there, staring up at the North Post, snow began to fall softly.

THE NORTH POLE WAS ABUZZ THE NEXT MORNING. THE North Post, a central beacon of life there, was shining at full capacity once again. Many of the younger elves couldn't remember a time when the post shone that way, and many of the older elves had tucked it away as a deep memory, one they were not quite confident was real.

But since it was back, the elves couldn't stop talking. Rumors abounded. Maybe Ms. Claus's strength had finally fully matured. Perhaps the Cheer source she had tapped into was somehow different from others. Or maybe it was just part of a natural cycle within Cheer that they had all been unaware of.

Holly contemplated many of those questions as she sat on her front porch, drinking hot cocoa and staring at the North Post. The elves who had been awake the previous night had quickly run home to their families in the tree houses, spreading the news about the post. That morning, Merriment Square was even busier than a normal day when Ms. Claus was in residence. While the Kringles were subtler about their curiosity, the Keyblers chatted animatedly with one another.

In the light of morning, the North Post was still unbelievably bright. It seemed as if their home had only been lit by lanterns until suddenly, it had been wired with electricity. Holly's childhood memories flashed through her mind. The North Pole had quite literally been brighter, one of the many reasons why her time with her parents had felt different from her time without them. She hadn't noticed until it went away and came back again.

Holly swirled the heavy mug in her hands. It showed four reindeer dashing across the sky, pulling a golden sleigh. Her mind was running through every hypothesis she could think of.

The Cheer cycle had been shorter. Her watch had filled almost immediately. And the Cheer she'd delivered had been brighter than ever before. *Why?* She tried to consider all the variables that had changed since the last Cheer cycle.

She had visited a small town. Well, it had hardly been the first time she'd visited one of those. She'd attended other festivals in rural areas as well as weddings and retirement parties.

Oregon. She'd been to Oregon, too, mainly to the coastal towns.

A fall festival. She had attended those before. *Was this one different somehow?* Not likely, other than the fact that she had been way more involved with it than she normally would be. But her Cheer meter had been skyrocketing before the festival even began.

Emerald Hollow. Holly paused on that variable for a moment. She'd never been to Emerald Hollow before, and she had to admit there was something inviting about the town that she couldn't quite put her finger on. Plus, their hot cocoa was the only one she had tasted that could rival the one made at the North Pole. But after she'd walked around the town and tested her watch, it didn't seem that the town itself was impacting the Cheer.

She let her mind go to the one place she had been avoiding: *Ash*. Her watch had first started kicking off when she met him, and it always seemed to feel extra warm every time she was around him. *But what could that mean? Is he just full of more Cheer than everyone else? Does his Cheer somehow repel negative emotions from others? And even if those things are true, why would that make the light in the North Post glow more brightly?*

It didn't make any sense, and things that didn't make sense bothered Holly immensely. She took another sip of her hot cocoa, but she barely tasted it. Her eyes roved over Merriment Square, looking but not seeing.

The elves weren't as invested in the *why* and *how* of Cheer as she was. Clementine had come on as elf mayor when Holly had taken over as Ms. Claus, and while she had intimate knowledge of all the North Pole's many operations, Cheer was one thing that was a bit of a mystery to them all.

Clementine had always said she was okay with that, as long as the Cheer kept functioning as it always had. The end result was what was important to Clementine, not the many paths to getting there. Those were Holly's domain. And the new path, the strange, unexpected synapse, had lit a fire under Holly to unravel it.

Someone had to know what was causing it. She set the mug down on the polar-bear-shaped wooden table next to her and stood quickly. *Time to go see Lumi Kringle.*

Chapter Fifteen

Lumi Kringle was the oldest living elf in the North Pole. While all elves and Clauses had longer lives than humans because of magic, Lumi's life had been particularly long. Though Holly hadn't seen Lumi since she was a child, and she barely remembered what she looked like, she knew that if anyone had the answers she was seeking, Lumi did.

Holly trod through the dense forest, slipping softly along the little wooden paths that hung a few feet in the air, connecting the tree houses. The snow that was a constant companion of the North Pole sparkled on the ground below.

The treehouse Holly was seeking was older and larger than most of the others in the elf forest, and Holly spotted it easily when she reached the far end of the woodland. A wreath made of evergreen branches, sprigs of holly, and a few white winter flowers that were found only at the North Pole hung on the oval door. Inside the wreath was a small hand-painted sign that read "Home is where the Cheer is." Holly raised her hand to knock, but the door swung open before her knuckles could make contact with the ancient wood.

"I've been expecting you." A soft, willowy voice greeted Holly as Lumi emerged from behind the door. She had short, curly silver hair and warm tanned skin and wore a thick silver sweater that seemed to be made of hundreds of ribbons or possibly small, billowy feathers. Her feet were enveloped in large white slippers. "Come on in. Let's have a seat. All the neighbors will start gawking if you stand there too long."

The woman's voice made Holly's skin prickle with recognition, and her brow furrowed as she followed the elf into the living room. She sat down on a large, plush cushion. In the better light, Holly studied Lumi's face more closely and gasped.

"Lia!" she exclaimed, thinking her mind must be playing tricks on her.

Lumi smiled. "I wasn't sure if you'd recognize me. I'm told I look quite different when I'm blending in with the humans."

"But... Lia lives in Finland! How do you even get there?" Holly's mind whirled. One of the few humans she'd struck up a friendly acquaintance with wasn't a human at all—she was an elf.

"I have my ways. Let's not worry about that now. Did you come here to find out about the comings and goings of elves?" When Holly shook her head, Lumi continued, "My grandelves have been bringing me treats at all hours of the day. They're experimenting with a new recipe for you. Would you like some?" Lumi indicated a tray piled high with cookies of all shapes and sizes.

Holly picked up a sugar cookie, struggling to process that who she'd thought was her one true human friend wasn't actually a human. *What else don't I know?* Her understanding of Cheer and elves, two things she'd always had a reasonable grasp on, was starting to implode.

She chewed the cookie as Lumi took a seat and couldn't help but savor the cloudberry-coconut treat. She'd never tasted anything quite like it. The longer she looked at Lumi's face, the easier it was to see her old friend Lia there.

"Now, let's get down to the reason you're here. We all saw the North Post last night," Lumi prompted, and Holly nodded, setting the rest of the cookie down in her lap. She would have to push aside her hundreds of questions about Lia and Finland for the moment.

"It's the strangest thing. I feel like I remember the North Post being like that when my parents were still here, but I was never really sure until the bright light came back last night, and I was hoping you could tell me more about it. Your memory of those days might be a little better than mine." In addition to her unusually long life span, Lumi Kringle was known to have a good memory. And apparently, she had some powers and a double life that Holly knew nothing about.

"Yes, I do remember it. Your father's time as Santa Claus was long, and he was very successful in the role," Lumi began.

"I always thought he must have been stronger than me somehow. I don't remember him being gone as much as I am. He only had to collect a little bit of Cheer each cycle, and it powered the North Pole easily. Or I thought maybe the sources of Cheer have gotten weaker over the years. I couldn't test either of those theories, though." Holly furrowed her brow.

Lumi—*Lia*—smiled at her gently, the corners of her golden eyes crinkling. That expression was so familiar to Holly, even though the hair and ears were different from the woman in Finland, and Lia had always hidden her eyes behind glasses. Some expressions couldn't be masked.

"Holly, dear, you've thought that all this time? That your father was more powerful than you?" She shook her head and sighed. "You are just as powerful as any Claus who has come before you. But sometimes there are... extenuating circumstances that determine the power of the Cheer."

Holly perked up. She was finally going to get some information about how Cheer worked.

"What do you mean? What extenuating circumstances?" Holly pressed. She sat on the edge of the cushion, the half-eaten cookie forgotten in her lap.

"I'm afraid I can't explain it, Holly. It must be experienced," Lumi said quietly, and Holly could sense she was holding something back. "You've come across an example in Emerald Hollow. That's a wonderful thing."

Holly's posture had started to stoop as she began to realize Lumi wasn't going to give her any answers outright.

"I don't understand. What have I come across?"

Lumi shook her head. "I know this is frustrating, Holly. I can't explain it completely right now. But Cheer was never meant to be a commodity for Clauses to collect. It's found all over the world, sure, but part of the mission is experiencing all the good the world has to offer. Up until now, you haven't been able to slow down and experience any of that. Am I right?" Lumi rested a hand gently on top of Holly's.

Holly wanted to beg, to insist that Lumi tell her what she knew. *What do my experiences have to do with whatever is going on with the North Post?* But from the set of Lumi's features, she wouldn't hand over the answers so easily. After all, they'd been friends for years. Holly recognized the expression in Lumi's eyes, one of compassion but also resolve.

"So what do I do now?" Holly's brain was working at a hundred reindeer paces per minute. Lumi knew something, but she couldn't or wouldn't share it. Holly hoped that she would explain more in time. But for the moment, Holly was on her own. She let out a deep breath, trying not to let frustration overwhelm her. She'd gone there for answers, but all she'd received were more questions. *Isn't that just like a Kringle elf?*

"I think you know what you need to do," Lumi said gently, and Holly looked up to meet her golden eyes. "But I'll lay it out for you anyway. You need to return to Emerald Hollow. The answers will come to you there."

HOLLY SOAKED IN HER BATHTUB THAT NIGHT, HER MIND whirring in frustration. She thrived when she had a testable question to experiment with. Just blindly searching for answers when she wasn't even sure of the question was a recipe for distress. She had already tried searching Emerald Hollow for answers. Nothing explained why her Cheer meter had stayed so high there.

Holly stared into space as the northern lights danced outside the wall-length window. She had barely noticed the lights that evening. Thinking about Lumi again, she replayed some of her visits with Lia in Finland. *Were there signs I missed?* She tried to remember their first meeting. *Did I seek her out or the other way around?* Of course, the third option was that magic had drawn them together.

She sighed and tried to focus on what had impacted her Cheer and the North Post. Her thoughts drifted to Emerald Hollow again, and she made up her mind. *If there's something to find,* Holly thought, *I'll find it.*

After Holly climbed into bed, she lay awake for a few more hours. She tried to lull herself to sleep by following the gentle swirling of the snowflakes on her watch. Humans couldn't see the movement, but she could, when she slowed down enough to pay attention to them.

Holly rarely took off her watch and only at the North Pole, just to see if she could still catch the trail of snowflakes and trace the pattern to unlatch it. But really, there was no need to remove it. Its magic caused it to be self-cleaning along with her wrist. It never rubbed or chafed. So she wore it always, like it was a part of her. Slowly, the snowflakes began to blur, and in the early hours of the Arctic morning, Holly fell asleep.

Chapter Sixteen

Holly woke up with a renewed sense of purpose after having a dream about her parents and their many days together at the North Pole. She didn't have to go experimenting in Emerald Hollow just yet. The Cheer she had brought in would easily power the North Pole and its operations for the rest of the cycle. In another few weeks, she would return to Emerald Hollow for the Christmas faire.

She had a whole cycle in between when she could collect Cheer elsewhere. Holly hadn't had that much time to spend at the North Pole since before she had taken over as Ms. Claus, and she intended to use it well.

She slipped on a brilliant white jacket as soft as clouds. It came down to her knees, covering the tops of her soft wool leggings. Then she tugged on her favorite white boots.

"Good morning, Clementine," Holly said a few moments later in Merriment Square. "What's on the agenda today?"

Clementine studied Holly, appearing startled by the question. "The agenda, Ms. Claus?"

Normally, Holly itched to get back out into the world, collecting Cheer. She never lingered around the North Pole. But Holly remembered her dream as well as what it felt like to help with the fall festival in Emerald Hollow. The sense of community had felt fulfilling, and she wanted to replicate that. The North Pole was supposed to be her home, after all.

"What's going on around here? I've decided to stay for a few weeks and get up to speed on everything. We're into the Advent season now, so I'm sure there's lots happening." Holly looked around the bustling Merriment Square. Elves were everywhere, walking between gazebos, studios, and tree houses. Some of the younger elves were ice-skating around the North Post.

Clementine raised an eyebrow but began to speak, not needing to look at her clipboard. "Each of the studios is in its second-to-last stage of production. All narratives have been fully designed and tested, and now we're working on the mass production. In a few more weeks, we'll start on all the finishing details that make each Dream unique. Then it's assembly-line packaging and preparations for loading into the bag."

Holly nodded as if she understood every detail. "Great. So what can I do?" Holly stopped studying the ice-skating Keybler elves and turned to look at Clementine, whose ears shot forward then returned to normal quickly.

"What can you *do*, Ms. Claus?" Clementine swallowed and gripped her clipboard more tightly. She looked down at it as if searching for a way out of the conversation.

"You know, what can I do around here? What did my father do when he was home during a Cheer cycle?" Holly asked, and Clementine's eyes grew soft. Holly knew that her parents' memory was a soft spot for the elves, and she loved them for it.

"Your father? Well, he was just... Santa Claus," Clementine

said, uncharacteristically shrugging. "He went around, checking on things and spreading cheer. Not Cheer, but cheer. Lowercase *c*. The elves loved when he came around, watching what they did, asking questions. He was not as inquisitive as you, Ms. Claus, but I think he asked to make the elves feel noticed."

Holly took a moment to process that. It all jibed with the image she had in her mind of her father. And to her surprise, it also made her think of Ash and how he ran the Emerald House. He was always there, hands on, offering help and letting others do their thing when he wasn't needed. She had a suspicion that the last part wasn't easy for him. But he'd trusted her with the fall festival decorations, something precious to him, and that had meant a lot to her. She shook her head. *Why am I thinking of Emerald Hollow right now?*

"And my mother? What did she do?" Holly asked, trying to refocus. Of course, she'd spent time with her parents growing up, but most of her work days had consisted of doing studies with her elf teachers or working on experiments on her own.

"Oh, she had all kinds of hobbies. She liked to work on things that would improve the North Pole. She designed the current Dream packaging system. Added the ice rink for the younger elves." Clementine waved her finger in the air as if she were checking items off a list. "Developed a new lighting system in the forest to connect the North Post power between the elf homes. All kinds of things. She stayed very busy, your mother."

Holly remembered her mother's inventive mind. Maybe that was where her scientific inclination had come from. *Why haven't I ever tried to do North Pole improvement projects? Because I've never had the time for that.* She was always too busy chasing Cheer.

"Well, then, thank you, Clementine," Holly said, resting her hands in her coat pockets. She could do projects. *But what needs to be done? I'll take a survey. Find out from the elves what's needed around here and go from there.*

She smiled, glad to have a purpose and feeling the same compelling force she felt when chasing Cheer. It was time for Holly to learn the ins and outs of the North Pole.

Chapter Seventeen

Ash hung up from a call with the Hallmark rep and scratched at his stubble a little too forcefully. Everything was in place for the Christmas faire. He had hyped up the town pretty heavily in their application and needed to deliver.

He ran through his mental checklist. The vineyard deal needed to be tied up, and he had to figure out all the logistics for the Christmas faire, monitor the daily operations at the Emerald House, and make plans with the chamber of commerce to revitalize the empty buildings on Main Street.

He glanced at the picture of his family on the desk, which had been taken when he was eight years old, and he and his parents had gone to cut down a Christmas tree for the house. If it weren't for that picture, he wasn't sure he would remember all the details of his mother's smile. But there she was, frozen in time, laughing as if she had no plans to leave.

His dad's theory was that she'd gone because the town was just too small for her, and she had bigger dreams. That idea still bothered Ash. *Why couldn't she see the potential this town had?* With enough effort, it could be a destination, not just a detour from the interstate. Ash was determined to make it happen.

His cell phone rang, and he answered the call with a smile.

"Hey, Sof. Everything okay? Why are you calling on your day off?"

"Did you see the article in the *Oregonian* about the fall festival?"

He could practically hear the squeal she was struggling to suppress. His heart rate kicked up, and he switched over to his phone's search engine. A few clicks later, he saw the article.

"They raved about it. Said it was like something out of a fall fairy tale and that Emerald Hollow might be on its way to becoming the state's premiere holiday festival destination." She finally let out the squeal, and Ash grinned.

"This is incredible." He continued to skim the article.

"I wish we could send the link to Holly as a thank you. You don't have her contact information, do you?"

His heart skipped at her name, and not for the first time since she'd left, her vibrant smile jumped into his mind immediately. He'd checked the registration records after she checked out, but oddly, there was no address or phone number in the system. "I don't."

"Too bad. Well, she's planning to come back for the Christmas faire, right? We can thank her then."

"Yeah, that's what she said. I owe her big time. I still don't know how she did all that. It was like… magic." Ash glanced out the window and saw a massive eagle soaring over the treetops. He walked over to the window to watch it. The large bird's wings stretched wide, sailing seemingly without effort.

Sofia snorted. "More like extremely hard work. Holly has some badass skills. You should talk to Hallmark about hiring her as their set coordinator. How'd that meeting go, by the way?"

Ash pulled his eyes from the eagle and thoughts of magic, struggling to focus on business. "Everything's set up. They're sending their rep, who will take pictures and explore all parts of the Christmas faire then take off. Some kind of council will vote on the entries."

"Wow. It's nerve-racking but exciting too. What do you need help with? I can start spreading the word."

"I've got things under control for now," Ash replied, though the to-do list in his brain was growing longer by the second.

"You don't have to handle all this yourself. It's not possible. Besides, the Christmas faire is for and from the whole town, Ash, not just you."

"I know. I know. It's just better if I keep a handle on the logistics for now. I'll let you know when I have some projects to go around."

"You'd better. Now, go get some sleep. I feel like you've been working nonstop these days."

"I'm fine, Sof. See you tomorrow."

"*Adios.*"

He hung up the phone and glanced out the window again, but the eagle was gone.

Chapter Eighteen

Weeks passed, and the Advent season was in full swing, with Christmas less than two weeks away, and the elves were working with perfect efficiency. Holly wasted no time collecting information from them and putting it into action. She had spent hours each day in the studios, studying the elves as they worked on the delicate liquid-like orbs containing Dreams and finding out what, if anything, she could do to help improve their work lives.

The elf schools needed new seating cushions, and Holly had commissioned them. Some of the studios could benefit from modernized conveyor belt systems, and Holly approved the upgrades. Auryn, Holly's young elf assistant, had stepped in to help whenever she needed him, and she'd made sure that jingle pops were plentiful for him and his sister.

In the meantime, Holly had taken a quick trip to Costa Rica, soaking up Cheer from locals and tourists alike. She had been able to gather Cheer much more quickly than on her last trip there, and negative emotions still weren't affecting her meter. Her watch hadn't vibrated incessantly like it had so many times in Emerald Hollow, but there was no denying that gathering Cheer was easier.

Holly was mostly happy with the theory that many of the elves seemed to have adopted—her Cheer had fully matured, and she could operate as her father had. They could be right, but the question still lingered in Holly's mind, nagging at the corners of her thoughts when she wasn't fully immersed in a project. Lumi had told her she needed to return to Emerald Hollow. She'd promised Ash and Sofia she'd help with the Christmas faire. And something else was drawing her back as well, something she couldn't explain.

When Holly emerged from her home on a sparkling December morning, Clementine called, "Good morning, Ms. Claus. We're preparing the sleigh for your return to Emerald Hollow, as requested." She was suppressing a grin, and it took Holly a moment to pick up on her excitement.

"What is it, Clementine?" Holly looked around in confusion. Snow swirled gently across the ground. Merriment Square was nearly empty, which was odd.

"Come with me."

Holly followed her through Merriment Square to the large Jingle Bell Hall, where elves held events and celebrations.

The doors swung open, and hundreds of elves yelled, "Surprise!"

Holly's jaw dropped. The hall was crammed full of elves, Kringles and Keyblers alike, many of whom she recognized as having worked alongside the last few weeks.

"They wanted to wish you well on your last Cheer cycle before Christmas," Clementine explained, and Holly turned from surprised to touched.

"We've prepared all your favorites for breakfast." A young Keybler elf wearing a tall baker's hat ran up to Holly excitedly. The hat slipped down over his eyes, but his pointed ears still poked out the sides.

Holly felt a well of gratitude for her elf friends, warmth expanding in her chest. She followed a sea of elves as they guided her to a seat of honor, and the baker elves brought food to Holly and all the other elves in the hall.

Together, they dined on one of the best meals Holly had ever tasted. Some of the elves had set up instruments in the corner, and a Kringle band played Christmas music while the others ate and chatted happily. For a moment, Holly was reminded of listening to music with Sofia in the café at the Emerald House. The feeling of contentment she'd experienced in both situations was similar.

By the time Holly was seated in her sleigh that afternoon, she was refreshed and ready to investigate Emerald Hollow again. She needed to experience for herself whatever Lumi Kringle had been hesitant to explain.

Her reindeer crew consisted of Dasher, Gale, Ivy, and Clove again. The four had been given a break when she went to Costa Rica, but Ivy and Clove had apparently begged to return to Emerald Hollow, as they'd grown fond of the forest there, and Dasher and Gale had insisted on going to supervise them again. Auryn had assured her the other reindeer didn't mind staying home for another cycle. They were busy preparing for the Reindeer Games, which occurred each year during evergreen season.

Clementine waved goodbye as Holly's sleigh rose from the snowy field near the stables, and Holly took one last look at the North Post. Its light shone brightly over Merriment Square, powering all of the North Pole. Holly's hair whirled softly in the wind. Maybe her time as a successful Claus had finally arrived. Perhaps life was going to be easy from then on. The golden sleigh slipped away into the evening sky.

Chapter Nineteen

The vibrant autumn leaves that had clung to the trees when Holly previously visited Emerald Hollow were piled on the ground in brown-and-gray clumps. The air was colder, too, though it didn't bother her. Winter had clearly fallen on the Oregon town, and again, Holly had the odd sensation that she felt at home there, despite the absence of snow.

She was both nervous and excited to see Sofia and Ash, wondering whether they would be glad to see her again or if they'd gotten back to their normal small-town routines, which didn't involve her. Maybe they had forgotten they'd invited her back. It was unlike her to worry about what humans thought of her, and she frowned before spotting the Emerald House as she rounded the corner. The sight of it being lit brightly from within instantly calmed her.

Holly approached the reception desk and asked to check into the same suite she had before. She had come back a little earlier than planned, but the worker easily obliged, Holly's magic taking care of the details.

Surveying the cozy lobby, she noticed the fall decorations had been replaced by red, green, silver, and gold holiday baubles, and garlands of greenery were draped perfectly over counters, fireplaces, and windowsills. With all the festiveness in the building, Holly was surprised not to see a Christmas tree.

"Holly!"

She turned to see Sofia emerge from the restaurant. She was wearing a festive apron, and her hair was piled high in loose curls.

"You came back!" she exclaimed, pulling Holly in for a hug.

"As promised." Holly returned the embrace with a smile.

Sofia studied her, and Holly looked down at her own outfit, confused. She was wearing a fitted red coat over dark jeans and black snow boots, and her hair was down in simple waves.

"You look gorgeous. Does Ash know you're here?" Sofia asked, tugging Holly aside as a small family stepped up to the front desk to check in.

"I don't think so. I just arrived." Holly looked around the lobby again. Her pulse had kicked up a bit at Ash's name, but she changed the subject. "It looks like the Emerald House is all ready for the holidays."

"Oh yeah. Ash likes us to get everything out the first week in November. Usually, the tree is up before now, too, but he's been so busy, and he insists on using a real one. We would have been glad to have you while we were decorating," Sofia teased. "The town talked of the fall festival decor for days afterward. A local journalist's photos of the festival went viral, and we've already started to receive reservations at the Emerald House for next year's festival. The exposure also seems to be leading to an increase in reservations for the Christmas faire. Of course, all this has Ash running around at a hundred miles an hour to prepare for the influx of visitors."

"Well, I'm here now, and I hope I can help." Holly felt a prickle of concern. Ash could obviously handle himself, but it seemed he tended to take on too much. She had witnessed that kind of unchecked willingness to please in humans before, and its effect on Cheer was strongly negative. She didn't want that for Ash.

"And thank goodness. With the predicted increase in crowds, expectations are high. Plus, there's the Hallmark contest. It's putting us all a little on edge, especially Ash. He will be relieved to have the extra help."

At that moment, a familiar black-and-white dog appeared at Holly's side and rubbed his head against her thigh, licking her hand lovingly.

"Comet!" Holly exclaimed, excited to see the dog again. She squatted to give him a nice scratch behind his ears, and his tail swished back and forth.

"His ears must have been burning," Sofia said.

Holly knew before she looked up that Ash had joined them. Her watch was vibrating nonstop. She stood to see he was wearing jeans and a flannel button-up shirt in deep green. His skin was less tanned than when Holly had last seen him, but his dark hair and bright smile were just as she remembered. He still had a five-o'clock shadow.

"You're back!" Ash said in his usual welcoming tone.

His demeanor calmed Holly, and she forgot that she had ever felt nervous about seeing him and Sofia. He could make anyone feel comfortable, and she realized it was his own kind of magic. The thought made her smile.

"And ready to get to work. What do you need for the Christmas faire?"

Ash laughed and rapped a knuckle casually on the reception desk. "That can wait until tomorrow at least. You're a guest here. Were you planning to have dinner here at the restaurant?"

"Oh, I hadn't thought about it yet. But yes, most likely. I just need to drop off my bag in my room first." Holly clutched the straps on her backpack. She'd nearly forgotten it was there.

"Sof, when are you off?" he asked then addressed Holly. "Maybe the two of us could join you. We have a special tradition I'd like to introduce you to."

"You read my mind," Sofia said. "My shift ends in thirty."

"Perfect. Does that work, Holly? Get settled in, and meet us back here in the lobby in half an hour?" Ash paused to fist-bump a young man who walked by and said hello.

"Sure. See you in half an hour." Holly gave Comet one last scratch behind the ears then retreated down the hallway to her small suite. She was delighted to find that it, too, had been decorated with lights and greenery for the winter season.

She quickly unpacked her few belongings then sat on the bed to study her Cheer meter. It had been buzzing wildly as she'd met with Sofia and Ash in the lobby, and she realized she was going to have to focus on tuning it out during the extended moments of charging. If her watch was going to act like that the entire time she was in Emerald Hollow, she would have to let the sensation become a part of her, which was the opposite of what she was accustomed to doing. All her adult life, Holly had to pay close attention to the Cheer meter and be prepared to move at any sign of a change in frequency.

If she didn't have to constantly anticipate running from negative emotions, perhaps she could focus on letting the watch be a part of her that complemented her but didn't control her. The idea felt foreign, and she was still hesitant to trust it. Lumi Kringle said she had to experience something. *But what? And what will happen if I don't experience it?*

$$Chapter\ Twenty$$

Holly emerged in the lobby and turned toward the restaurant, but Ash called her name and held open the front door instead.

She raised her eyebrows at him, confused. "We're not eating here?" she asked, slightly disappointed. The food at Emerald House was some of the best she'd ever had outside the North Pole.

"Not inside, at least." Ash's eyes were sparkling, and Sofia grinned as she grabbed her coat to join them.

Then Holly noticed a large picnic basket in Ash's hands and a silver thermos in Sofia's. They walked down a path around the side of the building and into the back garden. The white gazebo had soft white light on all sides. Holly gasped when she saw it. It reminded her so much of the one in Merriment Square when it was decorated that way.

Ash smiled at her expression.

"We like to eat out here every now and then," Sofia explained as the three of them climbed the few steps into the gazebo. It had been draped with garlands of greenery that matched those inside.

Ash pulled a brown tablecloth from the picnic basket and spread it over the table.

"The food's all here. I remembered what you liked last time and asked the cooks to make it. I hope that's okay," Sofia said.

Holly nodded in disbelief. *Sofia remembered my favorite dinner order?*

The three of them took their seats, and Ash and Sofia worked together seamlessly to set up plates, mugs, silverware, paper takeout containers, then all the food and toppings.

"Sofia said you like the hot chocolate here." Ash poured some from the carafe into a white mug he had pulled from the basket. Steam flowed out with the liquid and quickly dissipated in the chilly air.

"It's the second-best hot cocoa I've ever had," Holly admitted then took a sip and closed her eyes in delight.

"Second best?" Ash laughed and looked from Sofia to Holly. "Where do we find the best? I might need to try it and take notes."

"At the—back home," Holly said. She had years of practice in avoiding talking about the North Pole but was so comfortable with Ash and Sofia that she was slipping.

"In Canada?" Ash asked. "Putting us Americans to shame, are they?"

"I have to admit you're giving us a run for our money. And honestly, I have extremely high standards for hot cocoa. That I keep ordering yours should tell you how good I think it is." Holly took another sip before opening one of the takeout containers and spooning some of the food onto her plate.

"It's an old Hayes family recipe," Sofia said, buttering a piece of toast. "They won't share it with anyone and say there's a secret ingredient."

"Nutmeg," Holly said nonchalantly.

Ash's eyes widened with surprise. "That's an interesting guess," he said slowly, though his expression was suspicious.

Holly simply shrugged and twirled her pasta on her fork. She and Ash stared at each other for several moments. The flecks of gold in Ash's eyes seemed to dance in amusement or maybe curiosity. Goose bumps that had nothing to do with the winter air slid over Holly's arms.

Sofia looked between the two and cleared her throat. "So, Holly. We're glad to have you back. Is everything well back home?"

Holly finally finished spooling her pasta and held it just above her plate. "Oh yes. I took a little time off work to take care of some things around town. It was a lot of fun, actually." She smiled as she remembered her going-away breakfast with the elves.

"You took a vacation to take care of things around town?" Sofia asked, raising her eyebrows. "Ugh, you sound like Ash."

"Somebody's gotta do it," Ash said jovially then took a large bite of his burger. After he'd swallowed, he changed the subject. "What are you up to tomorrow?"

"No specific plans. I was going to explore the town a little more. And of course whatever you need to get ready for the Christmas faire. I'm here to help." She finally took the bite of her pasta.

"Careful," Sofia said. "With your results from the fall festival, we may ask you to do all the decorating again."

Ash shook his head at Sofia, and Holly wasn't sure what discreet conversation he was trying to have with her.

"I'm kidding, of course," Sofia added.

"What do you need done?" The decorating had been fun, and it would be more of a nice exercise than a burden for her to take that on again.

"Well, it's kind of a big ask, so feel free to say no, but the float that usually pulls Mr. and Mrs. Claus in the parade is kind of falling apart. It needs to be repainted. I'm planning to do it—"

"He's planning to do everything himself, and that's impossible." Sofia rolled her eyes.

"I can paint," Holly said confidently.

"Are you sure? I just need a little assistance. You won't have to do much."

"Show me where all the materials are tomorrow." Holly buttered a roll. "Seriously, I need to pay you back for this incredible dinner."

"All your meals are on the house this week, if you help with painting. That's my least-favorite task."

"I will hand-make all her meals myself, if it means I don't have to paint," Sofia added. "But that's enough work talk. Holly, are you seeing anyone?"

The question was so sudden that both Holly and Ash jerked their heads around in surprise.

"Seeing anyone?" Holly was generally good at interpreting expressions in cultures all over the world, but sometimes they were a little vague, and she wanted to make sure she had it right. It had come out of nowhere.

"Yeah, like, are you dating anyone? Either seriously or casually?" Sofia popped a berry from her fruit salad into her mouth. She eyed Ash delightedly, who was looking uncomfortable for once, and seemed to be trying to suppress a grin.

"Oh. No," Holly said. "I don't have time for that. Work takes most of my focus."

"I see. I'm surrounded by workaholics." Sofia let out a disappointed sigh.

"What about you?" Holly asked. "Are *you* seeing anyone?"

Ash grinned, and Sofia grimaced.

"No, but not for lack of desire. This town's just too small for all that. The only decent single guy left is Ash, and no offense, but he's just a little too young and idealistic for me."

Ash tossed a roll at Sofia, and Holly grinned, though her mind was swirling. Sofia couldn't be more than a few years older than Ash.

"What about a tourist?" she asked, watching the two of them in amusement. "You probably meet lots of people at the restaurant."

"That's true, but I've met more toads than princes, I'm afraid." Sofia pursed her lips. "But enough about me. Why don't we discuss why the town's most eligible bachelor is still single?"

Ash narrowed his eyes at her. The conversation had been like tossing a beach ball of embarrassment around the table, landing on one person for a moment, to everyone else's delight, then being tossed away by the holder with relief.

Holly perked up a little, wanting to hear the answer.

Ash cleared his throat. "Haven't dated the right woman yet. Now that we've got that out of the way, what do we want for dessert?"

The rest of the evening passed with pleasant small talk. Holly burst into laughter more than once as Sofia told tales at Ash's expense. To his credit, he never looked more than mildly embarrassed. He laughed along, occasionally interjecting to half-heartedly defend himself. Holly's watch vibrated wildly throughout their dinner and warmed her wrist. She tucked her hand into her coat pocket after they finished eating.

When dessert wound down, the three of them loaded their dinner containers and dishes into the picnic basket, and Ash carried it as they walked back to the Emerald House.

Holly glanced toward the woods and spotted Ivy watching them through trees, just as the reindeer had the first evening Holly and Ash had walked down the forest path together.

"Didn't that look like a fawn?" Ash asked, frowning. "That's odd. It's not their season. Must have been something else." He shook his head and continued to walk up the path. Meanwhile, Holly stood stock-still, unable to breathe. She glanced in Ivy's direction again, but the reindeer had disappeared into the forest.

Chapter Twenty-One

Holly woke up early the next morning and went outside to check on the reindeer. She'd snuck a roll into her coat pocket during the gazebo dinner, and she held out her hand to give each of them a piece. Ivy shook leaves off the top of her head as she emerged from the forest to greet Holly and claim her treat. Clove licked her lips in satisfaction.

Holly eyed Ivy suspiciously. "What were you doing last night?" Holly had settled down since the initial shock of Ash's seeing the reindeer, but it still made her nervous. Emerald Hollow was full of unknowns, and the frustration of not having an explanation was grating on her.

Ivy looked up at her with her big eyes. Holly let out a sigh. The reindeer weren't to blame. As far as they knew, humans couldn't see them. They weren't used to having to work to stay hidden.

"I know," Holly said, petting the young reindeer's head. "It's okay. Things are just a little strange around here. I think the four of you should try to stay hidden in the forest during the daytime, just in case."

She let out a breath and decided to change the subject.

"Painting Santa's sleigh is on the agenda today. Not ours," she added quickly when Dasher looked toward the golden sleigh stashed deeper in the woods. Though the sleigh was supposed to be invisible to anyone's eyes but hers, after Ash's comment, she wasn't certain about anything. She'd covered it with a few branches that morning for good measure. "It's for Emerald Hollow's holiday parade."

Holly chatted with the reindeer for a few more minutes, soaking up the sunrise. The reindeer seemed content to nestle their heads against Holly's palm. It still felt strange to be still, not constantly dashing from place to place to capture Cheer or to avoid losing it. *Is this something that could continue if I unlock the secret of the Cheer at Emerald Hollow? Is that something I would even want?*

A low whistle snapped her out of her thoughts, and she turned to see Comet loping toward her. "Hello, puppy," she said, walking toward him. She threw a quick look over her shoulder and was relieved to see the reindeer dashing into the woods.

Once Comet reached her, he rubbed his head against Holly's hand eagerly. A few moments later, Ash emerged from around the corner.

"There you are!" he called to Comet, who didn't even glance up from his love session with Holly. Ash smiled when he saw her. "He usually comes immediately when I whistle. Apparently, he likes you more than me."

"Maybe he smells the re—the roll I was just eating."

"You're out here early. What time do you want to get started on the sleigh? I can take you over and get you set up whenever you're ready. Should we grab some coffee to go?" Ash was talking in that overflowing way he had a habit of, all of his questions coming out one after another.

"Oh, I don't drink coffee. But I'd love a hot cocoa," Holly said, and Ash raised his eyebrows.

"How do you survive without caffeine?" He looked at her as if she were a living miracle.

"Too much of it makes me feel weird," Holly replied, thinking how overstimulated she typically was from the signals of all the emotions around her. She'd added caffeine on top of that in the past, and it had been a disaster. She wrinkled her nose at the thought.

Ash put his hands up in a show of surrender. "All right. All right. Hot chocolate, it is. And three espresso shots in a mocha for me." He rubbed his hands together.

Holly wondered if that explained his seemingly endless energy and enthusiasm.

"Aren't you cold? Do you want my jacket?"

She was wearing a thin brown sweater and jeans, while he was bundled up in a Carhartt jacket. Holly hadn't expected to see anyone that morning, so she hadn't taken her usual care to dress appropriately for the weather.

"I'll grab my coat when we go inside," she said quickly.

Once they were inside, she went to her room to gather her jacket, beanie, and scarf while Ash ordered their drinks from the café.

Her watch was humming pleasantly, and she checked to confirm the Cheer meter was already at capacity for the cycle. Unlike when she'd come in the fall, she wasn't in a rush to return to the North Pole and discharge it. Something about the Cheer in Emerald Hollow had led to the brightest light the North Post had given off in years, and she had to figure out why.

Holly almost felt like she could hear Lumi Kringle whispering in her ear, telling her to *experience*. She decided that the best course of action was to simply go with the flow in Emerald Hollow, against everything she knew about gathering Cheer. If an opportunity was presented to her, she would take it. She would live like a resident and see where that got her. And at the moment, that meant painting a sleigh.

~

Ten minutes later, Holly and Ash were in a small workshop on the Emerald House property, situated between the main building and the woods. The workshop was laden with scraps of wood, metal, boxes, tools, and old paint.

"We do lots of projects for the house and the town activities out here," Ash said, reading Holly's thoughts.

"Is the sleigh in here too?" Holly peered around the piles, searching for anything that looked like a sleigh and not seeing anything.

"That and all the other float supplies are behind that wall there." Ash pointed at a tall wood wall that covered half the space.

He walked toward it, and Holly followed. Her eyes immediately landed on a dilapidated wooden sleigh in the middle of the makeshift room. The red wood on every panel was chipped.

"It got left outside for a few days after the parade last year by accident." Ash looked a little guilty, and he scratched the back of his neck. "We got a bunch of snow during that time, and the paint didn't hold up too well."

Holly nodded, glancing at the cans of paint and boxes of decorative supplies. The building must be where Ash stored all the seasonal decor that didn't fit in the storage room inside the hotel.

"We load up the sleigh on that flatbed trailer when it's time for the parade." He gestured through a window in the back of the workshop to a trailer parked outside.

"Do you decorate the trailer too?" Holly was taking in everything around her, her brain doing inventory automatically.

"Not usually. No time," Ash said reluctantly then let out a breath like a low whistle. "I'd meant to have the sleigh sanded already but haven't gotten around to it yet. I'll get that done today so you can start painting tomorrow." He waved his hand toward what Holly assumed was a sanding device. "But in the meantime, you can see what supplies we have here and let me know if there's anything else you'll need."

Holly nodded and began to sift through the boxes while Ash put on safety glasses and plugged in the power tool. From the corner of her eye, Holly spotted some large conical shapes wrapped in glittery garland in the other corner of the room. Things were piled in disarray, so it was hard to tell, but it looked like there were tons of them.

"What are those for?" she asked.

Ash stood up from plugging in his equipment and smiled. "Those are for the holiday maze. With the Hallmark rep coming out this year, and since we're in the running for Best Small-Town Christmas Faire, some of us on the council had the idea to build a large holiday maze in the clearing where we had the fall festival. The walls of the maze are going to be made mostly from those trees there. People can enjoy the maze and Christmas village in addition to the parade and tree lighting." His face lit up as he explained, so Holly knew it wasn't just something he did as part of his job or to help his community. He was invested.

"That sounds really fun." The elves would enjoy a holiday maze.

"We've had various volunteers working on those trees for months. It was cheaper to make them and decorate them ourselves than to order in bulk. Most of the supplies have been donated by local businesses."

"I'm sure it's going to look spectacular," Holly said.

Ash shook his head and laughed. "I'll settle for functional this first year. But I'll admit that with the Hallmark rep coming out, the pressure is on. We have to put on our best display ever."

"We'd better get to work, then."

Chapter Twenty-Two

Ash gave Holly a pair of disposable earplugs then settled in to work on the other side of the wood wall from where Holly was sorting through boxes. He wanted to avoid getting any spray from the sanding on her. The panels had been sanded before, and he wasn't sure how many more seasons they'd be able to eke out of the sleigh before needing to build a new one.

The hours passed quickly as he worked, his mind jumping rapidly between the various tasks he needed to do. He had vendors to confirm, things to finalize with his employees for the Emerald House booth—all the normal, day-to-day operations at the house, which were ballooning with the influx of visitors at the restaurant plus all the dealings with the vineyard and the orchard.

They'd been impressed with the sales at the fall festival, but they were still dragging their heels on an exclusive. The Christmas faire was a way bigger draw, and Hallmark was in the mix. If every-thing went well, he had a feeling they could finally get an exclusive deal going on some of the vineyard's local-favorite labels.

Around noon, he took out his earplugs and turned off the sander. Flexing his hands, he stretched out the muscles in his forearms. Holly popped her head around the wall, her arms full of fresh greenery. He jumped a little when he saw her.

"You're still here! I figured you'd take inventory then take off for the day." He watched as Holly stuffed the greenery into a large plastic tub and gently closed the lid.

"I've just been working on a few things for the float. Are you ready for a break?" she asked, straightening up. She'd shed her black puffer coat at some point, and she grabbed it from a nearby sawhorse.

"You read my mind. Lunch sounds great." Ash hadn't realized how famished he was until he'd stopped working. He slipped off his work gloves and tossed them onto a bench. "I've probably got a couple more hours of sanding this afternoon, but she'll be ready," Ash continued as the two of them carefully made their way out of the crowded workshop.

He tried to clear a path in front of them, worried Holly might trip on something. *When did the workshop get so disorganized?* He added the task to his mental to-do list.

They continued up the path to the Emerald House. Ash glanced out at the forest as they walked. An eerie feeling filled the air, and it was strange that it hadn't snowed yet. They normally had a few good dustings by late December, and it didn't bode well for the local agricultural industries the next summer, including the orchard and the vineyard. Holly caught his eye and smiled at him, and his shoulders relaxed.

He felt so relieved she had come back. She'd promised to return for the Christmas faire, but a small but overpowerful part of him worried he might never see her again. Women like her didn't return to places like Emerald Hollow—not yet, at least. Her presence calmed him.

At dinner in the gazebo the night before, the lights had danced in her hair, and the conversation between the three of them had flowed easily. For a short while, his never-ending to-do list had paused in his head, and he'd been fully in the moment. He wanted more of that.

Ash followed her into the house, and they were soon settled into a booth in the restaurant. The place was bustling with the lunch rush.

"Hey, Tyler. I'll take my usual," Ash told the server when he came to greet them. The young man placed a mug of coffee in front of Ash, and he inhaled deeply, nodding in thanks.

"The club sandwich and chicken noodle soup, please," Holly said.

Ash watched her as she spoke to Tyler, the light from the window highlighting her face.

"That's my favorite soup here," Tyler said to them. "She has good taste, Ash."

He was a high school student who had been working for Ash for about a year and was in the running for a big scholarship. If he got it, Ash was sure he would go off to college and eventually get a job in a larger city. Ash was happy for him but still wished people with talent like his didn't have to leave to find work.

Tyler elbowed Ash stealthily before leaving the table. Ash shook his head and suppressed a grin. Great, the staff were already starting rumors.

Ash cupped the mug of black coffee like it was the first he'd seen in weeks. The smell had him perking up already. He noticed Holly watching him then, a soft smile playing on her lips.

"What?" he asked, also smiling and unsure why.

"Don't wait for my drink to arrive. I know how you feel about coffee."

He raised his mug toward her in gratitude. "Thanks. This will get me through the next round of sanding." He took a sip of the warm liquid, everything about the sensation causing him to both relax and perk up. Some of the tension in his head slowly started to subside.

Holly looked at her watch, her brow furrowed. *Is she late for something?* He had seen her looking at it a few times before. When she saw him noticing, she tucked her hands under the table.

Tyler returned with their orders a few moments later and whispered in his ear, "Sofia wanted me to let you know that Lucas is here."

Ash sat up, the coffee suddenly feeling cold in his hands. *What is he doing here today?* The tension instantly returned.

"Everything okay?" Holly asked, studying him. He tried to smooth his facial expression and took another sip of his coffee.

"Yeah. We just have an unexpected guest." He nodded his thanks at Tyler, who left them with their lunch plates.

Ash flexed his hands again, still trying to work out the tension from holding the sander. "The Christmas faire is going to be here before we know it. I'm really glad we're taking care of Santa's sleigh now, at least. The chamber of commerce is having a meeting in the café tomorrow night, and most of the vendors will be there. You're welcome to join, if you feel like it. Fair warning—you may get suckered into volunteering more than you already have. I'll try to tell them you already have your hands full with the sleigh, and maybe that will keep them off you." He watched Holly's face as he spoke, hoping she wouldn't feel overwhelmed. Their little town could be a lot.

But she simply nodded and let out a delicate laugh. It sounded like music to his ears after the news about Lucas.

"Thanks for the warning. Don't worry. I won't volunteer for anything I can't handle."

She always told him she could hold her own, and from what he'd seen, she was right.

"After the miracle you worked at the fall festival, I'm not sure there's anything you can't handle."

They picked up their sandwiches then and began to eat, with Ash occasionally interjecting to say hello to someone walking through the restaurant. As old friends and acquaintances walked by, he found himself wanting to introduce Holly to each of them. Once he realized he'd introduced her to three people during the half hour they'd sat there, he decided he might need to take it easy.

"People are so friendly here," Holly mused. "It reminds me of home." She glanced out the window, which was covered in frost despite the lack of snow. It seemed her thoughts drifted for a moment, and he assumed she must be thinking of Canada. He had a feeling he would love her home too. *How magical does a place have to be to produce a woman like this?*

"Emerald Hollow has that effect on people." He thought of all the good people who were part of his life. Then he thought of the one who wasn't. "Though not everyone is taken by its charms." He quickly stood and bussed their table before Holly could inquire about what he'd meant. *Why did I share that last part?* It seemed like his brain had no filter around her.

He remembered that Sofia had told him she'd shared with Holly the fact that his mom had left when he was young. She'd felt bad about sharing his private information and said the words had just flowed out of her unexpectedly. He didn't blame her. He'd trusted Holly immediately, as well. He collected himself as he carried away their dishes then returned to the table.

"I'm heading back to the workshop to finish sanding. If you want, I can call you when I'm done, and you can get started with the painting whenever you'd like. Did you determine whether there are any other materials you need? I can send someone to the hardware store." His mind was sparking on all cylinders again, fueled by coffee and lunch. Even as he spoke, he was scanning the restaurant and lobby, making sure there was nothing that needed tending to. *And where did Lucas wander off to?* He should see why he was there.

"It's fine, Ash. Everything I need is in the warehouse."

He smiled at her casual use of his nickname. Everyone who knew him around Emerald Hollow called him Ash, but he loved how quickly she'd adopted it.

"Great. What's your phone number? I'll text you when I'm done sanding."

He pulled out his phone, and Holly shook her head, a panicked expression flashing across her face. He wanted to ask her if she was okay, but he spotted Lucas in the café, which momentarily distracted him.

"Oh, I don't have a phone with me currently."

He turned back to Holly, and her expression was back to normal—calm, open, beautiful.

"Maybe I'll just check in at the warehouse in an hour. Or you can leave a message for me by calling the lobby. I'm just going to run an errand, then I'll be ready to start painting."

He studied her for a moment longer, still feeling like he had missed something important, but he shrugged, letting it go. If there were things she didn't want to share, he didn't want to force her. He'd just done the same when the conversation had almost veered to his mom.

"Okay, then. I'll call the lobby. See you in a bit." He gave her a soft smile then watched as she exited the house. When she was out of sight, he took a deep breath and entered the café.

"Hey, Luc." He kept his tone even and casual. Lucas didn't intimidate him, but their history was murky. And Lucas's visits were never for social calls, at least not anymore. "What can I do for you today?"

Lucas had been his friend as a child. He was a couple of inches taller than Ash, but Ash always felt that their eyes were level with one another. Lucas's beard had grown out a bit since he'd seen him last, and the dark hair was a strong contrast to his pale skin. He sensed that something else was different, too, but he couldn't quite put his finger on it.

"Ash." Lucas nodded at him, his voice curt. "Just came for a cup of coffee. That's still allowed, right?"

"Of course," Ash replied, though he didn't trust the explanation.

"So that's it. Just here for a cup of joe."

Ash tried not to roll his eyes. He didn't have time for Lucas's theatrics.

"All right, then, man. See you later." He turned to go.

Lucas gripped his arm. "Wait. You holdin' up today? I know it's the anniversary of—"

Ash took a step back, shaking his arm free discreetly. *So he came here to remind me of Mom?* He'd actually forgotten what day it was. The anniversary explained why she had been on his mind when he was talking to Holly. But Lucas didn't care how Ash was doing. They had severed ties years ago.

"Whoa," Lucas said, putting his hands up dramatically in surrender. "Didn't mean anything by it."

Ash thought he smelled alcohol on his breath. It was barely one o'clock in the afternoon. Concern creased his forehead, but he shook it off. Lucas had come to cause a scene, and he wouldn't give it to him.

"See you later," he said before he could change his mind.

His childhood friend pulled a wry smile, and Ash turned away, anxiety rippling down his back. He needed to get outside and back to work.

Chapter Twenty-Three

Holly's previous interactions with cell phones had been nebulous. She only ever saw them from the outside. Humans stared at them all the time. Sometimes, they brought joy and laughter. Other times, they brought stress and anxiety.

Her father had known what it was like to collect Cheer before the advent of cell phones, and she always wondered if people's emotions used to hold steady for longer in those days. They didn't have constant sources of information to interrupt whatever they were trying to do.

From Holly's point of view, cell phones made it much harder for humans to be in the moment. But she was sure they had their uses, and on that chilly winter day in Emerald Hollow, she found herself in need of one.

The clerk in the cell phone store was trying to be helpful, but Holly hadn't given her much to work with. They needed some information that she couldn't provide: a home address and a credit card.

"Sorry. We can't set up a phone plan without those." The clerk looked at Holly apologetically. She seemed surprised, and Holly imagined it was a reaction to meeting someone Holly's age who didn't know how cell phone plans worked.

"Oh. Well, I don't really need a plan. Just a phone with some... What do you call them? Minutes. I just need to be able to make calls and texts," Holly said, desperately trying to find a work-around. The conversation with Ash in the diner had shaken her. Based on what she knew of adult humans in America, not having a cell number was a red flag.

If she was going to stay and unlock the secrets of Emerald Hollow's Cheer, she needed to be able to fit in. She felt like she'd been doing that pretty well until the moment in the diner and hoped Ash hadn't noticed her panic. She refocused on the clerk, who was still looking perplexed. *Why isn't my magic helping to get around the contract rules?*

Then the clerk smiled as if she had an idea and walked over to a display of pay-per-minute phones. "We do have these. You can pay a certain amount up front then load more money onto it when you need it. They're kind of old school, though. No data, no apps. But you can call and text."

Ah, there was her opening. Whether it was magic or just the store's policies, she would be able to get a cell phone. "Perfect!"

"Let's get you set up."

Five minutes later, Holly was returning to the Emerald House with a basic flip phone that was likely designed for preteens. Apparently, her magic hadn't thought she needed a smartphone. But for the first time in her life, she had a phone number and someone to give it to. Holly smiled as she continued up the frosty sidewalk to the Emerald House, the workshop, and Ash.

THE RECEPTIONIST IN THE LOBBY NOTIFIED HOLLY THAT Ash had called. He'd finished the sanding and needed to run a few errands, but she was welcome to go to the workshop whenever she was ready. "He left it unlocked and said feel free to let yourself in. He just asked that you lock the padlock when you leave. Oh, and he said to tell you he's sorry he missed you." The receptionist's voice was neutral, but Holly thought she saw a slight pull at the side of his mouth.

"Okay. Thanks. I'll head down there now." Holly tried not to read into the clerk's expression. She contemplated it as she walked. It seemed like most of the Emerald House staff were in on some kind of private amusement she didn't understand.

The workshop was unlocked, as promised. She left the padlock dangling in the latch as she slipped inside then closed the door behind her. The sleigh looked completely different from when she'd first seen it. The chipped paint had all been cleared away, leaving a smooth, pale wood surface behind. Holly opened up the first can of paint, grabbed a roller, and prepared to spend the rest of the afternoon working on the sleigh.

A few minutes into her work, she looked around and noticed an old radio on the workbench. She plugged it in, and it immediately started playing a local radio station. The current song was a classic Christmas hit, and Holly smiled. *Perfect.* She got back to work.

Holly was completely in the zone while decorating, and the afternoon flew by. She could feel her magic working, assisting in the manual labor. Occasionally, her mind drifted to Ash, and she wondered what errands he was taking care of.

After a few hours of work, Holly neatly packed up the materials she'd been using, arranging them in such a way that they were perfectly prepped for the next day's work. She was on track to have the sleigh and float completed by the end of the day.

Ash didn't know she would be decorating the float too, and she got a little thrill at the idea of surprising him. His reaction to the fall-festival decor had been priceless. She flicked off the radio, slipped out of the workshop, then locked the padlock. She was still humming a Christmas tune as she walked back to the Emerald House.

Chapter Twenty-Four

Sofia was working in the restaurant when Holly returned. She slid into the booth that had somehow become her favorite, and Sofia brought her a hot chocolate before she had to ask.

"How's it going out there? I can't believe you agreed to paint the sleigh. Props to you, because I already wormed my way out of helping with that one a while back." Sofia grinned and tucked a loose curl behind her ear.

"It's going well. I should have it done tomorrow. Ash said there's a chamber of commerce meeting tomorrow night. Are you attending?"

Sofia rolled her eyes. "He looped you into that, too, did he? Well, okay, yes. I'm going. I'm actually a vendor at the Christmas faire. I sell jewelry."

"You make jewelry?" Holly asked, delighted. If Sofia was a maker, she had that in common with the elves, especially the Keyblers. No wonder Holly liked her so much. "I'd love to see your work."

Sofia pointed at her ears, which were currently sporting studs shaped like gingerbread men. They had buttons and all. Holly remembered the guitars she'd seen dangling from Holly's ears in the fall.

"Wow, those look professional!"

"They're not half-bad. But I'm sure you could whip up some earrings, too, if you wanted, Miss Crafty." Sofia's mouth twitched.

Holly grinned. It was so easy being around Sofia. She was like an old friend Holly had never had.

Sofia returned to the kitchen, and Holly sipped her hot chocolate as she watched the goings-on around her, a feeling of something like contentment slipping around her like a warm coat.

HOLLY HUNG OUT IN THE CAFÉ BY HERSELF FOR THE rest of the evening. The fireplace was warm, soft holiday music was playing, and people rotated to and from the bar, ordering glasses of wine or appetizers. Holly sat where she had a view of the lobby and partially into the restaurant. She had a book open on her lap to appear occupied, but mostly, she was just people watching. Everyone seemed so happy at the Emerald House. She subconsciously checked her watch a few times, but the gauge was as steady as ever, and her habit of checking was becoming way less frequent.

Occasionally, Holly glanced around the lobby, hoping to see Ash pass by. Her stomach sank a little in disappointment as the clock struck nine, and she hadn't seen him at all. She popped her head into the restaurant and said goodbye to Sofia then quickly walked down the trail to see her reindeer one more time before going to bed.

"This is all very strange, Dasher," Holly said, sneaking them their final treat for the night. "I used to be quite content with just being around humans to collect Cheer. Now, I'm actually enjoying spending time with them, and I'm sad when they're not around. I don't know how to feel about it."

Dasher nuzzled her hand in response. Clove and Ivy were rolling on their backs in happy amusement, while Gale glared at them in disapproval.

"It seems we're all enjoying this little town." Holly eyed the forest, where the reindeer had spent the day exploring. "What do you think, Dash? We don't usually stay in one place so long. Are you eager to get back to our nomadic lifestyle?" Holly watched his eyes, but Dasher just nuzzled her hand again.

She sighed. "I just need answers. How is the Cheer different? And why here? Why Emerald Hollow? Why Ash?" She leaned her head against Dasher's and stared up at the stars.

Ash showed up at the restaurant a few minutes before ten that night to help Sofia close up the kitchen. They liked to do it together at least once a week, when Sofia was on the closing shift.

They worked seamlessly, each taking the chores the other didn't like. They'd bonded a lot over the years. There was nothing like talking and joking about small-town problems while mopping the floor together to strengthen a friendship.

"What were you up to today? I barely saw you," Sofia said as she finished counting the money in the cash register.

"I had to run out to the vineyard for a meeting," Ash explained.

"You were out there again? What's going on over there?"

"Just business." Ash grabbed some baking trays from the drying rack and began to put them away. "Was everything okay while I was gone?"

"Yep. It was busy but otherwise fine. Holly came in for dinner then hung out in the café for a while. She's really sweet. I can't believe she worked on that sleigh all afternoon."

Ash paused, turning toward Sofia, who had begun to mop the floor. "She worked on it all afternoon? She didn't have to do that." He began grabbing dishes again. "I don't know how I'm going to repay her. I'm swamped this year, and the Christmas faire is a priority for me. I can't believe she's so willing to help with everything."

"Neither of us has ever met anyone like her, and you know it. I've seen the way you look at her." Sofia sloshed the heavy mop back into the bucket.

"Even if what you think is true, and I'm not admitting that it is," he added when her face split into a satisfied grin, "there can't be anything between us, Sof. Her life is somewhere else. She's going home after all this is over." He reached out to take the mop bucket from her. Mopping was her least favorite chore.

"Have you asked yourself why she's here? Why she has stayed this long?" Sofia released the mop without argument and picked up a towel from the countertop.

"Simple. She really loves our hot chocolate." He grinned, and Sofia snapped his thigh with the towel.

"Not everyone leaves, Ash." Her voice was soft, and Ash knew she was alluding to his mother. He didn't think she knew about the anniversary.

"Not everyone." *But some do.* He pushed hard on the bucket as he walked past her to mop the floor on the other side of the counter, keeping his head down so that she couldn't study his face.

Sofia let out a small sigh. "Chicken," she muttered before returning to wiping down the glass display counter.

Maybe I am, but chickens don't get their hearts broken by women with dreams too big for this town.

Chapter Twenty-Five

Holly woke up early the next morning, planning to spend most of the day working on the sleigh and the float. When she came out of the hallway, Ash was in the lobby. She was in the middle of slipping a scarf around her neck when she saw him, and she paused.

The early-morning light was cascading through the front window, lighting his face. As he looked down at some papers on the reception desk, his forehead creased. When he looked up, he spotted her, and his expression instantly relaxed.

"Hey! So sorry I missed you yesterday. Did everything go okay?" He came out from behind the desk, and Holly caught the faint scent of something woodsy.

"Oh yeah, the decorating's going well. I was just heading to the workshop to get started again."

Ash glanced at his watch. "I guess you're an early riser too. An employee called in sick, so I have to work the front desk today, but I'd like to treat you to dinner this evening. Come find me whenever you're hungry, okay? I'll be off at five."

Holly nodded and smiled. Her stomach had done an odd little flip at the invitation.

"I just want to thank you for all your hard work on the sleigh. I seriously don't know if it would get done without you."

He sounded so sincere, and Holly's stomach flipped again.

"Something tells me you would have. But dinner sounds great. See you tonight." She finished arranging her scarf and pushed through the front door, cold morning air that she barely felt encompassing her.

HOLLY PUT THE FINISHING TOUCHES ON THE SLEIGH, returned to her room for a shower, then went to the lobby to meet Ash. The day had gone by quickly, as she'd gotten into the zone of decorating and building again. Still, occasionally, her brain interrupted her and reminded her that Ash had invited her to dinner. He'd been careful to say it was a thank-you for all her hard work, and she tried to make herself think that was all it was to her too.

He'd seemed tense that morning, before he caught her looking, and she was worried about that. Even though her Cheer was still full for the cycle, she was starting to get invested in the lives of the humans in Emerald Hollow. None of that had to do with collecting Cheer or her research into why the Cheer there was different. The feeling unsettled her.

Lumi Kringle had told her to experience, and she was trying. Though she'd thought that would mean just going through the motions of life in Emerald Hollow, she was realizing it wasn't that simple.

Someone couldn't just be around other people all the time, getting to know them, without becoming invested in their well-being. That wasn't a typical role for a Claus, and she wasn't sure if getting so involved was the right or the wrong thing to do. All she knew was that she couldn't help herself.

Holly sighed, trying to stop her thoughts from bouncing around. There was no point lingering on it. She slipped her room key into her pocket.

The lobby was busy when she entered it. People were beginning to arrive early for the Christmas faire. Scanning the room, she wondered about the emotions of all the people in it. She blinked, startled. That used to be a daily, minute-by-minute occurrence for her, but it was becoming a rarity. Instead, her personal emotion detector mainly focused on Ash, and she didn't need the help of her Cheer meter to read him. She spotted him coming out of the restaurant and forgot about everyone else in the room. He smiled, his eyes tender when they landed on her.

"Ready?" Holly asked, slinging her small purse over her shoulder. She began to head toward the restaurant.

"Woah, not so fast." Ash gently took her elbow and guided her toward the large front doors. "While I know we have the best diner in Emerald Hollow, I think you deserve something extra special after working on that sleigh all day. How do you feel about Italian food?"

Holly thought of the many authentic meals she'd had in Italy over the years. Locals and tourists eating in Italy was usually a safe bet for gathering Cheer, especially if they were enjoying a meal with wine. "I love it."

She stepped through the door, which he was holding open, then they went to the parking lot and climbed into Ash's truck. As he walked around his side to get in, she buckled her seat belt and studied the space around her.

Holly didn't ride in vehicles often. If she needed to go somewhere beyond walking distance, she took the sleigh. The truck was clean and clutter free, and the woodsy smell that Holly sometimes caught a hint of on Ash was also subtly present. She suppressed a smile.

"This is a nice truck," she observed once Ash was inside.

"Thanks. I've had it for a couple of years now. The four-wheel drive is nice in the winter, though we haven't had any snow yet this year, which is strange." Ash deftly navigated the large truck out of the parking lot and began to travel down a street in the direction Holly had gone to explore the shops in the fall.

"Does snow help or hurt the Christmas faire?" Holly gazed out the window at the quaint buildings.

"That's a good question. I would say having snow on the ground helps because it adds to the ambiance, and that's what people are coming for. And precipitation in the winter is really important for the local ecosystem and recreation in the summer. But too much snow or a large, fresh storm can prevent people from getting here. There's only so much our single snowplow can do at once. So it's a balance we want, I guess." He turned the truck onto Main Street.

Holly nodded thoughtfully. "Balance... yes. Balance is good," she murmured, thinking of the importance of balancing the emotions in her Cheer meter.

"Here we are." Ash parked in front of a picturesque Italian restaurant nestled between two boutique stores on the main road. The front windows had been painted with blue and white snowflakes.

After they got out of the truck and entered the restaurant, the smell of basil and fresh bread hit her instantly. Ash gave his name for the reservation, though the host clearly knew who he was. If the Emerald House were a central vein, Ash would be an artery.

"Everyone knows you here," Holly said with a smile as they took their seats at a small square table in a candlelit corner. The walls were painted like an Italian hillside vineyard, making the place feel both cozy and upscale, with soft music coming from unseen speakers.

"Yeah, well, that's just how things go in this town. I was born and raised here. My dad started the Emerald House when I was a little kid, with an old partner of his. It was just the restaurant back then. When I was a teenager, we added the hotel rooms for more of a bed-and-breakfast vibe, then I added the café when I bought the place. All that has caused us to interact with a lot of people in the town over the years. The Emerald House has hosted small weddings, baby showers, birthday parties..." Ash explained all that as he glanced over the menu.

Holly hadn't touched hers because she was too intent on his words. She studied his face as he looked down at the menu. The usual openness and easiness were there, but a touch of strain was underneath it. He hid it well, but Holly could sense something there that wasn't pleasant for him.

"You bought the Emerald House?" Holly asked after sifting through all he had said and settling on one thread for a follow-up question.

Ash lifted his eyes to meet hers. "Oh, you mean from my dad? Yeah. Well, kind of. My dad and a business partner built the original restaurant together. His partner still owned a stake in it when my dad decided to retire. Or technically, the partner's son did. My dad's business partner passed away about ten years ago."

"So you had to buy out your dad's old business partner's son?" Holly was still studying Ash's face. His expression was neutral, but his fingers tightened slightly on the menu.

"We were planning to be business partners, but he didn't really believe in the Emerald House. He thought it was from a bygone era and couldn't compete with all the chain businesses being developed in nearby towns at the time. I had big plans to expand the café, and I'm still planning to build a multipurpose room in the back for larger conferences and parties. He didn't agree with any of that and wanted to sell it to corporate developers." Ash took a deep breath and closed his menu. "I didn't have much capital, obviously, since I was in my midtwenties and just getting started. So I took out a small-business loan and bought him out with that."

"I see." Holly didn't want to push too far, so she opened her menu for a quick look then stacked it on top of Ash's.

His words resonated with her. Ash had received a Dream, and that Dream involved the Emerald House. He was one of those rare ones who were willing to chase that Dream with those purposeful, everyday actions. It didn't surprise her that he and his former business partner had parted ways. His partner's Dream must have been a different one. Or worse, he might have been one of those who thought he wasn't deserving of a Dream. Holly frowned.

"You know what you're having?" Ash asked then took a drink of his water.

"Yep, the hot caprese." Holly tried to refocus on being present in the Italian restaurant. She couldn't control what humans did with their Dreams and only ensured that they received them by maintaining sufficient Cheer levels at the North Pole at all times. Beyond that, she had to allow the humans to be humans. That had always been easy before, but with Ash, it was hard to keep her distance.

"That's a good one," Ash said with a smile. "Do you want to order some wine? I'm more of a beer person myself, but wine pairs well with Enzo's food."

Holly smiled and shook her head. "No, thanks. I don't drink." She couldn't tell him that alcohol interfered with her magic, so she left it at that.

Ash nodded as if what she'd said was perfectly normal then signaled to the server that they were ready to order. A man emerged from the kitchen suddenly and told the server that he would take their table. He appeared to be in his sixties and had thick dark hair that was beginning to gray. His skin was golden, and he smiled broadly at Ash and Holly.

"Ash, hello! Welcome, welcome. And who do you have with you this evening?"

Holly picked up on his Italian accent.

"Hi, Enzo. Great seeing you. This is Holly. She's staying at the Emerald House, and she's helping us out with the Christmas faire."

"Holly, what a beautiful name. Welcome." Enzo hooked his thumbs through the front pockets of his white waist apron.

Without thinking, Holly replied in Italian, *"Piacere di conoscerla."*

Enzo's eyes widened with surprise, and he turned to Ash. "She speaks Italian! Is that why you brought her here?" He seemed pleased and turned back to Holly without waiting for a reply.

They continued a short conversation in Italian, then Enzo took their orders and returned to the kitchen.

"You speak Italian? What are the chances I'd take you here for dinner? I'm impressed, and so was Enzo." He leaned back grinning.

"He seems like a nice man," Holly said, swirling her water in her glass so that it made a gentle rippling motion inside the rim.

"He is. I've known Enzo since I was a little kid. We sometimes collaborate on catering projects. Now that he knows there's someone who speaks Italian in town, I have a feeling we'll be seeing more of him at the Emerald House. Did you learn it for work? Or is your family Italian?"

"For work. Italy's a country I visit a lot," Holly replied, purposely avoiding details. She didn't know how she would respond if Ash asked if she spoke any other languages.

"You'll have to tell me how the food here compares to the real thing, then. Enzo's parents were both born and raised in Italy, so I think it's pretty authentic, but I don't have much to compare it to."

Ash looked around the room, and Holly followed his gaze. A few other couples and small groups were seated in the one-room restaurant, but all were far enough away that they could have a conversation without hearing anyone else.

"It smells authentic." The room was giving her a pleasant feeling, and she wondered if it was relaxation, something she wasn't used to experiencing as she chased Cheer around the world, constantly on the go. For the moment, she was enjoying the slower pace.

"So, tell me more about your family," Ash prompted then took a bite of melon wrapped in prosciutto, which had been brought as an appetizer.

"Oh, well." Holly tensed, her mind working quickly. "I don't have any family in the American sense of the word. But I have a... tight-knit community. We take care of one another like family."

Holly thought she detected a hint of concern in his expression.

"You don't have any family?" He set down the prosciutto.

"Well, I did. But my parents have both passed on. I didn't have any siblings." Holly had always thought of the elves as siblings, but she couldn't explain that to Ash.

"Holly, I'm so sorry."

Ash touched her hand, causing a warm jolt like she'd experienced when he'd touched her arm on the street. She tried not to jump away from him. If Ash noticed it, he didn't react.

"It's all right. They were ready to go." Passing on was different for Clauses, and humans couldn't understand. "What about your family?" she asked, ready to change the subject.

"Well, I have my dad here. He lives about an hour away, in a cabin on the river. He's living his retirement fantasy, waking up and fishing every day."

An older version of Ash standing on the riverbank in waders, fishing as the sun came up formed in her mind, making her smile.

"You already know about my mom from Sofia. And I don't have siblings either. I know what you mean about community, though. This community has been my family ever since I can remember."

"And now you take care of them," Holly said.

Ash's eyes widened with surprise. "Yes, I guess I do. Or I try to. I just want to give back a little piece of everything I've received. I want to make this place the best it can be. It has so much to offer."

Holly nodded. As someone responsible for the Christmas Dreams of humans all around the world, she understood that better than most. "That's a big responsibility." She sensed that the weight of it was more than he would admit and wondered if that was true for herself as well.

"Sometimes. But I always get more than I give, you know?" Ash said then took another bite of bread.

"I do."

Just then, their meals arrived. Holly thought she and Ash were kindred spirits in many ways. She felt she'd had a glimpse into his soul in that moment. But with all the half-truths and layers of magic she was operating under, he could never fully glimpse hers. Still, though her watch was vibrating uncontrollably, during the rest of their meal, Holly briefly forgot her Cheer meter existed at all.

Chapter Twenty-Six

The remainder of the evening passed pleasantly as they ate and chatted more about their backgrounds and interests. Holly had a tendency to answer questions very succinctly, almost as if she were trying to tell him something without telling him everything. He wanted to know everything about her, but he tried not to ask any follow-up questions when it seemed like she wanted to move on, and she seemed grateful for that.

An hour later, by the time they finished dessert, most of the restaurant had cleared out. Enzo approached their table, grinning. He'd always been friendly, but he'd been extra attentive that night, stopping by their table now and then with a quick word for Holly.

That she spoke Italian had been a surprise. She had so many layers to uncover, and he wondered what there was in her past or possibly even her present that caused her to hold back. Everything he'd seen of her was incredible. He couldn't imagine there was any part of her that wasn't worth sharing.

"You two have had a lovely night, yes?" Enzo leaned casually on a nearby chair.

Ash glanced at his watch then looked around to notice they were the last two patrons in the restaurant. "Whoa, I didn't realize what time it was. Sorry about that, Enzo. Dinner was great. Holly, are you ready to get out of here?"

Holly nodded and stood as Enzo slid her chair out for her. She said something to Enzo in Italian again, and Enzo beamed at her.

"Come back any time, you two," he called after them as they left the restaurant and headed for Ash's truck.

Ash held the door open for Holly and hoped she wouldn't be too cold in the truck. He should have gone out to start it before he'd paid the check. Time had flown by with her, and he'd forgotten about everything else.

"I think you may be Enzo's newest favorite customer. He's probably going to try to get you to move to Emerald Hollow," Ash said jokingly after he climbed into the driver's seat and started the engine. He quickly switched on the seat heaters and adjusted the temperature dial.

He noticed Holly had gone quiet. Maybe he was talking too much. Or maybe she was tired. Italian food often had that effect on him. He hesitated. The soft, spicy scent of cinnamon had crept into his truck with her, and it distracted him. "Sorry for keeping you out so late. I hope you don't have to be up too early tomorrow."

That line of thought had him sitting up straighter. His overflowing to-do list had somehow completely exited his mind while they'd had dinner, but it was back in full force. The next night was the chamber meeting in the café, and he had a few things he needed to prepare for.

"No problem. Thanks for dinner." Holly's voice was kind but quiet, and she stared out the window.

He wanted to take her hand and ask her if she was all right. *Why did her demeanor suddenly change?* He had a feeling she was keeping him at arm's length, and he realized he needed to do the same.

Ash had asked Holly to dinner without even taking a moment to consider it. He'd just told Sofia not to get her hopes up about what he was sure his best friend was thinking, then he'd gone right ahead and asked Holly on what likely appeared to be a date.

He couldn't control his actions around her. Spending time with Holly calmed him, and he craved that feeling, but that was an unfair expectation to put on someone. Holly's life was in Canada. And his life would always be in Emerald Hollow. Someday soon, she was going to leave, and it might be for good.

Chapter Twenty-Seven

"Are you ready for this chamber meeting? They can get a little wild," Sofia said.

Holly raised her eyebrows. "Wild how?"

"Oh, you know. People see the Emerald House as a second home. Sometimes they cut a little loose here. And we're serving my famous spiked cider. I'm sure we'll try to get the important business out of the way early, because after that, there's no telling what might happen." A mischievous twinkle lit Sofia's eyes.

"This town is full of surprises."

Holly was wearing a different sweater dress from the night before along with leggings and boots again, while Sofia had donned a bedazzled pair of jeans and a brown sweater that perfectly matched her eyes. Sofia's hair was pulled up in its usual ponytail, caramel streaks glinting in the light of the hallway.

"It has its charms," Sofia said, turning to wink at Holly. "So, how was dinner with Ash last night?"

"It was very nice. The man who owns the restaurant, Enzo, is really sweet. And the food was delicious."

Sofia rolled her eyes. "Everyone knows the food there is great.

What I want to know is how was dinner *with Ash*?" She pursed her lips and raised her eyebrows.

Holly elbowed her gently in the side. "Why are you making those strange faces? I already told you it was very nice."

"You don't have any juicy details to share?" Sofia was relentless.

"Well, he did tell me about buying this place and some of the circumstances around the sale. It sounds like it was a little contentious. I don't know if that's juicy, since you already knew about it, though."

Sofia stopped walking to grip her arm. "He told you all that? Wow. I mean, Ash is really outgoing, and he talks to everyone, but he doesn't usually share those kinds of details easily outside his immediate circle. He must really trust you."

Holly was taken aback by Sofia's words and the seriousness of her tone, so antithetical to her usual flippancy. But she couldn't dwell on it for long because they entered the café before Holly could respond. The small area was already bursting with people. Most were older than Holly and Sofia, but a few business owners in their late twenties or early thirties, like Ash, were scattered around. Holly spotted him across the room, chatting with an elderly white woman in an eggshell-blue puffer coat.

"Oh, look. The spiked cider is already set up." Sofia indicated a few different punch bowls and pulled Holly behind her as she approached them. "Some of the ciders are alcoholic and some not. Help yourself."

Holly watched Ash across the room as she absentmindedly served herself some of the regular cider, which was warm and instantly soothed her dry throat. Ash seemed to occupy his own space in the place, confident in his skin, and comfortable with everyone. He smiled when his eyes briefly met hers, then he looked away almost shyly to speak with someone else.

"This is good," Holly said to Sofia after taking another sip of the cider.

Sofia grinned. "Told you. Okay, let's knock out the business first before I have too many of these. The sign-up tables are over there."

Sofia led her to a table covered in small stacks of paper that handled the logistics of the Christmas faire. Holly looked them over. People could sign up for a vendor booth space, choose its dimensions, register a float, and fill out all the other little details that made the Christmas faire run every year.

It seemed like a well-oiled machine, and Holly thought again of the North Pole. She wondered what the elves were doing and how Advent season was going. Her watch was still humming away, as Cheerful as ever, and Holly trusted that everything was going well back home.

Holly followed Sofia as she signed up for a booth space for her jewelry and stopped to talk to various townspeople as they went. Sofia introduced them each to Holly, who was surprised when many responded with some variation of "Holly! The one who did the fall festival decor? I've been wanting to meet you."

"Told you they'd try to suck you into volunteering if you weren't careful." A familiar voice sounded at Holly's side, and she turned to see Ash standing next to her, holding a bottle of beer. His eyes sparkled mischievously.

"It's fine, really. As long as they don't have me working at a food booth. That's not my forte. That's more of an—" She'd been about to say, "Elf thing." She took a swig of her cider, which was nearly gone.

"Well, be honest. What do you think of everything? This is as Emerald Hollow as it gets. If this doesn't scare you away, nothing will." Ash's walnut-colored eyes were bright as he looked around the room.

Holly's chest felt warm, and she was more relaxed than usual. It seemed she was getting used to being around humans in a normal capacity, not just searching their emotions for those that would supply Cheer and those that would harm it.

"Scare me away? No way. I love this place." Surprised by the words tumbling out of her, she tucked her hair behind her ear nervously.

Ash's face only brightened more. "If I didn't know how much you love your friends in Canada, I might try to convince you to stay." His voice was relaxed, but his eyes scanned the room as he spoke, not quite settling on her.

Holly remembered the comment he'd made outside the Italian restaurant, when he'd joked about Enzo convincing her to stay. She'd gone quiet then, completely still. The words had jarred her. Holly had never moved anywhere—*couldn't* move anywhere. Her home was at the North Pole. But she didn't seem to be having such a strong reaction to the implication now. Her mind was comfortably taking in the music and the people around her.

"Are you keeping tabs on everything?" Sofia demanded, suddenly breaking free from another conversation. "Just relax, Ash. Most of the business is done. Now it's party time."

Sofia held up her glass to Holly. "And I need a refill. How about you?"

"Yes!" Holly exclaimed and followed Sofia to the drink table. She filled her glass again and scooted closer to Sofia just as Sofia let out a little gasp.

"What?" Holly tried to see if one of them had spilled their drink.

"Lucas," Sofia whispered, narrowing her eyes.

Holly followed her gaze toward the door. A tall, thin man about her and Ash's age had stridden into the room. He had pale skin and bright-blue eyes and was wearing a puffer vest over a long-sleeve shirt, jeans, and boots.

"Why do you look like you've swallowed a snowflake?" Holly asked, though she was picking up on something unsettling as well. The man's clothes fit in with those of the others, but the way he held himself didn't feel right to Holly. His eyes looked tired but also oddly focused.

Sofia paused, seeming to wonder at Holly's strange phrasing, but recovered and whispered a response. "He was Ash's old business partner. They didn't end on the best of terms. But you know about that now."

Holly turned to the man with more interest than before.

"So he's the one who didn't believe in Ash's vision for the Emerald House?" Holly took another large drink of her cider.

"It's not just that. He gave Ash a hard time during the buyout, and he still seems bitter that Ash's vision has panned out. Lucas lives a few towns over now but drops in every now and then to rain on everybody's parade. It's not a coincidence he's here tonight, during the chamber mixer." Sofia took a huge swig of her cider, set her cup down heavily on the table, and stood up straight, looking as if she were ready to stride right over to Lucas.

"Are you going to talk to him?" Holly hoped the answer was no.

"Somebody's got to see what he's up to." Sofia marched toward the door, and Holly followed her warily, feeling like a young reindeer navigating their first complicated flight pattern. Confrontation was something she'd rarely encountered in her days as Ms. Claus, and she knew instinctively that it wouldn't be something she was good at.

Before coming to Emerald Hollow, if she encountered a negative situation brewing, she got out of there as quickly as possible, striving to maintain her Cheer levels. But based on the fiery expression on Sofia's face, it seemed it wouldn't be necessary for Holly to do much other than provide backup. She took a deep breath and followed her friend.

Chapter Twenty-Eight

"Hellooo, Lucas," Sofia said.

Did she have another cider when I wasn't looking? Or maybe it really was as strong as she'd indicated. Holly gulped, feeling light-headed.

"Sofia," Lucas said, barely turning to look at her. He was searching the crowded café.

"Looking for Ash?" Sofia asked, planting herself in front of Lucas so he had to look at her.

He smirked. "Just wanted to say hello. The party's open to the public, right?"

"Not really." Sofia placed a hand on her hip.

"Then who is this? A new chamber member?"

"Holly is none of your business. She's here as my guest."

"I see," Lucas said, studying Holly more closely. "Emerald Hollow doesn't get a lot of new young women very often." When he smiled, a shiver ran up Holly's spine.

"Yeah, maybe she and your wife can be friends. Can I help you with something?"

Lucas's eyes darkened, then he gathered himself. "I'm just going to get some cider and make some small talk. Is that okay with you? I think I have a right to be here, seeing as my dad used to own the place."

Sofia rolled her eyes. "Your dad and Ash's dad built the place together. Yeah. We all know that. But Ash bought you out, fair and square."

"Like I said, I'm just here for the cider."

"All right." Sofia relented, pivoting out of his way. "But I'm watching you." She formed a *V* with two fingers and moved it from her eyes to Lucas's.

He put his hands up in fake innocence. "Do your best, Short Cake."

Sofia scowled as he walked toward the drink table.

"Short Cake?" Holly asked, confused and worried about the whole interaction.

"Old nickname." She shrugged. "I guess I can't keep him out. Chamber events are technically open to the public. But I should warn Ash he's here."

Holly followed Sofia as they waded through the crowded space to find Ash. She felt a strange buzz from her watch and looked down to see that the hand was spinning erratically. She stared at it in confusion. The Cheer level was still full, but the hand was completely out of control.

"Ash!" Sofia burst out in a loud whisper, pulling him from another conversation. "Heads up. Lucas is here."

Holly looked up from her watch, still confused, in time to see a muscle in Ash's neck tense.

"Did he say why?" he asked, glancing toward Holly.

"No idea. But it can't be good." Sofia seemed to relax a little since she had warned Ash. She swiped some carrots and dip from the table nearby.

"Okay. Thanks for letting me know, Sof. I'll keep an eye on him."

Holly wanted to follow up and see if everything was all right, but she was having a hard time concentrating. She trailed Sofia absently to the counter in the window. Her watch hand was still spinning nonstop.

"I feel strange." Holly took a seat on the barstool behind her.

"Strange how?" Sofia asked. Since she had confronted Lucas, she was blowing off steam by loudly crunching on a carrot.

"My head's a little fuzzy." Holly rested her elbow on the countertop and put her head in her hand.

Sofia looked at Holly then at her glass. She grabbed it and took a sip. "That's because you've been drinking the spiked cider."

Holly's eyes flew open. "What? No way! I was drinking the nonalcoholic." She looked at her glass in horror.

"Sorry, love. I make both versions, and I can personally attest that that one's alcoholic. I can see why you couldn't tell, though. The recipe is perfect." She beamed with pride.

Holly smacked her arm. "Sofia! I don't drink alcohol!" She put her hand over her watch, willing the spinning to stop.

"You can switch to water now. Don't worry about it."

Holly tried to relax, since she didn't technically need her magic at the moment. She didn't plan on needing a free meal or a new place to stay. Those things were already taken care of. And the alcohol didn't seem to have affected her Cheer levels. She let out a breath.

"Candy canes," Holly murmured, still stunned that she had been drinking alcohol unknowingly.

"Candy canes?" Sofia scoffed. "Is that some kind of Canadian expression?"

Holly chastised herself for the North Pole slip. She blamed it on the spiked cider. "Sure. We say it when we're embarrassed or disappointed. I guess it's kind of like shucks."

Sofia laughed and rolled her eyes. "That is way too sweet for me. You should say bloody maple or hockey sticks or something like that."

"I'll take that back to the Canadian government and see if they'll get on board. But seriously, no more cider for me."

The room seemed louder than ever before. All the members of the chamber were chatting and laughing. An empty bowl of cider was replaced with a new one. Just then, Holly's eyes landed on Ash, who was having a tense conversation in the corner with Lucas.

She nudged Sofia. "Do you think everything's okay there?" She pointed at where they were standing, huddled close.

Sofia narrowed her eyes. "Why can't he leave it alone?"

She jumped off her barstool, and as Holly followed her toward Ash and Lucas, she spotted Enzo making a beeline toward her. *When did he arrive?* Holly's heart rate sped up. She wouldn't be able to speak Italian with her magic incapacitated. Though she was comfortable with a few general greeting phrases, she wouldn't be able to hold a conversation.

Her magic had been confined once before many years ago, in Costa Rica, when she'd sat down to enjoy a delicious drink she thought was a mocktail. When her magic was affected, it defaulted to the language she'd last used. In Costa Rica, she could speak Spanish just fine under the influence of alcohol. But when she'd overheard what she assumed were French tourists at the café, she couldn't understand them.

Holly whispered into Sofia's ear that she needed to use the bathroom then ducked through the crowd. She went into the restroom and splashed cool water on her wrists and neck then rested briefly against the counter, looking in the large wood-framed mirror, which was adorned with boughs of greenery.

She sipped the glass of water she'd carried in with her. *This isn't the kind of mistake I make often. Am I getting careless here in Emerald Hollow? What would the elves think of me?*

"Nothing bad has happened yet," she said to her reflection then exhaled deeply.

But the night was still young.

Chapter Twenty-Nine

Holly tried to focus on the positive as she readied herself to leave the restroom. Her Cheer meter was still full, and she was having a good time. Sofia was beginning to feel like a friend, something Holly had never had before. She smiled as she thought of the fire in Sofia's eyes when she jumped to Ash's defense. Then her forehead scrunched in concern as she thought of Lucas. Ash was one of the kindest, hardest-working people she had ever met, and she didn't want any trouble for him.

She straightened and walked back out of the bathroom, ready to return to the café. A movement in the shadows of the lobby caught her attention, and she heard the sound of shuffling paper, so she drew back against the wall. She leaned in closer and saw a figure flipping through the hotel ledger. Ash did most things digitally, but he still kept an analog calendar under the front desk for employees to reference.

A tall man was standing behind the desk, flipping through the calendar. At first, Holly thought it was just an employee checking their shift and was ready to move on, but then the man turned slightly, and the light from the moon shining through the front window lit his face. It was Lucas.

"Can I help you find something?" Holly asked, stepping out of the shadows.

Lucas jumped a little but recovered quickly. "No, I was actually just leaving," he said smoothly, a smile curving on his face. "It was Holly, right?"

"Yes." She glanced toward the café to see if she could spot Ash or Sofia.

"Nice to meet you, Holly." He put an emphasis on her name that made goose bumps run up her arms. Then he grabbed an apple from a bowl on the counter, tossed it into the air, and caught it. He gave her a little wave and walked out the front door.

Holly let out a breath and entered the café, seeking out one of her friends. She spotted Ash first. He smiled when he saw her, but his face fell when he noticed her expression.

"Are you okay? What happened?" He placed a hand gently on her arm and led her out of the crowded room into the lobby.

"Yes, I'm okay. I just saw Lucas, though. He was going through your calendar behind the desk."

Ash's eyes moved to the desk and narrowed.

"At least, I'm pretty sure he was. I'm not thinking entirely clearly right now."

"He's probably just being nosy. Thanks for letting me know. You sure you're okay?" He studied her face, doubt pinching the middle of his forehead.

"Yes. Had a little too much cider, but it's wearing off now."

Ash raised an eyebrow. "I thought you didn't drink."

"Not intentionally. I was serving myself from the wrong bowl."

Holly laughed at the silliness of it all, and he did, too, seeming to relax.

"I told Sofia her cider was dangerous, but she keeps bringing it back every year." He glanced toward the café. They were silent for a moment, then Ash spoke again. "I just saw Enzo. He was hoping to talk to you."

Holly's eyes widened. "Oh! I'm kind of avoiding him, actually. My... Italian isn't very good when I drink." Holly tried to stick close to the truth, as always.

Ash laughed. "Understandable. I'm sure he'll be fine if he doesn't talk with you tonight. I was actually just getting ready to go let Comet out. Do you want to come? Fresh air might help if you're not feeling well."

"Are you my accomplice in hiding from Enzo?"

"Accomplice, escape artist. Whatever title you want to give me." His eyes sparkled, and Holly's cheeks heated.

They walked together down the hall toward Ash's suite, and it dawned on Holly that he lived kind of like she did at the North Pole, attached to all the action, ready to jump to work at a moment's notice while still being removed, living his life differently from everyone else in the building.

They collected Comet, who greeted them enthusiastically, and followed the path toward the woods, chatting about the evening's events.

Ash filled her in on who was who in the chamber. "The woman in the blue puffer jacket is Esmeralda. She leads a lot of events for the chamber, and we're working closely together on the Christmas faire."

Holly nodded, listening as he rattled off a few more names. About ten minutes into their walk, Holly spotted Ivy and Clove peering at her excitedly through the trees.

"What the—" Ash came to a stop to squint at the trees. "Those look like the fawn I thought I saw the other night. But they don't look like the deer around here."

"You can see them?" Holly asked. She had warned all her reindeer to stay scarce after the previous incident. Apparently, Ivy and Clove had forgotten that instruction. Her heart raced.

"They almost look like the reindeer one of our vendors brings down for the Christmas faire, but they haven't confirmed they're coming this year. It seems a little early for them to be here, if so."

Ash was oblivious to Holly's internal struggle, and he strolled over to the reindeer and held out a hand tentatively to Clove. Clove hesitated, her eyes flashing to Holly's, then she stuck out her tongue and licked Ash's hand. Holly gasped. Ash turned back toward her and smiled.

"Don't worry. They're friendly. The ones brought in for festivals are always accustomed to people," Ash said, completely misreading Holly's surprise as fear.

Behind Ash's back, Clove gave Holly an apologetic look, almost as if to say, "I couldn't help it."

Holly frowned. *Why isn't their invisibility magic working in Emerald Hollow? Has anyone seen them aside from Ash?* She had still been feeding them magic lichen at regular intervals. *Does this have to do with the spiked cider?* But that wouldn't explain how Ash had seen Ivy the first time.

Holly's thoughts jumped around too quickly, and she glanced at her watch. It was spinning a bit less rapidly because of the water and the fresh air, but it still wasn't fully back on track.

She felt lucky that Ash had come up with his own rationalization for why the reindeer were there, but that didn't mean others would. She made a face behind Ash's back that she hoped would signal to Ivy and Clove that they needed to disappear and stay out of sight, and the two young reindeer turned and ran.

Comet, who normally stayed right near Ash's side when they went for a walk, had been barking at Ivy and Clove and looked ready to give chase.

"Comet, stay," Ash commanded, and the dog stopped near him, though his back legs were quivering with a desire to run.

Holly tried to relax her breathing.

"I'll have to check on the vendors tomorrow. The reindeer shouldn't be loose in the woods like this." He returned to the trail, and they continued to walk. "You and Sofia seem to be getting along well. She's going to be really sad when you leave."

Holly's chest seized. She didn't know when it had happened, but the thought of leaving Emerald Hollow pained her. Sometime in the last few days, she had stopped searching for the town's mysterious source of Cheer and was instead just enjoying being there. She was *experiencing*, like Lumi had told her to do.

It took her a moment to realize she hadn't responded to Ash's comment. "Sofia is great. She's the best friend I never knew I needed." Holly tried not to focus on what would happen after the Christmas faire, when she had to return to the North Pole, deliver Dreams, and get back to her regular routine. *But what is my regular routine? Dashing around the world, chasing Cheer? Do I enjoy that?* She certainly loved succeeding, constantly changing variables to try to maximize her Cheer collection. But she wasn't sure she'd been truly happy.

They continued the walk back to the Emerald House mostly in silence. The usually talkative Ash seemed comfortable just to walk with her, and Comet trotted along between them, occasionally turning to sniff in the direction the reindeer had gone.

Holly's watch hand still twisted a little too quickly, its normal pattern disrupted, as they strolled through the evergreen trees. Holly thought her brain felt exactly the same way.

Chapter Thirty

Ash woke up early the next morning, as usual. He planned to be productive, and he had a meeting with the vineyard owners in an hour. Stopping in the restaurant to grab a coffee to go, he said good morning to Sofia, who was working a rare-for-her early shift.

Sofia just nodded sleepily.

Then Holly entered the lobby. The smell of cinnamon drifted to him.

"Ew. Why are you both such early risers?" Sofia asked, slipping an apron over her blue sweater. "I wouldn't even be close to awake right now if I weren't filling in for Tyler." She rubbed her eyes and yawned dramatically.

"Where are you heading off to so early?" Ash asked Holly, shrugging on his jacket and ignoring Sofia's sleepy theatrics.

"I like going for walks in the mornings. It's so peaceful," Holly said.

He saw her surreptitiously take a few oranges from the lobby fruit bowl and slip them into her jacket pocket. Smiling, he wondered where she was going with them.

"How about you? Taking Comet for a walk?" Holly asked once the oranges were firmly out of sight.

The dog was wagging his tail eagerly at Ash's side.

"What? Oh. No. I'm sure he wishes I were, but I have to run a few errands this morning." "A few" was an understatement, but he had a clear plan for the day and was confident he could get everything done as long as he didn't have any unexpected pressing issues come up, which certainly wasn't guaranteed.

"I can take him for a walk. I'm going anyway," Holly offered, and Comet's tail thumped loudly on the floor.

A weight lifted from his mental load. He'd felt guilty about not having a ton of time to walk Comet lately. Though he still tried to throw the ball for him each night, their morning walks had been getting less and less frequent.

"Really? He would love that. He doesn't usually use a leash with me, but you should probably have one just in case he tries to run off. Here." Ash reached behind the lobby desk and pulled out a long blue leash. Snowflakes were engraved in the fabric. "Are you sure you want to take him? That's really nice of you."

"Of course. It's no problem." Holly took the leash from Ash and clipped it on Comet's collar. "We'll probably be back before you. Where should I take him?"

"Oh, he's free to wander around the lobby. Thanks, Holly. You're a lifesaver. And be careful out there. It's a little icy this morning. We've put down salt on most of the paths, but we may have missed some areas."

"Come on, Comet. Let's go," Holly said, gripping the leash and opening the front door.

Comet trotted eagerly in front of her. Holly turned and gave Ash a little wave then headed down the path in front of the house.

He watched for a moment, making sure she seemed steady on the slippery ground. She looked perfectly fine, but he made a mental note to do an extra pass with the salt on the path she tended to take to the woods.

He glanced at the spot in the lobby where the Christmas tree usually went, kicking himself for having put it off so long. He would have to make that a priority the next day. Maybe Holly would even want to help. The thought had him smiling as he grabbed his truck keys and went to open another bag of salt.

"ALL RIGHT, COMET," HOLLY BEGAN AS SHE AND THE shaggy dog made their way down the icy path. "Last time, you barked at the reindeer, but let's try to be cool this time, okay?"

The slick ground, which would be treacherous for most people, was no different from walking on a grassy field or dirt path for Holly. Her steps were steady, and soon, they had reached the clearing where the reindeer were waiting for their morning treats. Comet tried to bound toward them, but Holly held firmly on to the leash.

As they approached, Comet didn't bark but instead began to sniff incessantly. Holly cautiously let him approach each reindeer, and mutual sniffing occurred between the five animals. Holly didn't think the reindeer had had much, if any, interaction with dogs, though they were always friendly with the penguins at the North Pole. At last, all parties seemed satisfied to be around one another without going crazy, and Holly doled out the oranges and magic lichen.

"What's on the agenda today, Dasher?" She scratched the face of her most senior reindeer. "Are you tired of Emerald Hollow, or are you enjoying it here?" Dasher nuzzled his face into her hand, and Holly took it as a sign of contentment.

"Yeah, me too." She let out a breath.

As she conversed with the two elder reindeer, Comet was busy making friends with Ivy and Clove. She looked up to see the three of them chasing one another playfully in the clearing.

"Would you look at that. Ash would get a kick out of this." She wondered what errands he had to run that morning and if there was anything she could do to help.

"Dash, Gale, for once in my life, I'm getting to live completely in the moment."

Gale wiggled her ears, and Dasher blew out a little whinny.

"I don't even know what to do with myself other than try to be productive while I'm here. I guess that means more prepping for the Christmas faire." Holly's mouth relaxed into a smile as she thought of all the dusty boxes of decorations in Ash's workshop. She didn't have to sit around and wait for his instructions. Instead, she would surprise him by tackling a few projects on her own. The thought of lightening his load made her smile even wider, and she straightened, seeking out Comet's leash. He was still jumping and running playfully with Ivy and Clove.

"Come on, boy. We'll visit them again soon." She clipped the leash back onto his collar and started up the trail.

Chapter Thirty-One

Later that evening, Ash returned to the Emerald House through the side door and headed straight to his apartment for a shower. The vineyard meeting had gone on longer than he'd expected, pushing back everything else he'd needed to do into later and later time slots.

He'd managed to finish all his errands, but he was arriving back at the house later than he'd intended. Though grateful that he had a reliable staff, he still felt guilty when he was out all day. The sun had already been down for a few hours.

Comet rushed down the hallway to meet him as he unlocked his door.

"Hey, buddy." He knelt and gave Comet a thorough scratching behind both ears. "Have you been roving out here all day?" Then he remembered that Holly had walked him that morning, and he'd told her she could leave him in the lobby. Comet jumped in front of him and went into their apartment, heading straight for his food bowl. Ash looked at the clock on the microwave. His stomach twisted in guilt again.

"Sorry, boy." He usually fed Comet an hour earlier. He

scooped an extra-large serving of the dog food and placed it in Comet's bowl, hoping that would make up for the late feeding. Comet scarfed down his food, just like always. *Dogs. They can forgive you for almost anything.*

He showered, played tug-of-war with Comet, then went to the restaurant for dinner, leaving Comet in the apartment.

When he arrived, he was surprised to find Holly sitting in her usual booth. Her plate was nearly empty, and she had her hands wrapped around a mug. So he wasn't the only one having a late dinner.

She smiled when she noticed him, and he slid in across from her. "Hey, I was hoping I'd bump into you. I wanted to say thanks again for walking Comet. He didn't try to run off, did he?"

"No, he was great."

Holly's warm expression instantly made him feel better about his day.

"So," Ash said, shifting in the booth a bit and trying not to look uncomfortable. He had thought about his plan again on his drive home and had committed to going for it. Though he had recently convinced himself to stop spending time alone with Holly, some unknown force seemed to be directing him to do exactly the opposite.

He cleared his throat. "There's this tradition I do every year. My dad started it when I was growing up. A couple of weekends before the Christmas faire kicks off, we go hiking to our favorite mountain lake. Just to clear our heads. We also cut down a tree for the lobby. I'm super late this year, but I'm finally doing it tomorrow. I was just thinking that—since you're new in town and haven't gotten to see all the surrounding beauty—you might want to come with me."

His heart rate sped up, and he watched her face with trepidation. A Christmas-tree cutting was more involved than a dinner, and he didn't know if that type of thing would interest her. But for some reason, the idea of her coming with him had caught on that morning, and he hadn't been able to shake it since.

"Is that an invitation?" Holly asked, her eyes sparkling.

As always, he was completely taken aback by the constant flush in her cheeks and the air of quiet calm yet total uniqueness of presence she brought whenever she was in the room. He realized why he wanted her to go with him. She made everything feel magical, and he needed a little magic at the moment.

"Sure is." He cleared his throat again and tried to draw on some of his casual confidence, which seemed to falter when he was around her. The look on her face was encouraging, so he relaxed, his chest expanding.

"Then yes, I'd love to."

"Great! So we'll leave around eight, if that's okay. And I'll pack lunch. Do you have some comfortable hiking shoes?" He thought she might not have any hiking clothes at all.

"Yep, I'll be good to go." Holly seemed bursting with energy that evening, and he wondered what she had done after walking Comet.

"Hey, Ash. Got a moment? I wanted to ask you something about the vendor booths." Ash was startled to see Jordan, an Emerald Hollow local, standing by the booth. He'd barely registered anyone else in the restaurant after he'd spotted Holly. The day felt like it would never end, and he was suddenly eager to get to the next one.

"Jordan, hi. Sure thing. Just a moment." Jordan nodded and stepped away.

"Okay, then." Ash slapped his hands on his thighs and rose from the booth. He studied Holly again, wanting to rest in that feeling of whatever joy seemed to be coming from her. "See you in the morning."

"See you then," Holly replied, her eyes meeting his one last time. They still sparkled, but there was an almost imperceptible squint as if she were trying to analyze something about him. He'd never noticed anyone else looking at him that way. Sometimes he wondered if she could see right through him.

Then her face relaxed, and she picked up her mug and took a sip. Sure it held hot cocoa, he tried to suppress a knowing grin as he went to talk to Jordan. Dinner would have to wait a little longer.

Chapter Thirty-Two

Ash and Holly met early the following morning, both of them decked out in comfortable winter hiking clothes, and Ash sporting a large gray backpack. Holly watched as Ash carefully double-checked that they had everything they needed. Once he seemed satisfied, he opened the back door of the truck for Comet to jump inside, and they climbed into the front seats. Holly was secretly excited about riding in a vehicle again.

"How far is it to the trailhead?" she asked as Ash shifted the prewarmed truck into drive. The heated seat was already warm beneath her.

"The drive's about thirty minutes, then the hike to the lake is about forty minutes from the trailhead."

As Ash navigated out of the parking lot of the Emerald House, Holly studied him. He was wearing a gray-and-blue beanie, a puffer coat that seemed thin but Holly was sure was well insulated and warm, and some comfortable-looking dark-gray pants. The whispers of a beard were forming a hint of a five-o'clock shadow. He'd packed them each a thermos, his with coffee, hers with hot cocoa. She picked up the cup, which she had been balancing on her thighs, and took a sip.

"And you've been going out here since you were...?"

"For as long as I can remember. Probably three or four. There're pictures of my parents taking me up there in a backpack."

"I love traditions. People don't always appreciate their power, but they hold memories, hope, and the promise that some things will always be there, even if everything else changes over time." Holly took another sip of her hot cocoa and looked out the window at the thick green forest.

She was in a great mood that morning and looking forward to their outing. She'd barely resisted telling Ash about all the Christmas decorations she had made when she saw him at the restaurant the previous night. The town was in for a surprise when they saw their updated streetlight baubles, overhead garlands, maze decorations, and of course, Santa's sleigh.

Besides, they were on their way to get a *Christmas tree*. That was one of her favorite human Christmas traditions and one they'd emulated at the North Pole. She'd never cut one down before, though. All Christmas trees at the North Pole were living. Being part of the tradition for the first time had her almost giddy.

"I've never thought about it that way, but you're right. For me, it's a chance to reset. Remember where I came from and why I'm doing all this."

"It's therapeutic," Holly suggested.

Ash nodded. "Yeah, I guess it is. My dad had to stop coming a few years ago when he started having some knee issues, but I've kept it going myself."

They drove on in comfortable silence for a little while, enjoying their hot drinks. Ash obviously knew the road well, and he took every turn expertly. Before long, they turned onto a dirt road Holly would never have noticed and rattled down the bumpy path until they reached a small oval clearing.

"This is the trailhead," Ash said, pulling his truck toward the edge, then put it in park.

They climbed out of the truck, and he removed his backpack from the back seat, sliding it on. Comet jumped out and instantly put his nose to the trail.

"Ready?"

Holly nodded. "This is beautiful."

She admired the forest and the clear winter sky as they made their way up the thin dirt path into the woods. The trail had a gentle incline, and Ash had a flush to his cheeks before long. Holly felt sure she did too. Walking alongside Ash felt good... natural.

"So, what's the status of the Christmas faire?" she asked. "Have all the vendors been sorted?"

"Yeah, as much as they can be. We're getting down to the wire now, a week out. No more additions. Most people sign up months in advance, but we always hold a few spots for last-minute add-ons. We got one last night at the restaurant when I was sitting with you, actually. Did Sofia tell you she's having a booth?"

"She did. I'm excited to see her jewelry."

"Sofia's really talented. Her booth was pretty popular last year."

Ash followed the trail as it turned sharply to the right, and Holly was close behind him. No one else was in sight, and only the occasional rustling in the trees indicated any animal life was around.

"I can't wait to see it. I've still got a little work to do on some of the decorations, but they're coming along."

"You're still working on those?" Ash came to a halt and turned to look at her. "I mean, I thought you were just working on the sleigh. You didn't have to do any more than that."

"It's fine," Holly said, nudging the back of his foot to get him to keep walking.

He gave her a stern expression but acquiesced. She smiled behind his back. He had no idea.

"I feel like we're taking advantage of you. You're supposed to be a guest here, enjoying the place like a tourist."

"Do I seem like a tourist?" Holly asked, amused.

"Not at all." He laughed. "You fit in here really well."

Holly had the feeling he was about to say more, but he didn't and quickened his pace a little.

"Well, thank you. I love it here."

"Have you ever thought about staying?" Ash asked.

Holly's chest constricted. She was glad he was walking in front of her and couldn't see her expression. *There's that idea again. Staying.* But it was impossible. She never stayed anywhere.

"Oh, I don't know. I live in Canada, and it's... Well, it's complicated. But I do love it here. I meant that. If I didn't live in Canada, I could see myself here."

Ash paused to take a swig from a water bottle. "Are you thirsty?" He offered her another bottle that was strapped to the side of his backpack. Their hands touched as she took it from him, and a buzz of electricity creeped up her arms then ran down her spine, and she shivered. When she drank, the water was pure and sweet.

They walked a little longer, making small talk. Before Holly knew it, they emerged from the thick trees and into a clearing with a mountain lake glistening in the winter sun. The far edges were frozen, but the part nearest to them was a deep blue that reflected the forest behind it. Her breath caught.

Ash smiled. "Pretty cool, right?" He walked closer to the lake, where a large log was lying across the meadow, slipped off his backpack, and dropped it to the ground. Then he walked closer to the lake and started studying the earth, the frost crunching under his feet. Comet took off around the lake.

"What are you looking for?" Holly asked, joining him.

"Smooth, flat rocks," he said, seeing one that met his standards and picked it up. He gripped it softly and tossed it in a halfway underhand motion, sending it skipping perfectly across the lake.

Holly smiled in delight. "I'm guessing that's one of your traditions too?"

"Yep. Well, when the lake's not frozen. Want to try? I'm guessing Canadians are expert rock skippers."

"Not exactly. Well, some probably are, but not me. I've never actually tried it," Holly admitted. She found a rock that seemed similar to the one Ash had selected and gave it a toss. She wondered if her magic was working on the rock, because it soared across the water, skipping perfectly seven times.

Ash whistled. "First time? Are you sure about that?"

"Beginner's luck." She shook out her hands, feeling the buzz of her watch. She had hardly noticed it during the drive or the hike, but it had been active. "So, why isn't the lake frozen all the way across?"

"It will be later, probably. I'm hoping we'll get at least a dusting before next week. Not too much but enough to set the tone for the festivities."

Holly knew what he meant. The forest was stunning, and it would look magical when the trees were frosted in snow like at the North Pole.

She watched Ash as he looked out over the lake and the forest, suddenly completely taken aback by his presence. She had seen beautiful men before, all over the world. But no one had drawn her eye like he did. Something about Ash, not just his looks, caused a little piece of her to melt inside, like a piece of chocolate when it was stuffed next to a freshly toasted marshmallow.

Holly suddenly had a strong desire to show Ash her home and the northern lights. She let herself daydream about it for half a second then squeezed her eyes shut tightly, realizing it could never happen. Shaking herself, she wished there were snow around that she could sink her toes into to cool her off. Whatever was going on inside her brain needed to send itself back into whatever merry little cabin it had emerged from.

She opened her eyes to see him examining her face.

"Everything okay?"

"Yeah. This place is just... really beautiful. It reminds me of home a little bit."

"Really?"

They stared at each other for several moments. The chocolate began to melt again, and she squeezed her fingernails into her palms. She could sense his interest, and for a second, she thought she could tell him more. Then she took the toasted marshmallow that was plaguing her heart and mentally squashed it.

"Yeah. There's a lot of forest there too. And it's so peaceful." She'd never wanted to open up to a human like that before, but Ash made her feel so comfortable. He had a way of bringing down her carefully crafted walls. It would be safer to change the subject. "But this is really stunning. Do you ever come in the summer?"

"Yep." Ash tossed another rock across the water. They both watched it skip. "The lake's good for fishing. It can get pretty busy, believe it or not. We get a lot of fishermen at the house, and many of them hike out here that time of year."

"That sounds wonderful. I can picture this field full of wild-flowers."

"You'll have to come back in the summer and see it in person." He didn't look for her reaction but instead reached into his back-pack for the tin of fruit, cheese, and crackers he'd packed for breakfast.

A traitorous warmth started to creep into Holly's chest again at the thought of seeing the place in the summer, and she took the second small tin from Ash and tried the grapes first. He poured some steaming liquid from another thermos and offered Holly the lid. She caught the fragrant scent of apples.

"Apple cider?" she asked in surprise then took a sip and savored the sweet but sharp taste.

Ash nodded, his mouth full. "They're from a local orchard. The people also own a vineyard."

The two ate a few more bites, watching Comet dash around the lake, then Ash spoke again.

"It's not public knowledge yet, but I've been working on partnering with the winery. We'd serve their wine and cider exclusively at the Emerald House and offer tours of the vineyard and orchard for our guests. I was thinking about coming up with some kind of transportation system to take people to the vineyard straight from the House. I'd like to host some themed nights in partnership with them as well. But there are a lot of details to work out. It's part of the reason I've been so busy lately."

"That sounds amazing, Ash." Holly set her snack tin down on the log beside her. She thought of his Dream again and was glad he was one of the ones who chose to chase them. "I can see why you're successful with the Emerald House. You have a big vision for it. It really feels like the center of the community."

Ash's face lit up. "That's great to hear, because that's been my goal from the start. That's how my dad and his business partner originally envisioned it too. But we have to adapt with the times, and that means taking risks. I have a lot of other ideas for expansion, as well, but I'm trying to tackle one thing at a time."

"That seems wise,"

"Part of it's banking on this Best Small-Town Christmas contest. Even being listed in the top contenders would bring a lot of tourism to our town. I'd be able to justify the additional invest-ment to my lenders. And maybe it could give our local economy a jump start. I just know that if Main Street could be revitalized, the town could really be something special." Deep passion filled Ash's voice, and Holly could tell it meant more to him than he was saying.

"Then I guess we'd better make sure this Christmas faire is one to remember." Her chest tightened. She would do anything she could to make the Christmas faire the best the town had ever seen. To her, the town was already something special.

His eyes rested on hers for several moments before she finally looked away.

"Well, what do you think? Ready to find the perfect tree?"

"Born ready," Holly replied, grateful to break the tension. Besides, her magic had already helped her zero in on numerous Christmas-tree-ready firs on the hike in.

"I like the confidence, because I've spent over an hour deciding before. Did you already see a good one on the way up here?" He slung his backpack over his shoulder and whistled to Comet. "We'll have to get one close to the truck so that we don't have to carry it too far."

They made their way back down the trail, enjoying quiet conversation and watching Comet dash in and out of the trees. Holly tried to savor the time, wondering if she would ever again get to enjoy time like that in nearly magical woods with a human who seemed to be so much like her. When the truck was in sight, Ash pulled out his keys to unlock it.

"Where should we look first?" he asked, grabbing the small chain saw from the truck bed.

Holly's watch was humming underneath her jacket and gloves, and she pointed about fifty yards away. "I have a good feeling about that stand of trees."

Ash followed her lead, and they tramped across the frozen ground, Holly gracefully, Ash heavily. She circled the trees for a moment then paused.

"That one." She raised a hand to point at a symmetrical pine about fourteen feet tall. It was tucked between a few other trees.

Ash whistled. "I would never have spotted that one. It looks perfect."

He fired up the chain saw and had the tree on the ground within a few minutes. They put on gloves, and together, they carried it back to the truck and loaded it in the bed.

"Fastest Christmas tree harvest ever," Ash said appreciatively, closing the tailgate, then brushed his hands together to clear them off. "I might need your help again next year."

He winked, and Holly's cheeks heated against her will. Though he was complimenting her magic, not her, she couldn't help but feel fulfilled by the praise. Ash was the heart of Emerald Hollow, and she had been able to help him. It felt better than she could imagine, and her watch hummed, creating heat.

"Just my secret talent, I guess," she said, aiming to diffuse the thick cloud that had suddenly filled the air around them. Ash was standing so close to her that she thought if he listened hard enough, he might be able to hear her heart beating. She took a step backward.

"You have a lot of those." Ash smiled, called to Comet, and loaded the dog into the back seat.

"Thanks again for bringing me here, Ash," she said as they got in the truck. "This place is really special. I appreciate your sharing it with me."

For once, Ash didn't say anything. He just gave an almost-bashful smile, put the truck in gear, and hit the road.

Chapter Thirty-Three

"How was your date? I mean hike?" Sofia asked, a sneaky gleam in her eye, as she slid into a tall chair at the café counter that evening.

Holly nearly spit out her tea. "It wasn't a date." Holly raised her chin and didn't meet Sofia's eyes.

"Oh, *sure*. Two people going alone to a romantic location that means a lot to one of the two people? If that's not a date, I don't know what is." Sofia slurped her hot toddy, looking triumphant.

"It wasn't a date, Sofia. I don't date." Holly tried to stick to the facts, but she suddenly felt panicked. She tapped her watch nervously. It hummed steadily. *If Sofia thinks it was a date, does Ash?*

"You don't date? Ever?" Sofia looked aghast then waved a hand. "Do you like him? Please say you like him." Sofia's face was so full of hope that Holly couldn't help but smile. "I knew it! You like him!"

"Shh! I enjoy his company, if that's what you mean. But I'm leaving soon."

"Sorry." Sofia lowered her voice. "But this is the best development this town has had in *a while*. Ash is like the hottest catch in town, but he's never seemed interested in anyone here. He's always been so focused on his business." She took another sip of her drink then pointed at Holly. "Then you come along, and it's like *bam*, he's smitten." She wiggled her eyebrows.

Holly's jaw dropped, but she caught herself and closed it, taking a deep breath.

"Things like time and place can be worked out," Sofia added more gently.

Holly shook her head. Time and place didn't even operate in the same dimension for Holly and Ash. Still, the thought that he might be feeling something like what she was feeling sent a little thrill through her. Anyone would be lucky to have Ash, and Holly couldn't deny that something had shifted, at least for her, on their outing in the woods.

Of course, she could sense that they'd been growing closer. It had been obvious. But that didn't mean he was developing any significant romantic feelings toward her. *How could Ash, who's so invested in this place, be interested in someone like me, who, as far as he knows, lives in Canada and has no intentions of moving?*

Holly shook her head a second time. "That can't be right, Sof. He knows I'm going back to Canada." Holly gripped her mug of hot tea a little too firmly. She was regretting not ordering her usual hot cocoa, her comfort drink.

"I'm just telling it like I see it." Sofia shrugged then shifted on her barstool to let someone squeeze between the counter and the couch in the small space. "So, are you interested in a piece of jewelry for the Christmas faire? Maybe some earrings? I'm happy to make you something."

Holly relaxed at the change in conversation. "I would love that." She had never worn earrings before because they weren't strictly necessary for blending in with the locals in most places.

"Great! What design do you want?" Sofia asked, pulling out her phone to open her photo album.

"Surprise me," Holly replied.

Sofia slid the phone back into her bag and nodded as if that suited her, then she returned to her hot toddy, staring out the window of the café.

"I can't believe it hasn't snowed yet. Usually, we've had a few different downfalls by this late in December." Sofia tucked a curl behind her ear.

Holly frowned at the echoing of Ash's observations, hoping her magic wasn't somehow interfering with the weather. But she discounted the thought. If anything, her magic would make snow fall, not the other way around. *Wouldn't it?* "Well, we've got a few more days until the start of the Christmas faire. Maybe we'll get some by then."

"There's nothing in the forecast currently. I've been checking. But I hope you're right. Christmas won't feel the same without snow."

They both eyed the twinkling lights in the café window, which were shaped like snowflakes, and looked at each other with a laugh.

"Well, if that's all the snow we get, I guess it'll have to do," Sofia said, raising her mug to Holly's.

"Cheers," they said simultaneously, their glasses giving a little *clink*.

They sat talking by the window until long after the last customers had left the café.

<h1 style="text-align:center">Chapter Thirty-Four</h1>

The Christmas faire was only days away and would run throughout the week, with the major events, including the parade and the visit from the Hallmark rep, happening on Christmas Eve. The whole town and especially the Emerald House was abuzz with excitement and last-minute preparations. Ash was running on adrenaline and caffeine.

He pulled up to the Emerald House and parked his truck on the frosty but still snowless ground. Though he had given up any hope of it snowing, he still checked the weather app three times a day, just in case.

He noticed Holly through the window. She was having lunch and chatting with her server, Tyler. He couldn't help stopping to watch her. The sun always seemed to hit her hair just right, no matter where she was. She fit in so easily in Emerald Hollow and seemed like one of the locals, perched comfortably in the booth, her favorite order memorized by the whole staff, a hot cocoa always in hand.

Still, even with that ease, she stood out. Ash had a hard time taking his eyes off her when she was around. She seemed to glow no matter the circumstances, and her smile could have been stitched together with pure joy. A smile like that was rare, and Ash was discovering he would do anything to be the one putting it on her face. He had been trying unsuccessfully to shake off that desire.

It had only gotten worse since the Christmas-tree-cutting trip. That outing hadn't felt so perfect since he'd been a kid, making the trek with both of his parents. He could envision her going there with him every year, and that was not something he could allow himself to hope for.

After Christmas, she would go back to Canada, where her life was. As much as she fit in, he had the nagging sense that she was hiding something or at least keeping something close to the chest. *What kind of secret did Mom have that caused her to disappear one December evening, leaving Dad and me behind?* He pushed away that question, as he always did when the memory of his mother threatened to steal his joy.

Holly turned to look out the window, her conversation with Tyler having come to an end, and spotted Ash, her pink lips pulling together into a sweet smile. He gave her a bright one back then walked into the house, glancing at the Christmas tree in the corner.

Holly had selected one that fit perfectly in the tall lobby, and the staff had worked together to dress it with ribbons, tinsel, and ornaments. A bright silver star topped it all off. He thought it might be the best tree the Emerald House had ever had. More than one customer had told him the place looked magical. He entered the restaurant and asked Tyler for a coffee then closed the few steps to Holly's booth.

"Okay if I sit?"

"Of course. Usually, you don't even ask." The corners of her eyes crinkled as her smile widened.

He gave a rueful laugh. "I guess I act like I own the place. How has your day been?" he asked, meeting her dark-green eyes. If a forest could be held in a gaze, that was what Holly's eyes would hold.

"Nice. I've just been working on a few things for the Christmas faire. Nothing much. Just some finishing touches."

Holly had been giving as much to the Christmas faire preparations as he had lately, and that kind of support and care for the town wasn't something he took lightly. "I really don't know how to repay you for everything you've been helping us with. Is there anything I can do for you?"

Holly's enthusiasm was wonderful, but part of him was waiting for the other shoe to drop. She'd already said she was going home to Canada after the Christmas faire. *What will life look like around here then?* It was hard to imagine not bumping into her around the house, bright eyes and a smile always greeting him. He tried not to think about it.

"Anything you can do for me?" Holly repeated, seeming startled by the question. She tilted her head.

While Ash could tell that she was clearly self-sufficient, he wondered if she ever relied on others. Her job took her all over the world. *Does she ever relax and let anyone take care of her?* He wanted to place his hand on top of hers, but he held back.

"Just keep serving this incredible hot cocoa, and I'll never need anything else," she said after a moment. Her cheeks were glowing.

Ash raised his coffee cup to her mug, and the ceramic clinked softly.

"Cheers. I promise that as long as you're here, the hot chocolate will be too."

Holly gave a satisfied smile and took another sip of his old family recipe. He loved how much she loved it.

"So, I just had an idea," he continued, sitting up straighter in the booth. "I have some work to do this afternoon, but what are you up to tomorrow evening?"

"I don't have any plans." Holly leaned toward him slightly, her shoulders rounding forward.

It seemed like an invisible string stretched between them, connecting them as confidants. Warmth bloomed in his chest.

"This is pretty last minute, but in the past, I've thrown an ugly-Christmas-sweater party here at the House. It slipped my mind this year with everything I have going on. You know how I feel about traditions, though. Should we throw the party tomorrow night? I mean, should I? You can just show up, as a guest, of course," Ash added hastily, not wanting her to think he was trying to add something else to her already overflowing plate of generosity.

"But on such short notice?" Holly asked, a small furrow forming between her eyebrows.

"It's Emerald Hollow. I just need to tell one or two people, and word will get around. All we really need is some appetizers and drinks and maybe a few things for door prizes."

"But what about you? Do you have time to handle setting up a party?"

It finally dawned on him that she was worried about him, not the guests. Her brow was knitted in concern, and it made his heart ache in a happy way.

"Don't worry. Everything I need is already here at the house. Maybe you and Sofia can help me with some of the logistics of the prizes at the party. Sofia knows what to do. It'll be great."

"Okay. That sounds fun," Holly said slowly, her forehead starting to relax.

"Great!" Ash felt a familiar jolt of energy, and he couldn't be completely sure if it was from the coffee, the thrill of hosting, or another feeling he didn't want to acknowledge. If he was honest with himself, he probably wouldn't have tried to throw it together if Holly weren't there.

But she was. He continued to try to deny it, but he wanted to spend more time with her. Any moment she wasn't around, he wondered what she was doing or if she needed anything. Time with her meant time when he wasn't thinking about anything or anyone else.

He also just wanted her to experience an Emerald Hollow ugly-sweater party before she left town. Her words about the importance of traditions had stuck with him during the entire Christmas-tree outing and since. Christmas was the season for traditions, and he didn't want to miss a fun one just because he was pursuing some new things. "I'll spread the word."

"So I guess I need to find an ugly sweater."

"Yep. But I can't help you there. It's a competition." Ash couldn't resist teasing her a little. He had a feeling she could give as good as she got. Ash was competitive, but until that moment, it had never been aimed at her.

Holly's eyes widened, and a surprised laugh escaped her. Sparkles danced her eyes.

Yep, I was right.

"Okay, then. You're on."

A delighted warmth filled his chest, and he gave Holly a wicked grin as he stood. The song "It's Beginning to Look a Lot like Christmas" was playing softly in the lobby as he entered, and he hummed along.

$$Chapter\ Thirty\text{-}Five$$

"So, did you hear about the ugly Christmas sweater party tomorrow night?" Sofia asked that evening when she and Holly met in the café after her shift. It was starting to become their custom. They sat at the counter seats facing the street again, not far from the fireplace, which warmed the whole room. Sofia was having a glass of white wine while Holly stuck to water.

"Yep. Ash told me today at lunch. Actually, I think he decided to do it while we were sitting there. Like the idea popped into his head right before he mentioned it to me. Is that normal for him?"

Sofia sighed. "I've seen this before. Sometimes when he's stressed, he can go into hyperdrive, so to speak, and basically overdo everything. He thrives on social interaction, too, so it's all a recipe for a last-minute party. I'll keep an eye on him. He can work himself to exhaustion."

Holly's forehead tightened. *Is running the Emerald House, leading the committee for the Christmas faire, entering a nation-wide contest, and managing this vineyard deal all too much for him?* Most people didn't know about the vineyard deal and probably didn't realize just how much he was doing on any given day. Ash excelled in disguising his weariness from most people, but Holly could sense it there just below the surface.

"I wish there were something I could do to help," Holly mused, staring out at the sidewalk in front of the Emerald House. A woman was walking by with two large black dogs, holding her jacket tightly closed against the cold air.

"You have helped a ton with the sleigh. Ash said so. That was a big weight off his shoulders. And you've been helping out with Comet when Ash is too busy to walk him. Trust me —your being here is really beneficial to everyone, especially Ash."

Holly nodded, still wishing there were something more she could do.

"So, do you have an ugly sweater?" Sofia continued.

Holly perked up. She'd thought an ugly sweater might show up in her bag via magic when she returned to her room after lunch, but it hadn't.

"Not yet. Do you have an extra?"

"Girl, I'm the queen of the ugly Christmas sweater. But I don't wear store-bought ones. I make my own. Kind of famous for it around here, actually." She flicked her hair in mock arrogance, and they both grinned. "I have tomorrow off work. Do you want to come over, and we can make our sweaters together? I'll pick up some sweaters from the thrift store in the morning that we can use as our base, then we can go through my craft box and deck them out."

"That sounds great," Holly said, excited to see Sofia's house.

"I'll pick you up around eleven. Prepare yourself—we're going to be listening to Christmas music all day."

"I specialize in Christmas music," Holly said. Sofia had no idea how much.

"I knew there was a reason we're friends," Sofia teased, and they clinked their glasses together in a toast.

"Here we are. Take your pick." Sofia spread two sweater dresses on her couch.

They were standing in Sofia's small living room, Christmas music already playing softly. Sofia had given Holly a tour of her home, which was an adorable two-bedroom house decorated in an eclectic yet elegant way that perfectly displayed her personality.

Pops of color punctuated all the practical furniture. A bright painting of a beach covered in colorful umbrellas adorned the living room wall, a blue light fixture hung from the ceiling, and a large blue-and-yellow rug covered the wood floor. A small Christmas tree in the corner was filled with blue, yellow, and hot-pink ornaments and tinsel. The star tree topper appeared to be homemade from wire, ribbons, and sequins.

"I found these two sweater dresses and noticed you wear them a lot, so I thought we could pair them with some tights."

Holly looked between the two. One was green and the other white. She thought about choosing the green one and dressing as an elf, but then she remembered Ash's challenge and snagged the white one. Sofia took the green one then led her to a circular dining room table surrounded by bins of various sizes.

"All my crafting and sewing supplies are in here. There's a ton of fabric and a bunch of Christmassy pieces from previous years, so help yourself."

Holly did a quick scan of the bins, and unsurprisingly, everything she needed was there.

"So, have you always lived in Emerald Hollow?" Holly asked as a Nat King Cole Christmas song began to play. She continued to sift through the craft and sewing supplies, occasionally pulling something out and setting it aside.

"Mostly. I grew up here, but then I was in the military for six years." Holly looked up in surprise, and Sofia nodded. "Got out to help care for my mom when she was sick. I needed a job, and Ash hired me at the Emerald House. He was just taking over the business completely at the time. And he pays surprisingly well for this area, which is part of the reason his employees are so happy, and he has low turnover."

Holly smiled at that bit of information. It jibed with her mental image of Ash.

"When my mom passed, I decided to stay here. I love this place, and working at the Emerald House is a great job while I build my jewelry business. My online shop is starting to do really well, though vendor fairs like the Christmas faire are where I do the most sales."

"I'm so sorry about your mom," Holly said. Even though she experienced death differently as a Claus, she knew how difficult the passing of a loved one was for humans. She had sensed grief in her Cheer meter many times. It was a complicated emotion, something deeper and longer lasting than other feelings. It changed constantly, taking on different forms, some more bearable than others.

"Thanks, Hol. Ash was great through it all. Gave me all the time off I needed. We've kind of been best friends ever since." She snagged a bag of pom-poms from the bin. "Ah-ha! Just what I was looking for."

They chatted for a few more hours in comfortable companionship as they worked on their dresses.

"You have some serious sewing skills," Sofia commented.

Holly tried not to feel guilty that she had magic at her disposal, while Sofia was the one using pure skill. "Oh. Thanks. Yeah, I've had a lot of practice. Crafting is big back home."

"Kind of like decorating?" Sofia asked. "I know you said you're in marketing, but you must have some experience in event planning or something. Or are you a competitive crafter in your spare time?"

Holly laughed. "It's just in my blood, I guess."

Sofia snorted. "Remind me never to challenge you to a contest." Sofia's phone beeped, and she glanced at the alert. "A big storm might be rolling in tonight. Not until after the party, though, it looks like. Still, I'm gonna throw some snow boots and a warmer jacket into my car just in case."

"Think we'll finally get the snow everyone's been hoping for?" Holly asked, feeding the hem of her dress through the sewing machine.

"They're currently predicting just high winds and rain, my least favorite combination. But you never know. Maybe we'll get lucky."

Sofia went and found her snow boots and placed them by the door, then they continued to work on their masterpieces until they were complete.

Holly finished her dress before Sofia was done with hers. "Do you have some baking supplies? I want to whip up something for the party."

Sofia stood and dug through her cabinets, pulling out all the basic baking ingredients and dishes. "Have at it."

Holly got to work, easily making a plate full of jingle pops, the only recipe she knew by heart. Her watch did an odd little blipping motion as she pulled the jingle pops out of the oven, and she thought fondly of Auryn. She would have to make him a fresh batch as soon as she got back to the North Pole.

The thought made her pause, standing there holding the tray of hot jingle pops next to the still-open oven door. She'd barely thought of the North Pole lately, as immersed as she was in Emerald Hollow. Closing the oven, she shook that realization away.

"Those look great," Sofia said once the pops had cooled. "They'll be a hit at the party."

Holly smiled in satisfaction, hoping Sofia was right.

Just then, "All I Want for Christmas Is You" came on through Sofia's speaker, and they began to belt out the lyrics.

"You should sing that to Ash. He'd love it," Sofia teased her after the song ended and they'd returned to their normal volume.

Holly threw a large pom-pom at her head.

"Okay, I think we're ready! Let's get a picture."

Sofia clipped her phone into a tripod and grabbed a remote that went with it. Holly, who had never been in a picture before, was startled. Sofia slipped an arm around her waist, and they leaned close to each other, smiling for the camera. As Sofia snapped a few more pictures, Holly relaxed and followed her lead. Then Sofia sorted through them and grabbed a photo printer from a nearby bookshelf.

Within minutes, a miniature photo had come out of the machine, and Sofia handed it to Holly. "We look fab."

Holly stared at the photo, a smile creeping onto her face. Sofia, whose green sweater dress had been turned into a Christmas tree covered in tinsel and pom-pom ornaments, was beaming next to Holly, who was playing an inside joke with herself by dressing as Ms. Claus.

Holly had added furry red fabric to the bottom and around the cuffs of the white dress, a vertical line of three bows down the front, and a fitted black belt made of tulle fabric. She had quickly stitched a collar shape around the neck, trying to throw in all the human stereotypes of Ms. Claus to make it obvious who she was. She tucked the photo into her purse.

"Wait!" Sofia exclaimed just as they were about to walk out the door and head to her Subaru. "You need a Santa hat with that." She ran to another room, grabbed a red-and-white tufted Santa hat, and placed it on Holly's head. The red portion was made of sequins. "There. Now it's perfect. Let's go, Mrs. Claus."

<h1 style="text-align:center">Chapter Thirty-Six</h1>

Holly and Sofia pulled up to the Emerald House just before seven. The parking lot was fuller than usual at that time of night, and others were entering the building in their ugly sweaters. Holly carefully cradled the plate of jingle pops as she looked around and caught sight of a necklace of flashing Christmas light bulbs around a woman's neck and reindeer antlers on a man's head.

"Ash was right. Good turnout on short notice," Holly observed, following Sofia through the heavy front doors.

"Never underestimate the power of word of mouth in a small town," Sofia replied.

A glass bowl labeled Door Prizes Entry and a roll of raffle tickets sat on a small table. Sofia picked up the pen and filled out a ticket for each of them.

Sofia linked arms with Holly. "Now, where is he? I can't wait to show him our outfits."

They made their way through the busy café, Holly stopping to put the jingle pops on the table with the other appetizers. Christmas music was playing from the speakers, and guests were already starting in on the spread of appetizers and drinks. Holly saw the man with the reindeer antlers take a jingle pop and smiled.

"How did he pull this together so quickly?" *Without magic,* she thought.

"Probably asked the kitchen staff to work on some appetizers during the slow time in the afternoon. Pulled some prizes out from the storage room. All the bones were already here for a party, so all he really needed was the people. And here they are." Sofia gave a half twirl, waving her hand across the swath of people. Holly thought Sofia might have been underestimating Ash's efforts, but she nodded and followed her toward the back room.

Sofia poked her head through the door. "There you are!" She stepped over the threshold, letting out a delighted laugh. "Would you look at this? Santa and Mrs. Claus!"

Holly pursed her lips, trying to hold back a smile, as she followed Sofia into the small room and laid eyes on Ash. He was dressed in a red sweater with Santa's face embroidered on the front. Like Holly, he was sporting a Santa hat.

"She wears it better," Ash said, his eyes lingering on Holly until the box he was holding started to slip, and he moved away to tuck it onto a shelf.

A flush creeped up Holly's neck, and she experienced a strange mixture of relief and disappointment when the charged moment ended.

"What are you doing back here working? The party's in full swing," Sofia said.

"I know. I just had to put away a few things to make more space. I figured the party wouldn't get exciting until you two showed up anyway." He winked, and Sofia swatted his arm.

"If you're referring to my spiked cider, I didn't make any this time around. It's a wine night for me. Holly brought a dessert, though. Something called jingle pops. I tried one before we left, and they are divine."

"I'll have to taste one. You two look great. Where did you get the dresses?" He looked between them appreciatively.

"We made them at Sofia's house today," Holly said, placing a hand on her hip to pose.

"Impressive. She introduced you to her craft box, did she?" Ash touched an ornament on Sofia's sleeve, and it gave a little jingle.

"She did. Now I know where to go if I get in a pinch when decorating. I guess we're all good at doing things on short notice," Holly said, nodding through the door toward the party.

Ash waved a hand casually. "That's nothing much. Besides, I was hoping to rope one of you into helping me with the ugly-sweater contest and the door prizes."

"I'm in," Sofia volunteered.

Holly nodded. She'd never helped with a contest before and was eager to get more experience acting like a local in Emerald Hollow.

"You're lifesavers. All right. I've gotta go check on things out there. But the first round of door prizes is being announced at seven thirty, and the final sweater results are at nine. Make sure to vote." He leaned in closer to Holly and whispered, "And may the best Claus win."

He pointed at each of them then disappeared through the doorway.

Holly's gaze trailed after him, her watch vibrating so hard that she thought it might fly off her wrist.

"That man can never stay still for two minutes," Sofia mused, taking Holly by the arm again. "But he's right about voting. Let's put our names down for the contest. You can vote for two people. That way, everyone doesn't just vote for themselves."

They found the table and signed up for the contest. An Emerald House employee who was working at the table snapped each of their pictures, did a quick printout using a printer similar to the one Sofia had at her house, and tacked their pictures to the bulletin board.

"Write your names underneath," she instructed.

Once done entering the ugly-sweater contest, they roamed around for a while, Sofia introducing Holly to townspeople she hadn't met yet and greeting others that she already had. They stopped by the appetizer table for snacks, and Holly was delighted to see that her jingle pops were all gone.

"It's almost seven thirty," Holly said, checking the large clock in the corner.

"Let's go," Sofia said and went to the front door to grab the crystal bowl.

They met up with Ash by the café counter, where a microphone was resting on a serving tray. Ash picked it up and tapped it on then opened his phone to turn down the music.

"Good evening, everyone," he said then gave the group a moment to get quiet.

A few conversations continued in the far corners of the room, but most people turned their attention his way.

"We're getting ready to do our first raffle drawing here. We'll have them every half hour until nine, when we'll announce the winner of the ugly-sweater contest."

A few people whistled in anticipation. Ash glanced at Sofia, and she raised the glass bowl into the air.

"Mrs. Claus, will you do the honors?" Ash asked, his eyes shining at Holly.

It felt strange to hear her last name coming from Ash, and she panicked before realizing he was referring to her sweater.

"Here goes." She reached into the bowl and grabbed a raffle

ticket then looked at the name scrawled across the top. "Enzo!" she pronounced loudly.

A few people clapped or clinked their glasses. Enzo made his way through the crowd to claim his prize. The rest of the party-goers returned to their conversations.

"Lovely to see you again, Holly," Enzo said, beaming.

He was wearing a sweater covered in tiny snowflakes and pizzas. Then he asked her what the prize was in Italian, and Holly responded, also in Italian, that he was receiving a gift card to the Emerald House. He clapped in delight, and Holly wasn't sure if it was more about winning or about her Italian.

"I didn't know you spoke Italian," Sofia said, looking impressed. "You're full of surprises. Next thing I know, you're going to tell me you speak Spanish."

"*Hago hablar español,*" Holly replied without thinking.

Sofia's jaw dropped. "How many languages do you know? Please don't say more than three."

"A few more. It's part of my work," Holly replied, eager to change the subject.

She and Enzo spoke for a while longer while Sofia and Ash mingled with the guests. Enzo told Holly about how he'd started his restaurant, and the details were surprisingly juicy.

"He is really interesting to talk to," Holly told Sofia half an hour later, when Enzo had claimed he was ready to head home and brag to his wife about his raffle winnings.

"Oh yeah, he's a character. Though judging by the length of that conversation, I'm guessing you know him better than I do now," Sofia said.

Holly felt a little warmed by that idea. She was getting to know humans on a level she'd never experienced before coming to Emerald Hollow, and spending time with them brought her more joy than she'd ever imagined. Then a knot formed in her stomach when she remembered it was all temporary. But she tried not to focus on that for the moment.

Holly glanced up sharply when a large group in the corner of the room began belting "Rudolph the Red-Nosed Reindeer." To Holly's surprise, Sofia dashed over to them and joined in, singing loudly. The group looked like a Christmas choir, perfectly in sync, swaying from side to side. Some people had even linked arms.

Ash appeared at Holly's side just then.

"Is this a tradition of the ugly-sweater party?" she asked. A nervous feeling she couldn't articulate was beginning to slide across her skin like wispy clouds over the cold ocean.

Grinning, Ash shrugged. "I have actually never seen anything like this. Especially Sofia. She's usually up for anything, but she *never* sings in public." He squinted a bit then and glanced at the food table. "Didn't Sofia say there was no spiked cider?"

Holly's heart rate sped up as she followed his eyes. Though there was no spiked cider, there had been jingle pops. Holly's mom's voice ran through her mind as she thought of a time when they'd baked jingle pops together. Her mom had told her that jingle pops were an old North Pole recipe made with love and magic. She couldn't have meant that literally, though.

Unlike magic lichen, jingle pops were made with baking ingredients that humans were used to eating. But maybe something about the recipe itself, the combination, was magical? Or perhaps Holly, a magical being, infused magic into the recipe when she baked it. Holly had thought she'd known a lot about magic, but her time in Emerald Hollow was teaching her how much she didn't know.

Holly turned back to the choir, who had finished the song and were beginning to square-dance together. She covered her mouth with her hands. Sofia had partnered with the man wearing reindeer antlers. She had definitely seen him take a jingle pop, and she groaned.

"What's up?" Ash turned toward her.

Hoping he didn't sense her panic, she replied, "Um, nothing. It's just very... entertaining."

Ash scratched the back of his neck, watching the dancers. "This is kind of strange. There are some people in that group I have never seen dance before. And how do they all know how to square dance?"

Cold fear gripped Holly and she took a deep breath. She crossed her fingers that the jingle pops wouldn't do more than put people into the holiday spirit.

"Maybe they're all just overtaken by the atmosphere," Holly suggested, praying that whatever magical shenanigans had taken over the room would wear off soon.

She and the elves had never had that kind of reaction to jingle pops. Then again, they were all used to being around magic every day. For humans, a tiny infusion would be a complete novelty. Holly continued to watch nervously, keeping her eyes peeled for any effects that extended beyond singing and dancing.

Finally, the dance ended, and the individuals sidled off to join their nonmagically influenced friends, laughing heartily. Sofia was practically skipping as she joined Holly and Ash.

"Wow, Ash. This is the best party you've ever thrown." Her eyes were bright, and they danced about the room as she looked for the next source of fun.

"Sofia, why don't you have some vegetables?" Holly suggested, frantically filling a small plate with carrots and celery. If anything could impact magic sweets, it had to be vegetables. Sofia didn't argue and crunched into a carrot with gusto.

"I was just getting ready to let Comet out. Do either of you want to come?" Ash asked.

Sofia shook her head. "I'm good here. You two go. Holly is Comet's new favorite person." She continued to eat from the plate Holly had given her.

Holly glanced around the room nervously, unsure whether she should agree, but things seemed to have settled down a little. "Okay, sure." She looked for a place to set down her drink.

"Bring it if you want. Do you need to stop by your room and grab a coat? It's getting colder out there by the second."

Holly followed Ash down the hallway, throwing one last look over her shoulder at the partygoers. Sofia was still near the appetizer table, eating. Holly tried to relax, but all she could do was wonder how much more there was to her magic that she had yet to understand.

Chapter Thirty-Seven

Holly forced herself to turn her attention fully to Ash as she walked with him out of the café and down the hall toward their rooms.

"Did you hear there's a storm rolling in tonight?" Ash asked. "I'm hoping it's finally going to snow, but it's not in the forecast."

"Yes, Sofia told me."

They stopped by her room, and she retrieved a coat and gloves then continued down the hall and around the corner.

"How do you like living here at the Emerald House?" Holly asked, curious to see his living quarters.

"It's great. Really convenient for work. And this place has always felt like home to me." Ash unlocked the door. His room was away from all the others, and there was a door directly across from his to the outside. A rug with paw prints on it lay in front of his entryway. He pushed the door open, and Comet rushed to greet them. Holly petted the dog as she took a look around, running her hand down the sleek white streak on his back.

She wasn't sure what she'd been expecting, but it wasn't what she saw. Instead of a hotel room or even a suite, it looked like the inside of a small house or apartment. It had a full kitchen and a spacious living and dining area, and she glimpsed a hallway to her left, where she imagined the bedroom and bathroom were. The place was sparsely decorated but very warm and inviting. Holly smiled, and Ash noticed her looking.

"Oh yeah, forgot you hadn't been here yet. There's a private patio out that door over there with a barbeque and a hot tub for when I need some time away from the rest of the house. But honestly, I don't spend a ton of time here."

"It's great," Holly said as Ash pulled on his coat.

They returned to the hallway, and Comet trotted ahead of them, wagging his tail at the prospect of going outside.

"How is everything going with the vineyard deal?"

"It's making progress. I was trying to close the deal before the holidays, but it looks like it's going to have to extend into January. Speaking of the holidays..." Ash pushed open the door, and they all walked outside. He took a ball out of his pocket and threw it for Comet, who went tearing through the grass to chase it. "Are you still planning to go home on Christmas Eve?"

"Yes. Obligations. You know how it is," Holly said, thinking *obligations* was a severe underestimation of the task of delivering Dreams around the world. Still, the idea of leaving caused her to feel a slight sense of panic.

"I do. My dad skips most of the festivities in town these days, but he comes to the house on Christmas morning, and we have breakfast together. It's the one day of the year that the restaurant and café are closed so that all our employees can be with their families. We like to feel as if we've rented out the whole restaurant, and we cook everything in the commercial kitchen together."

Holly could picture it, even though she didn't know Ash's dad.

"That sounds really special." She thought of all the elves having Christmas dinner together in the giant hall at the North Pole. She usually missed it because she was so tired from the Christmas Eve deliveries, and she tended to have a meal at home by herself. Comet nudged her thigh, his ball in his mouth. She took it from him and threw it.

"Wow, Comet. You're just gonna ditch me like that?"

Holly laughed.

"Seriously, you've really hit it off with him. Normally, he sticks to my side like glue."

"The feeling is mutual," Holly said, laughing again as Comet performed a roll in the grass. He reminded her so much of the young reindeer, and he had firmly worked his way into her heart in her time in Emerald Hollow.

"You know how I told you Comet is named after the cosmic snowball, not the reindeer?"

"Yeees," she said slowly. "What about it?"

"When I was a kid, I wanted to be an astronomer. I was pretty into stargazing. I would stay up and watch them for hours, until my parents forced me to go to bed."

"That sounds like me with the northern lights. I can never get enough of them."

Ash's eyes widened. "The northern lights? You can see them from where you live?"

Though she panicked for a second, she was pretty sure the northern lights could be seen from Canada, so she tried to relax, which was getting easier to do around Ash by the day. "Yep. They're amazing. It's like this sea of green that streaks and swirls in unpredictable ways. I think of it like Van Gogh's *Starry Nights* but better." Holly had learned about famous works of art in her human studies classes.

"That was one of my mom's favorite paintings," Ash said, turning from her to look up at the sky. "Maybe a love of the stars was something we had in common."

Holly simply waited rather than responding. Her parents had left her, but it had been in a different way. It had been their time. Ash's mom had left when he was a child, and she couldn't imagine what that would be like for a little boy.

"It was hard for a long time, but I'm happy with how things are going in my life now. We can only control ourselves and how we react to things, you know?" His voice was quiet and contemplative. He almost sounded like he was trying to convince himself. They stood side by side, and Holly thought she could hear his heart beating if she listened closely enough.

All the years Holly had been Ms. Claus, she had been in control of collecting Cheer. She'd felt competent and sometimes even powerful. But she hadn't really been in control. She'd always been at the mercy of other people's emotions. *What would it feel like to know that you could control your reactions without running away at the first sign of discomfort?* She leaned down to pick up the ball again and chucked it for Comet.

"Sorry, that was probably a lot. If I'm talking too much, just tell me to shut up."

"Not at all. Your words got me thinking. With my... work, I haven't really been in control of my reactions. It's hard to explain. But here in Emerald Hollow, I've been able to slow down for a while. I don't think I've been able to be fully in the moment for a long time, and I didn't realize how nice it would be."

"I'm glad this place has had that effect on you. That's how I see it too. And I hope you know that you're always welcome here.

Short-term. Long-term. Maybe you don't have to go back to the grind."

Holly could hear the sincerity—and the question—in Ash's voice, but she pushed it aside, staring at the night sky. He would never understand why she couldn't stay. It wasn't like with his mom. Holly didn't have a choice. Her responsibilities were beyond her. They affected the entire world, and he could never know about it. She was a Claus, and Clauses always put Christmas first.

"Maybe," she said softly, though she knew it was a lie.

"All right, buddy. Time to go back inside," Ash said after a few more minutes, looking at his watch then up at the dark storm clouds.

Holly thought of the reindeer. They were built for all sorts of weather and used to storms at the North Pole, but she made a mental note to check on them before she went to bed.

They all went back inside, Holly taking another quick glance around Ash's apartment as she picked up her glass. The whole place had the feel of him, just like everywhere in the Emerald House did. Without thinking about it, Holly shrugged off her coat and tossed it onto the chair next to Ash's, then they returned to the party together.

THE REST OF THE EVENING WENT BY QUICKLY AS THEY held two more drawings and mingled with the other residents of Emerald Hollow. The party was a roaring success, but Ash wished he could just be outside again, talking with Holly under the stars.

More often than not, Ash stood at Holly's side, introducing her to friends and neighbors, who often remarked on her job well done at the fall festival. Many people at the party seemed even more upbeat than normal, and he had to admit it was the most festive party he had ever hosted. Maybe Holly's presence had something to do with it. She had that effect on people. She was magic.

Sofia pulled him aside when he went to the back room for more supplies. "Looks like you and Holly are having a good time." She leaned casually against the doorframe.

Ash rolled his eyes at her. "What are you up to, Sof?"

"Nothing. Just making an observation."

"Mm-hmm. Sure. But yeah, we are having a good time. And so are you." Ash found what he was looking for and tucked the stack of paper cups under his arms. "Why are we running out of cups? Are people getting a new cup with every drink?"

"It may not be my cider, but that sangria is dangerous too." Sofia nodded in satisfaction.

Ash laughed. "I can tell. Did I see you *singing*?"

"I don't know what came over me. It was like I was possessed. Must be all the holiday spirit in the room. It's like a fever."

"Did you already vote for the ugly-sweater contest? Announcement's in ten."

"Not yet. Thanks for the reminder. I don't think Holly has yet either. I'll grab her to vote, then we'll compile the winners for you. Meet you at the counter at nine? By the way, Ash, this is the best party ever." She did a little twirl on the way out of the supply room.

Ash tried to suppress a grin. It really was a weird night but in the best way possible.

He followed her out, closing the door to the supply room firmly behind him. He caught a glimpse of Holly across the room, talking to Esmeralda. They were chatting as if they were old friends, and Holly looked radiant, her cheeks flushed, the end of her sparkly Santa cap falling loosely over the side of her face.

He couldn't believe he had brought up his mom unprompted. The words had come out of him as if by force. Even talking about something he found difficult to process, his mom, was easier when she was there. He smiled when she caught his eye then ducked his head to look away. He was quite glad he'd decided to throw the party, even if some of the guests were acting like it was their last night on Earth.

Chapter Thirty-Eight

"Here's how this works," Sofia said. "We examine the pictures or just look around the room for your favorite then find the name that matches. If they didn't stop over here and enter sometime during the evening, you can't vote for them. I've made that mistake before—too much sangria early on. Like I said, you can vote for two. We tally up the votes, then the two winners each get the title of the Ugliest Sweater, which they hold on to until next year. Kind of like the harvest-potato thing."

"Got it," Holly replied, reaching eagerly for the little note cards where she could cast her vote. "I'm voting for you and the man who has every reindeer sewn onto his sweater." Holly had gotten a kick out of that one and reminded herself to tell her reindeer all about it later that evening.

"Last chance to vote!" Sofia suddenly shouted toward the partygoers, and a few people quickly came to the table to cast their votes.

"Okay, let's tally these up," Sofia said to Holly after the final votes had been cast. She took out a piece of paper and drew a series of boxes on it.

Holly figured it was best not to interfere with her system and waited while Sofia read from the note cards and tallied the names. "Looks like we have our winners," she said after a few minutes.

Sofia sifted through a box under the table and pulled out two Christmas sweaters that looked like they had been made for infants. The front of each was embroidered with the words Ugliest Sweater. They were so stiff that they could stand up on their own on the table. She handed them to Holly. "Let's go give away some tiny baby sweaters."

They went to the café counter, where Ash, who had been eying their progress, was waiting.

"No ties this year?" he asked Sofia.

She shook her head. "Two clear front-runners this time." She cleared her throat and picked up a glass, clanking a spoon against it. "Listen up! We've got our winners for this year's ugly-sweater contest!"

Her words were met with a few cheers and whistles, and everyone turned toward the three of them, eager to hear the results.

"It looks like you all decided to go for a couples theme this year. Our winners are our very own Ash and Holly!"

Cheers went up around the room, and Holly glanced at Ash in confusion. There were sweaters in the room that were way more detailed than either of theirs. *Why did they vote for us? And why did Sofia refer to us as a couple?*

The cheers seemed a little more raucous than the situation called for. Holly and Ash accepted their sweaters with smiles, though Ash's neck was flushed. She thought she heard him whisper, "Couples? Really, Sof?"

"Now, finish your sangrias, call your sober drivers, and get outta here!" Sofia called to a chorus of laughter.

Many people gathered their coats and tossed plates into the trash, stopping only to congratulate Holly and Ash. Apparently, the people of Emerald Hollow knew how to take a hint, even with magic in the mix. Holly tried to laugh off their congratulations, but she couldn't help thinking they had all been in on the little ambush.

Holly assisted Sofia in cleaning up at the voting station, then she returned to where Ash was chatting with Collin, the man with the sweater covered in reindeer, as he cleaned off the counter.

"Great sweater. I voted for you," Holly said, deciding not to comment on the inaccuracy of some of the reindeer's appearances.

"Thanks. Your dress is great too. I think the whole party was pulling for you two, Mr. and Mrs. Claus," Collin said with a grin.

Ash coughed loudly then tried to suppress it. Holly squeezed her lips together to hide a smile.

"I guess it's time for me to get out of here. This was an epic party, Ash. Nice to meet you, Mrs. Claus." He winked, and Holly returned the farewell.

"Hey, Ash," she said. "I forgot I dropped my jacket off at your place after we let Comet out. It has my room key in it. Can I go grab it?"

"Sure thing. Here's my key. Just lock it up on your way out. I'd go with you, but..." He waved his arms toward the group of people around him who were eager to say goodbye and thank him for the party.

"Thanks. Be right back." Holly quickly made her way to his apartment, opened the door, and grabbed her coat. Comet bounded up to her, wagging his tail, and she spent a few minutes petting him and savoring the clean, woodsy smell of the space. Finally, she said goodbye to Comet and turned back to the door. When she opened it, she came face-to-face with Lucas.

"Oh, hello." Her heart rate increased at his sudden appearance.

"Were you looking for Ash?" Holly stepped into the hall and closed the door behind her then slipped Ash's keys into her pocket.

Lucas looked startled to see her but quickly put on a smile that Holly thought was meant to be reassuring. "Holly, right? Nice to see you again. Are you... staying with Ash?"

"What? No. I'd just left my coat there. I'm staying in one of the suites here. Is there anything I can help you with?" She was starting to feel uncomfortable, and she glanced down the hallway to see if anyone else was around, but it was empty. There were small dark circles under Lucas's eyes, and Holly took a step away from him.

"Nope, I was just leaving. Actually, I was stopping by to see if I could help with the Christmas faire. Do you know what kind of work still needs to be done?"

Holly perked up. The Christmas Cheer must be spreading through the whole building. Did Lucas have a jingle pop? She hadn't noticed him earlier, but the party had been busy. Maybe there was a chance for reconciliation between Lucas and Ash. No wonder he was nervous. Things hadn't been great between them for years. Perhaps she could help.

"Hm, you'd have to ask Ash to be sure. I think most of the details have come together at this point. We're putting the finishing touches on the sleigh and some of the other props out in the workshop. Do you want to come with me to the café? Ash is still out there, and he could answer your questions better than I could."

"No, that's okay. I'll catch him another time. Thanks, Holly," He grinned at her again then disappeared out the door across from Ash's rooms.

As the door opened, Holly heard the wind whipping fiercely.

Holly intended to tell Ash about seeing Lucas, but she got sidetracked by Sofia dragging her to the kitchens for a glass of water to share some elaborate story about her magical night. Just seconds into the story, Sofia stood up straighter and looked out the window. "Looks like it's starting to get nasty out there. I guess I'd better get going."

"I'll walk you out," Holly offered, thinking of sneaking some of the food down to her reindeer before retiring for the night. "Let me just find Ash and return his room key."

Sofia agreed, and they both turned back to the café. Ash was talking to the last two partygoers near the door, but he said goodbye to them when he saw her.

"Here are your keys," she said, handing them to him. "Do you need some help cleaning up?" She looked around at the bowls of leftover food and scattered paper cups.

"Nah, I've got it."

Just then, Sofia returned with her purse.

"Be careful out there, Sof. The storm's rolling in."

"I saw that. Holly's walking me out, so make sure she returns safely in a few minutes."

Holly gave a mocking smile at their concern. She hoped that meant Sofia was returning to normal, the effects of the jingle pops fully worn off. She and Sofia walked out to the car together, their arms linked to steady themselves against the wind.

"I'm getting really used to having you around," Sofia called over the sound of the wind.

"Me too." Holly squeezed her arm. "Drive safe, Sof."

They hugged each other, then Sofia climbed into the Subaru, the door slamming hard behind her. Holly watched her drive off then turned down the trail toward the woods, hurrying since she knew Ash would be expecting her back inside soon. Her reindeer came trotting up happily when they saw her, and she slipped them each some grapes.

"There's a storm coming in tonight. Best to bed down early."

They nuzzled against her in agreement, and she promised to come check on them in the morning. She pulled her coat tightly around herself to avoid it ripping in the wind and hurried back up the path to the Emerald House.

Chapter Thirty-Nine

"There you are," Ash said as she pushed open the heavy door into the lobby. "I was just getting ready to come check on you." He had his coat on but shrugged it off since she had returned. "Heading to bed?"

Holly glanced at the lobby and saw that there was still a little cleaning up to do, so she grabbed a trash bag from the floor and began scooping paper products into it. "Soon, once we're done in here."

Ash nodded at her gratefully, and they worked together for another fifteen minutes until the room had been cleared, counters wiped down, and the floor swept.

"You should probably be on the payroll at this point," Ash joked as he put the broom away in the kitchen.

Holly laughed. "Don't worry about it. I've enjoyed more than my fair share of hospitality here." She thought slightly guiltily of her free suite and all the free meals she'd consumed. She wasn't sure whether Ash was consciously comping those, or it was part of her magic.

"Well, I hope you'll be able to enjoy the Christmas faire as a guest. Before you go back home." He said the last part quietly and almost reluctantly.

Holly took a step closer to him.

How could I explain all this to him? Holly didn't really want to go back to Canada, which wasn't Canada after all. She lived at the North Pole and needed to check in there every month to deposit Cheer. Her lifestyle was otherwise nomadic, and she had never stayed in one place so long. *How could I tell him what Emerald Hollow is beginning to mean to me when I don't quite understand it myself?*

"Maybe I'll visit again after New Year's," she suggested, trying for a playful tone but realized she sounded sad. She would always be just a visitor to Emerald Hollow, someone who stopped by now and then but ultimately belonged somewhere else.

Ash stepped closer to her, gently touching her arm. Holly didn't jump that time. She was suddenly conscious of her watch, which she had barely noticed that evening, humming rapidly against her skin. Its warmth matched that of his hand on hers.

"Would you like to dance?" he asked, holding her hand up in the air as if about to promenade.

She nodded, surprising herself, and he called out a voice command to the speaker to turn on a jazzy Christmas song. He slid his other hand around her waist and squeezed her hand a little tighter. Holly'd had occasion to dance a few times, visiting weddings or concerts to collect Cheer, but never face-to-face with another person.

Instinctively, she knew how to step and sway. She'd always been a good dancer, assuming it was part of her magic helping her blend in, just like her inherent knowledge of local languages and cultures. If the wedding guests had to perform a traditional dance, Holly knew the steps and fell in flawlessly.

Her hair swished over her shoulder as she tossed her head

lightly, settling into a rhythm with him. Ash hummed along to the music, then they danced in silence for a few moments, Ash spinning her and reeling her back in slowly.

"What's really keeping you in Canada, Holly?" Ash asked softly.

Their faces were close, her head tilted toward his shoulder, so she couldn't see his expression.

"Your work? Your community? I understand those things better than anyone. But..." As he hesitated, their dancing slowed even further. "Is there anything... anything that's missing there?"

Holly leaned back a little and met his eyes, and their warmth melted her heart. "I don't know. I didn't think so until I came here. Then... I don't know. Everything sort of changed for me." She struggled with words again, realizing it was impossible to explain any of it to him. She felt dizzy at his proximity. He smelled faintly of oranges and pine.

He brushed her hair behind her ear, and her breath hitched, then he dropped his hand back to rest softly on her waist.

"Things changed for me, too, when you arrived."

Holly felt like there was a hummingbird inside her stomach. For a moment, she was blissfully happy. But a moment later, fear gripped her—fear of hurting Ash because their relationship could only be temporary and fear of what living as a Claus with humans might be causing. The jingle pop incident had turned out innocuous enough, but it could have been much worse. She was a Claus, and he was a human. Their lifestyles were incompatible and always would be.

She took a step back, gently releasing his hand. "I should get to bed before this storm gets too loud and keeps me awake all night." Holly shivered at the loss of his touch as he gently dropped his hand from her waist. She avoided making eye contact with him. The air was still charged with an electricity

Holly didn't think was her magic. "Thanks again for a really fun night."

"You're welcome," Ash replied, though she barely heard him, as she was already disappearing down the hallway.

The faint warmth she'd felt where his hands had touched her slowly dissipated, replaced with the harsh sounds of the storms outside and in her heart.

Chapter Forty

Holly woke the next morning to the wind still howling and rain coming down heavily, slamming the Emerald House with impressive strength. Reminded of the hurricane she had once experienced but managed to get away from with the reindeer, she felt thankful that Emerald Hollow was located well above sea level.

She got up early and went out to the reindeer again, Comet at her side. He'd been in the lobby when she entered, Ash nowhere in sight, and slipped out the door with her when she opened it. She tried to call the dog back in but gave up when he wouldn't listen.

"Stay close," she said to him as they scurried down the path toward the woods. Tree limbs had fallen during the night, and the parking lot of the Emerald House was covered in pine needles and other debris from the forest. The sky was a dark charcoal gray, and thunder rumbled nearby.

"This is some storm," she murmured, sighing in relief as the reindeer trotted out of the forest to greet her, looking perfectly healthy and warm. "Good morning, friends." She handed each of them a carrot, then Comet started to play with Ivy and Clove, the three of them running in circles in a blur of black and tan.

Holly hadn't brought an umbrella because the wind was too strong. Instead, she'd slipped on a parka and pulled the hood far over her face. Comet was getting soaked, and she wondered if Ash would be upset. Thinking of him made her mind flash to the previous night. She'd barely stopped thinking of it since. She remembered the feel of her hand in his and the soft touch on her waist. Then she had pulled back, snapping the thread of whatever was building between them.

Why was I so afraid? As she lay in her bed, watching the swirl of the snowflakes on her watch while the storm raged, she wondered if she'd overreacted. The jingle pop incident had turned out fine. So far, her magical abilities had only helped the town. She thought of the workshop full of decorations she'd been working on all week. Warmth filled her as she pictured herself showing Ash everything she'd made. He was going to be thrilled.

Maybe the town would have a shot in the Hallmark competition, the vineyard deal would go through, and Ash would see his Dream for the house and Emerald Hollow fulfilled. If she couldn't give him anything else, maybe she could give him that.

Holly was snapped out of her fantasizing by a loud clap of thunder. She whistled for Comet, and to her surprise, he came immediately and stood by her side. Saying goodbye to the reindeer, she snuck them each one last snack, then she turned back toward the Emerald House. Comet ran next to her, and she hurried toward the large building as the rain came down harder than ever.

When they reached the building, Comet shook water off him under the covered carport before they went inside, and Holly wondered in amazement if Ash had trained him to do that.

"Good boy," she said, contemplating where she could find a spare towel to dry him off even further.

Just then, lightning cracked, followed by an earsplitting clap of thunder. A moment later, all the lights in the Emerald House went out.

THE RESTAURANT WASN'T OPEN YET WHEN THE POWER shut off, and the café only had two early-bird customers. The few employees on shift gathered in the lobby and waited for Ash to arrive. Holly, who had forgotten all about trying to find a towel for Comet when the building had gone dark, gathered with them, ready to help.

"Good morning," Ash said, coming around the corner in a long-sleeve Henley and jeans.

Holly's breath caught at the sight of him. His hair was wet, and Holly wasn't sure whether he'd just taken a shower or he'd been outside without a coat on and changed his clothes. Judging by the hint of orange and pine when he walked past, she put her money on the shower. He didn't make eye contact as he walked by her.

"I just started the generator, but that's only enough to power the fridges so the food doesn't spoil and maybe the hot water tanks for a while. The restaurant will be closed until further notice. I just spoke with the power company, and a line is down. In this weather, it could be a while until things are working again. Restaurant team, you're all free to go, or stay here if you need some place warm and dry. I'll get all the fireplaces cranking." He turned toward the hotel staff, who were gathered near the check-in counter. "If any of you need to get home to your families, let me know. Otherwise, I'd like to keep you on to help with guest needs."

Ash was like a controlled whirlwind, handling everything and everyone around him. Holly stayed still, leaning on the lobby counter, barely able to keep her eyes off Ash as he took care of business. Her heart did a little flip each time she looked at him, though he was completely focused on the tasks at hand. Most of the employees gathered their personal items and headed to the parking lot.

Finally, feeling restless, she decided to get a jump start on the fires. The lobby had a massive fireplace, and the café did as well. With expert skill, Holly stacked the logs that were stored in a corner of the café, looked around to make sure she didn't have an audience, then sparked the fire with her magic.

Fire wasn't typically something that magic delivered, but apparently, roaring fireplaces fell under the cozy Christmas vibe. Within seconds, a full fire was forming in both hearths, and Comet's coat quickly began to dry as he lay down in front of the one in the lobby.

Ash returned, greeting the customers in the café and letting them know they were welcome to stay as long as they wanted, and if they needed any more coffee to help themselves to the remaining drip carafe.

"Hey," he said, finally coming toward Holly. "Who started these fires?"

"I did. Thought you had enough on your hands." Holly put her hands in her parka pockets, trying not to think about when she'd been close to him the previous night.

He seemed impressed but didn't say anything more about them.

"Looks like the power could be out for a few hours. All we can really do now is stay inside and keep warm." He glanced at her still-damp coat. "I see you've already been out there."

"Yep, and it's pretty fierce."

"I'm guessing other hotel guests will be waking up soon and coming out to see what's going on. I'll put out some dry food for breakfast and try to keep the coffee hot. Then it'll be music and board games in the lobby until the power comes back on, I think."

"Let me get the breakfast stuff out," Holly offered. "You can check on the guests and make sure your hotel staff who are still working today don't need anything."

"Are you sure? I can—"

"Don't worry about me. I wouldn't have offered it if I didn't want to do it. Besides, I don't know where the board games are." She winked.

His shoulders relaxed, and she hoped that any awkwardness between them had faded. He smiled in that easygoing way she was used to and tilted his head as if studying her. Someone called his name, and he turned away.

Chapter Forty-One

olly took her time learning her way around the kitchen. She almost never cooked at the North Pole. The elves took too much pride in serving her. Eventually, she figured out where the various dry goods were stored as well as a few serving plates and dishes. She made up some trays of bagels and spreads, fruit, and cheese, arranging them in a pleasing pattern.

Finally satisfied, she carried the two large dishes to a table in the lobby. It appeared most of the guests were up and in various stages of checking out or settling in. A couple of children made a beeline for the breakfast platters, and their father thanked Holly gratefully.

After all the single nighters checked out and others returned to their rooms, only one family with two elementary-school-aged children remained in the lobby. They had taken a weeklong vacation and were staying at the Emerald House through the Christmas faire.

"We'd planned to go visit my sister about thirty minutes from here today, but I don't think she'd want us driving until this clears up," the mother informed Holly, seeming to think she was a member of the staff.

"Of course. I think we have some board games around here. Is there anything else you need for the kids?"

"Luckily, they both like to read, and we have some crafting supplies in the room. Board games would be great too. All right if we just hang out in the café area? They might get cabin fever in the room, as delightful as it is."

"Absolutely," Holly assured her, thinking about the rest of the day. She should probably prepare something for lunch for the family if the power was still out then.

Ash reappeared then, and Holly and the family all turned toward him. He was carrying a stack of board games, and he set them down on the counter. "Help yourselves." He winked at the kids, who smiled at him shyly and began to sift through the games.

Next, Ash grabbed a bagel and smeared it with cream cheese. "This looks great. I see the guests are helping themselves. I didn't actually realize how hungry I was until I saw this."

"Can I challenge you to a board game?" Holly asked, hoping to make up for running out on their conversation the previous night. She wanted him to know that she still considered him a good friend. "Though I'll admit I've never really played before. Not any of these games, at least." She eyed the stack, from which the family of four had already selected a game called Sorry. Holly thought it seemed like a strange name for a game.

Ash's jaw dropped. "What? Do they have different board games in Canada?"

Holly was unsure of the answer, so she said, "My parents were fans of homemade games. We had some family heirlooms that don't exist on the market."

"No way! You had your own original board games? I would like to see those. But in honor of your introduction to average-people board games, I'll let you choose whatever you want." He grabbed a plate and added a few more morsels of breakfast to it then walked to the stack and leaned against the counter.

She felt the strangest urge to wrap her arms around him, and she quickly turned her attention to the board games. Studying the stack carefully, she said, "Hmm, are there any here that are better for two players?"

Ash looked through them before sorting them into two stacks. "There. All these are good for two players." He stepped aside so she could pick one and pulled out his phone. "I'm just going to check on Sof."

"Tell her hi from me. And we can make this a three player if she wants to join us." Having another friend there might help balance the gravitational pull she felt whenever he was in the room.

Ash passed on the message and spoke to Sofia for a few more minutes.

"All right, well, call me if you need anything," he said then hung up the phone.

Holly turned to look at him, waiting for him to fill her in.

"She says the power is off at her house, too, but that this is the 'perfect opportunity to stay home and work on my jewelry.'" He put air quotes around the words. "She wants to make a few more batches before the Christmas faire. So I guess it's just you and me."

You and me. She tried not to let the words have more power than they were intended to have.

"Which game is your favorite?"

"I'm actually more of a card guy. More action." He snagged a deck off the table. "We could keep it simple. How about a game of War?"

"War?" Holly asked, eying the cards warily.

"Don't tell me you don't have cards in Canada."

Holly laughed. "No, we do. But I've never played War." She didn't elaborate that she had a card game with the elves that didn't involve any numbers, and each card represented a different Christmas-related item. The object was to combine the cards to make a Christmas lyric then sing it. She smiled at the thought then got her head in the game.

Ash explained War, and it sounded simple enough, though he had to keep reminding her which face cards were of higher value.

"What is a jack?" Holly asked. She understood king and queen but was confused by that one.

"Um, I don't actually know. I think it would be like a courtier or something. Someone important in royal society," Ash said, laying down a ten and taking her eight.

"Why is the king of higher value than the queen? In some societies, the queen is the more important one by birth. Remember Queen Elizabeth?" Holly let out a little cry of frustration as she laid down a two. Ash's stack was growing much larger, while hers was shrinking rapidly. Apparently, her magic didn't care about her winning a card game.

"Those are just the rules of the game. But you're right. We can change them if you want. Next round, queen beats king."

Lightning flashed, followed by a roll of thunder. Out of the corner of her eye, Holly saw the little boy jump while playing the game of Sorry with his family.

"Those are close." Ash's brow furrowed as he glanced out the window. "Usually, storms like this are over in twenty-four hours."

Holly hoped he was right, not wanting the storm to impact the Christmas faire, which officially kicked off the next day. So far, it was only bringing lightning, wind, and rain, with not a snowflake in sight.

Ash won her last card, and she sighed. "I'm not very good at War."

"It's just luck. You could obliterate me in the next round."

They played again, that time with queen beating king. Once they tired of War, with Ash beating Holly in two out of three games, Holly wanted to increase her odds of winning.

"Can we play something involving strategy?"

His eyes lit up, and he thought for a moment. Comet came up to his side, and Ash scratched the dog's head absently.

"Let's try rummy. I'll walk you through it."

It took a few rounds before Holly was comfortable, but once she got the hang of it, she was unstoppable. Her scientific mind liked the probabilities involved.

"I can see why you wanted to play a game with some strategy. You just crushed me," Ash said.

Holly laughed. Winning a strategy game gave her a thrill similar to that of finding a Cheer jackpot. That made her think about the Cheer in Emerald Hollow again, and she frowned. When she looked up, she realized the family of four had retired to their rooms, and the café was quiet around them.

"I'm going to call the power company for an update," Ash said, standing to stretch.

Holly cleared away all the breakfast dishes while he made the call then looked to him for an answer when he hung up the phone.

"Not gonna be on for a while. It's a mess out there. I think I'm going to go out to the workshop to get some battery-powered lanterns. It's only going to get darker as the day goes on, and I want to be prepared if we're still without power this evening."

"I'll come," Holly said, reaching for her parka, which she'd slung over the back of her chair. It was fully dry, thanks to the roaring fire.

"You Canadians are thick-skinned," Ash said but didn't

protest. "I'm going to make Comet stay, though. I don't want him taking off at the sound of thunder."

Holly thought of the reindeer, assuring herself that the magic was keeping them safe. They bundled up in coats, hats, and gloves then braced themselves to enter the storm.

Chapter Forty-Two

"It seems less windy than it did this morning," Ash called over the wind as they ran toward the workshop. "Let's hope the worst is over."

The workshop came into view, and Ash gave a shout. Holly followed his gaze, and her heart sank. The large front doors were wide open. They rushed inside, and Ash worked on heaving one of the heavy doors shut. Once they got both doors closed, they stared at the mess. The boxes of decorations were smashed against the wall, soaked.

"The doors must have been open all night," Ash muttered in shock.

They wandered through the workshop, dazed, seeing ruined decorations in all directions. The garlands Holly had made by hand had been ripped apart by the wind, and the little bits of greenery were scattered all over the floor. She felt sick.

They turned the corner, and her heart dropped again when she saw Santa's sleigh. It had been somewhat protected from the wind and rain, but some creature had made the sleigh its home the previous night. The inside was covered in mud, and the fresh paint job was scratched. One of the panels had fallen off.

Ash picked up an overturned stool and sat down on it, silent. Holly had never seen him at a loss for words, and she, too, was speechless. Finally, he shook his head and stood, looking at the door.

"I don't understand." He ran a hand through his hair in frustration. "I'm sure I secured those. I lock them every time I leave, and I checked them again before the party last night because I knew a storm was rolling in." He returned to the doors and slipped outside then reappeared a few moments later with something in his hand.

"The padlock was lying on the ground out there." He looked completely bewildered, staring down at the lock.

Holly froze. Someone that Ash hadn't known about had been at the Emerald House the previous night. Someone had been lurking outside Ash's room. Holly had told him all the decorations for the Christmas faire were stored in the workshop. She felt like she had eaten one too many candy canes, her stomach twisting into knots.

"This is my fault," she breathed, blinking back tears. All their hard work was in tatters, and the look of sheer devastation and confusion on Ash's face cut her to the bone.

"What? No. Of course it's not." He stepped closer to her and took her arms in his.

She stepped back. "Listen to me. There's something you don't know. Last night, Lucas was here."

Ash looked up sharply, his eyes narrowed. "What? When?"

"I saw him toward the end of the party, outside your room. He was there when I went to get my coat. I... I told him the decorations and sleigh were out here in the warehouse. He was asking if he could do anything to help with the Christmas faire. I thought his intentions were good. I can't believe I didn't listen to Sofia's warnings about him. This is all my fault." Holly struggled to focus on anything other than the sprigs of greenery littering the soaking-wet floor. She didn't dare look at Ash's face, unable to stomach his disappointment.

The air had gone bitterly cold around them. Holly couldn't move. Then suddenly, she realized her wrist was cold. *Has the Cheer meter finally registered the strong emotions happening right now? Has the long rally of high Cheer finally ended?*

She looked at her wrist and let out a little cry. Her watch was gone.

Chapter Forty-Three

olly turned quickly, still grasping her empty wrist. She ran back toward the Emerald House, leaving Ash standing there outside the barn, calling after her. In a panic, Holly unlocked the door to her room and burst in, flashing through all the potential consequences of what had happened. Her Cheer meter couldn't accidentally come off because it wasn't designed that way.

If my Cheer meter is lost...

No, it can't be lost.

Suddenly, Holly remembered falling asleep the night before to the pattern of swirling snowflakes. She had a fuzzy memory of sleepily thinking of dancing with Ash and tracing the secret pattern.

Holly gasped. She'd unlocked the watch herself, before she'd fallen asleep. She searched around the bed then heaved a sigh of relief when she found the watch on the floor. Quickly clasping it around her wrist, she sat there, her back against the bed, her heart pounding. As she studied the screen, she noticed the watch face spinning erratically. *What does it mean?*

This could have been a disaster. This is *a disaster.* Maybe it had impacted her Cheer. All the decor being destroyed was bad enough, but it wasn't insurmountable, not for her. She could probably call up a Christmas supply company and request a large last-minute order, and her magic would ensure it was delivered to Emerald Hollow on time. Because she was Ms. Claus.

That was the problem. She was Ms. Claus, not a human. And she had almost lost her Cheer meter, the most precious, irreplaceable item on Earth. She hadn't even noticed for an entire morning. That was unforgivable. Holly hardly recognized the person she had become during her time in Emerald Hollow.

With the slow, agonizing sensation of a ship sinking toward the bottom of the ocean, she knew she had to leave. She had one aching moment of struggle, when the ship thought it might be able to stay afloat, but a final tug of the water collapsed it for good. She was never supposed to be in town in the first place. Ms. Claus had her place in the world, and it wasn't living with humans.

She didn't even remember to grab her backpack as she rushed out the door.

HOLLY PASSED THROUGH THE LOBBY IN A BLUR. SHE bumped into Sofia, not registering the pair of earrings Sofia had been holding out with a smile. At the look on Holly's face, Sofia's smile disappeared.

"Holly, are you okay? What's going on?" Sofia set the earrings on the lobby counter and moved to keep pace with Holly, who paused.

"I'm sorry, Sofia. It was a mistake to come here. I have to go." Holly started walking again, nearly to the front door.

"What are you talking about? What mistake?"

The Christmas tree stood behind Sofia, not lit up but still sparkling beautifully with ornaments and tinsel. The sight of it made her heart ache, and she closed her eyes.

"It's too much to explain, but I have to get home. I shouldn't be here. I don't belong here." Holly focused on holding back the tears that threatened to spill over.

"I don't know what happened, Holly, but I'm sure it wasn't your fault. Please stay. It'll kill Ash that you've left."

"I'm sorry, Sof. Please make sure he knows that. But I can't make his life any more difficult. I have to go." Holly clutched her Cheer meter tightly, worried Ash would appear any moment. She didn't want to face him.

Sofia simply shook her head, her mouth in a tight line. "You're running away." Her arms were crossed, but her voice was gentle. "That will hurt him more than anything."

"It's for the best. This could never have worked."

Holly had to go immediately. She had to protect Christmas. All the Dreams in the world were so much more important than what Holly wanted. And protecting those Dreams meant leaving the distractions behind. Emerald Hollow had been a distraction, no matter that it had been a wonderful one.

Holly reached for Sofia's hand and gave it a quick squeeze. Then she turned, pushed through the heavy doors, and hurried down the drive. She heard Sofia shout her name before it was muffled by the doors swinging closed.

A few moments later, the door whooshed again, then came the sound of footsteps running behind her. "Holly!"

Ash's voice nearly stopped her. Every ounce of her wanted to turn back, to run and tell him everything was going to be okay, but her duty to the North Pole propelled her forward, away from Ash.

Her thoughts began to spiral, building a pile of reasons she was in the right to go. The town would lose the contest, and it was possible the Christmas faire would be canceled altogether. Ash wouldn't get the funding from his investors for the vineyard deal. *How could I have been so naive about Lucas?* Sofia had warned her his intentions weren't good. *Do I have time to fix any of it?* The town was so much better off without her. She remembered the look on Ash's face at the sight of the destroyed decorations and gritted her teeth.

"Holly, wait!"

Though she could hear Ash's voice, it was far away. Holly ran to her reindeer and reached out to them before suddenly noticing Comet at her feet. He was looking from her to the reindeer, wagging his tail excitedly.

"I'm sorry boy. We have to go." She gave him a quick scratch on the head, her eyes welling. Wiping a tear from her eye, she left the dog behind.

Holly ran deeper into the forest to where the sleigh was hidden. The reindeer looked at her in confusion, Ivy and Clove whining at Comet, before Dasher realized what was happening and flipped into professional mode, getting them all organized to fly.

Holly climbed into the sleigh and raised the reins. She waited for it to rise in the air, but it didn't move. Her eyes flew to the reindeer, who were kicking their legs in frustration. She raised the reins encouragingly once more, but the reindeer shook their heads.

She froze. "What's going on? Can't you fly?" Dread suddenly formed in her chest. She climbed out of the sleigh in a panic, searching her pockets for magic lichen. They were empty. *When was the last time I fed it to them?*

She studied her watch again, fully panicked. The hand on the clock face was still spinning. She looked closer.

"No!" she gasped. The Cheer level had fallen to zero. *How is this possible? Is this because I took it off?*

She rubbed her fingers together in agitation as she walked around the sleigh in a circle, desperately trying to think of some way to give the reindeer her magic. If she didn't get to the North Pole soon, the elves wouldn't be able to finalize the Christmas Eve preparations. The Dreams wouldn't go out into the world. And it would be all her fault.

Chapter Forty-Four

Panic swelled in Holly's chest. She couldn't be stuck there. But there was no way to get back to the North Pole without her reindeer pulling her sleigh. She had failed everyone.

Her heart racing, she took a deep breath. *Think, Holly. Think.* She needed to get a message to Clementine to warn the elves.

Holly stopped pacing as she remembered something from her studies many years ago. Her watch could serve as a communication device with the North Pole in case of emergency, but she'd never had to use it before. She gripped her wrist behind her watch, studying it carefully. *How do I activate the emergency call?*

She tried poking, prodding, twisting, and turning, but nothing changed on the screen. She glanced over at her reindeer, tears pricking her eyes. Ivy and Clove's ears were drooping so low that they practically touched the ground. Even the normally stoic Dasher hung his head.

"Come on. Come on," she mumbled, tapping her watch face repeatedly in frustration. "Why aren't you listening to me?"

Then she froze. *Listening.* An old memory worked its way through the gears in her brain.

If you find yourself in times of need, "Listen" shall be your creed.

The old nursery rhyme had popped into her head like magic, and she thought of her mother singing that line to her almost absentmindedly.

Holly tried to relax her muscles and her mind. She closed her eyes and held her watch near her ear. There it was—a faint pattern. She'd never heard it before and strained to listen more closely.

Tick. Tick-tick. Tick. Tick-tick. Tick. She took a deep breath and placed her finger above the snowflake in the center of her watch then tapped along to the pattern she heard. *Tick. Tick-tick. Tick. Tick-tick. Tick.*

Almost imperceptibly, her watch started to glow. The face blurred, and moments later, Clementine's worried face appeared in the circle.

"Ms. Claus!" she exclaimed, seemingly out of breath. "Your house started shooting tinsel all over the front porch, and I rushed inside to see the round mirror above your fireplace glowing. Now here you are! What's going on?"

Holly was so relieved to have finally contacted someone at the North Pole that her legs gave way, and she sank to the ground, still gripping her watch. "Clementine, something is seriously wrong with the magic. The reindeer can't fly anymore. My Cheer meter is at zero. How am I going to get back to the North Pole? I can't go back without the reindeer!"

Clementine's ears shot up at Holly's frantic tone.

Just then, Holly remembered something else, and her pulse spiked. Maybe there was still a chance to get back to the North Pole. "Clementine, can you find Lumi Kringle?"

"Wait just a few moments. I'll be right back." Clementine's face disappeared from view.

Holly continued to tread deeper into the forest, not daring to look away from her watch face, and waited for what felt like an eternity.

When Clementine's face reappeared, Holly stopped pacing and stood completely still.

"She's here," Clementine said.

Lumi's face filled the watch, her golden eyes still striking through the tiny screen.

"Holly, what's going on? Clementine was too upset to explain."

"Lumi, how have you been getting to Finland? The reindeer can't fly. If there's another way for me to get to the North Pole, I need to know about it."

"The reindeer can't fly? What happened? Oh, candy canes," Lumi murmured, lines forming in her forehead.

"I don't know! Is there another way?" They were running out of time. She had to get to the North Pole then figure out what was wrong with her Cheer meter. "It's urgent!"

Lumi nodded. She hesitated then seemed resigned to speak. "It's called snow tunneling. Very few of us elves know how to do it. Only a few of the elder Kringles. It requires a lot of magic. But as a Claus, you should have the ability naturally."

Holly gasped. "Snow tunneling? I've never heard of it."

"Many years ago, the elder elves decided to keep it secret. We didn't need young elves running around the Earth, wreaking havoc and neglecting their duties at the North Pole."

"So how does it work?" Holly asked, shelving the rest of her questions. She wanted to know more about these elfcapades, but that would have to wait.

"You just need to have snow on both ends. Ideally a good bit of it. The more snow you have to tunnel in and out of, the less magic you need. Is there snow where you are?"

Holly glanced around, her heart sinking. Everyone had been saying it was strange that Emerald Hollow hadn't received any snow yet that year. She looked through the forest, up toward the steep mountains. There was snow at the higher elevations. She clamped on to the glimmer of hope. She could get there.

"I've got snow. What about the reindeer? Will I be able to snow tunnel with them?" Holly would never leave them behind, even in Emerald Hollow.

Lumi nodded. "I think you should have enough innate magic to do that. But, Holly…" She dropped her voice so that Holly had to lean in closer to hear her. "Please hurry. Things are… Well, they're starting to change here too. There's still snow, but it's melting quickly. I saw it starting to happen when Clementine came to get me. I don't know how much time you have to open a tunnel on this side."

Holly gasped. *What is going on? This is catastrophic.* She jumped to her feet. "We're on our way. How do I make the tunnel?"

Holly signaled to the reindeer to gather near her. Still attached to the sleigh, they jumped to attention. She listened closely as Lumi explained how to create the tunnel, trying to memorize her instructions.

"All right." She nodded. "I'll see you soon." Holly pressed her mouth into a line, trying to concentrate.

"One more thing, Holly," Lumi said, her voice serious. "Snow tunneling can have unexpected consequences. It can leave traces of magic, and we can't always control what happens. It's very important that no humans get near your tunnel. Do you understand?"

Holly was startled, but she nodded. "Thanks for the warning. I'll be deep in the forest." Holly was already walking rapidly, ready to hike, her reindeer at her heels.

"Then good luck. We'll see you soon."

<h1 style="text-align:center">Chapter Forty-Five</h1>

Once Holly had gone high enough into the mountains to reach snow, she stood still, gathering the reindeer close beside her. As Lumi had instructed, she held out her right hand, her palm facing forward, and began to make a circling motion.

She closed her eyes and concentrated fully on the North Pole, picturing an area between the elves' forest and the Mountains of the Whispering Winds, where the highest levels of snow gathered. She quickly prayed there was still enough snow on the other end to form the tunnel.

Holly opened her eyes to the sound of a soft whooshing, and snow was beginning to swirl in front of her. It became faster and faster, the whooshing louder, until a circle formed.

Snowflakes whipped her face as the vortex compelled her forward. Holly took a step toward it and felt as if gravity were urging her through the tunnel instead of planting her onto the earth. Her hair blew around her face.

"Let's go!" she called to her reindeer over the loud blizzard.

Together, they disappeared through the tunnel, and the forest in the mountains outside Emerald Hollow was silent once more.

Holly and the reindeer emerged in the place she had imagined, near the base of the elves' ski park. They all stood slowly, their legs wobbly. The trip through the snow tunnel had only taken moments, but it been like falling through a running washing machine. Her legs finally stabilized, and when she saw that the reindeer looked okay, she set off at a run.

When she made it to Merriment Square, Clementine was not the only elf to greet her. Hundreds of elves were there, awaiting her arrival and answers to what was going on.

Holly noticed that the North Post had dimmed. Whatever supercharged Cheer she had brought there before, it was quickly fizzling out.

The warm white lights that normally lit the arches over the path to Merriment Square were dark. She looked at her watch, and the Cheer level was still at zero. *This is unprecedented.* She sealed her lips together, trying to stay composed in front of her elves.

There was no reason to worry them yet. Holly had to block out the signs of disarray around her, including all the melted snow, and focus on what she needed to do.

She hurried down the path. Maybe she could still touch the North Post and transfer Cheer. The zero level on her watch had to be a false reading.

"I've got this," Holly whispered, gliding through the sea of elves toward the center of Merriment Square.

The elves murmured excitedly as they followed her. Holly approached the North Post and paused for just a moment before she placed her hand on it.

She reached out, touching the snowflake as she had hundreds of times before.

Nothing happened.

She pressed harder, willing her watch to transfer Cheer, but there was no familiar warm feeling on her wrist. The light of the North Post continued to dim. Holly suppressed a cry of frustration.

She hurried to her front porch, just barely avoiding running, Clementine at her heels. "Clementine, are there any reindeer that are able to fly?"

Clementine tapped her clipboard a little too quickly then pressed the jewel on her ring. "We have some emergency stashes of magic lichen, and we should be able to feed it to them. What are you thinking?"

Holly pressed her lips in a tight line, her mind racing. She'd been collecting Cheer without issue for years. She could do it again. An image of Ash's crestfallen face popped into her mind, and she heard him calling her name as she ran away. Squeezing her eyes shut, she pushed the thoughts aside and tried to ignore the knots that twisted in her stomach.

"I'm going to collect some Cheer."

Chapter Forty-Six

Holly spent less than ten minutes at the North Pole, quickly devouring a mug of hot cider as if it were a magic potion and checking on the defunct operations while four new reindeer and her sleigh were prepared for a late-night trip. Her mind was whirring. *Where can I go for the highest yields of Cheer tonight?*

She thought of a number of places where people would be celebrating the winter season, skiing, sledding, and baking. Festive holiday parties were probably happening right that moment. But all those reminded her of Emerald Hollow, of *Ash*, and she put them firmly out of her mind.

Australia, she thought. It was summer there. She would go soak up some Cheer in the sun. Her Cheer meter had crashed in Emerald Hollow, and Australian beaches were the farthest thing from Emerald Hollow she could imagine.

With her mind made up, she followed the path back to the stables, where Rudy, Sprig, Butter, and Peppermint were ready to take her wherever she desired. Clementine stood nearby, her hands tucked firmly into the pockets of her stylish white coat.

"I'm ready." Holly climbed into the sleigh for the second time that night, and for a moment, she was terrified it wouldn't rise into the air. She pictured Comet's sweet face and his whining as she left, but she focused on the reindeer in front of her, willing the image away, and prayed that the magic lichen the reindeer had been fed still held its power.

Holly's thoughts morphed from fear to determination. "I'll make a quick round, soak up as much Cheer as possible, then come straight back to feed it to the North Post. I can make multiple trips tonight if needed, as long as we can get operations going again." She could do it. She had never failed the North Pole, and she wasn't about to start.

Clementine nodded at her reassuringly, but Holly couldn't help but notice the tightening around her eyes. *This is fine,* Holly thought. *I'm back in my element. I'm an excellent Cheer collector. This is what I do.* She gave a little tap of the reins and only focused on what was in front of her as the North Pole disappeared below.

HOLLY TOUCHED DOWN IN AUSTRALIA ON ONE OF HER favorite beaches. She knew of a fairly secluded spot to land, and as soon as the sleigh hit the sand, she ran toward a more populated area. It didn't take her long to find people of all walks of life—couples lounging on towels or splashing each other in the water, families building sandcastles, and friends throwing a ball back and forth.

She glanced at her watch, eager to see the Cheer level start ticking up, but the dial was firmly stuck at zero.

Her heart sank.

She ran farther down the beach, flying by people who were laughing and smiling. They would have easily bumped up her

Cheer levels before. Her pulse raced, and she tapped on her watch face in frustration. *Could it be broken? Is that even possible?*

After fifteen minutes of futility, Holly returned to her sleigh and the reindeer. Her legs were unsteady as she climbed inside. For a moment, she simply sat there, hardly able to process that she couldn't collect any Cheer.

Rudy turned his head to look at her, his eyes wide. She thought of all the elves at the North Pole who were waiting for her to return with a watch full of the Cheer that sustained them all. They would be waiting for her to save them—to save Christmas.

She straightened her back and pulled a little too hard on the reins. There had to be another way. She must be missing something. As the reindeer flew back toward the North Pole, Holly prepared her questions for Lumi.

But she couldn't keep her thoughts off Ash. She'd created a mess at the North Pole and left behind one in Emerald Hollow. Tears formed in her eyes and were carried away by the cold night air before they could ever fall.

Chapter Forty-Seven

Ash's phone wouldn't stop beeping. Sofia wanted to know why he had asked her to call and pull out of the Hallmark competition. She would see the warehouse soon enough. They wouldn't get a second chance with Hallmark after pulling out at the last moment.

But the Christmas faire wasn't the only thing causing his stomach to feel heavy with dread. He couldn't stop thinking about Holly. *Where did things go wrong?* Maybe he shouldn't have shown his dismay in the warehouse. *Did that scare her off? Why did she blame herself?* She had been as invested in the Christmas faire as he had. He could never blame her.

But there was someone he could blame. He gripped the steering wheel more tightly. All those thoughts ran through his head as he cruised down the dirt road at greater speed than he'd intended. He hadn't been to the house since shortly after Lucas and Kara got married, not long before their business partnership dissolved.

The cabin came into view and was exactly as Ash remembered it. He took a calming breath and slowly parked, aware in spite of his hurt and anger that Lucas's son could be playing outside some-where. The front door opened, and Lucas emerged in a hoodie and sweatpants. He looked as bad as Ash felt.

"Did you do it?" Ash asked, slamming the truck door behind him.

Lucas closed the front door and stepped outside. The wind had died down considerably. While the storm system had passed, the storm between Ash and Lucas was just beginning. In fact, it was long overdue.

"Do what?" Lucas asked.

"Don't play dumb. Are you trying to tell me this isn't exactly what you wanted? What the hell, Lucas? What did I ever do to you that you would break in and sabotage my workshop like that?"

Lucas inhaled deeply, averting his eyes from Ash's face. "I just went in there looking for those old woodland figurines we'd carved as kids. I wanted to send one to my—well, it doesn't matter. What do you mean? What happened?" Lucas seemed genuinely confused, furrowing his brow, but Ash didn't buy the act.

"You broke in and left the place unlocked and the doors wide open. All night. During the biggest storm of the year." Ash was fuming. Holly's disappointment at seeing all her hard work gone down the drain still wrenched his heart. Then a look of pure devas-tation had crossed over her face, and she'd run away. Lucas hadn't just burned Ash or the town. He'd hurt Holly.

A dawning expression broke over Lucas's face. "How bad is it?" Lucas asked, coming down the steps slowly.

"Well, all the materials and decorations for the Christmas faire have been destroyed. Some of my tools are gonna be rusted too. Santa's sleigh got lived in by a raccoon, and you know how they are. So I'd say it's pretty bad, Lucas." The words tumbled out of him like hot magma, thick and dangerous.

Lucas cursed. "Ash. Man, I'm so sorry. I can't believe... I just swung in. I must have forgotten to lock it behind me."

Ash narrowed his eyes, not wanting to believe that all the destruction had been because of a stupid mistake—a forgotten lock. Holly was gone because of it. "You just swung in? How did you even get in there? That was trespassing, Lucas."

"I know. It was wrong. I should have just asked you. I'd had a little bit to drink, and I wasn't in a good place. I thought your old lock combination might be the same one you always used to use, and I was right. The doors were closed when I left. I swear. The storm must have blown them open."

Lucas looked miserable, and Ash blew out a deep breath. He sank onto a step on the porch and gripped his thighs. He almost had to laugh. Of course Lucas knew his old combination code. He'd used the same one since high school gym class.

"So this is really where our relationship has ended up? You having to sneak into buildings at the house and me having to assume the worst of you at all times? Why were you looking through my papers at the front desk?" Ash felt hollow. Lucas had been his best friend as a kid.

After taking a seat on the steps on the opposite side from Ash, Lucas kicked at the mud, casting his face toward the sky. "I don't know, man. Our differences were fine as kids. That's probably why we had so much fun together. But that didn't work when we tried to run the house together. You were always too independent for a business partner. I didn't dream as big as you, and you came up with all the good ideas. But you didn't let anyone help you. It was like you wanted to do it on your own. Like you had something to prove."

Ash's mind was swirling. *That's what Lucas thinks of me?* In his memory, things had gone down completely differently, with Lucas shooting down idea after idea until Ash had shouted in frustration that maybe he should just buy him out. On the spot, Lucas had agreed.

That had been the end of their business partnership and their friendship. Lucas stopped by a couple of times a year, seeming satisfied when something went wrong and trying to downplay successes when things went well.

"For a few years, I thought I had landed on top," Lucas continued, gripping tightly to a porch post. "Sure, the house was doing well, but you were alone, while I had my wife and kid. But now we're split up, and she's taken our son to live with her parents in Ohio." His face crumpled.

Ash felt frozen in place, shocked at this display of emotion. "Ah, Luc. When did that happen?" He dragged his hand through his hair uncomfortably as the anger drained out of him. All he felt was loss, and that was so much worse.

"About a month ago." It seemed like all the wind had gone out of Lucas's sails, and he slumped. "I'd just been fishing around the house lately, looking to see you struggling with something. I thought it would make me feel better about my situation. You were closing in on a deal with the vineyard."

At Ash's look of surprise, Lucas continued, "I've been doing some sales for them. I tried to drag that out, but I knew you'd get the deal eventually. Your plans were spot on, as usual. Then I saw that beautiful woman leaving your place, and I thought, 'Damn. He has it all now. And I've got nothing.'" Lucas put his head in his hands.

A deep knot of pain made itself more prominent in Ash's chest at the mention of Holly. "Yeah, well. I don't have her. Never did, and now she's gone." Ash stared at the forest surrounding Lucas's home.

"I don't know what I'm going to do, Luc. The Christmas faire's not going to be what everyone is expecting. Not even close.

It was my one big chance at reviving this town. So if you were hoping to see me struggling, you got your wish."

Lucas cursed under his breath again. "Well, that doesn't make me feel any better. And wishing anything bad on you was horrible of me." Lucas looked truly miserable, slouched inward, as if he wanted to disappear.

Ash shook his head. "What would our dads say if they could see us now?" He was still in disbelief at how the past few hours had played out. Holly, with her sparkling presence, glowing smile, and knack for knowing exactly how to help him, had disappeared, just like his mom had.

He remembered the snowy night when she had left just days before Christmas. He couldn't imagine how his dad had felt then or how Lucas was feeling. "Is there anything you can do to make things up with Kara?"

"I don't know, man. I haven't been the best husband lately. I've been spending too much time working and drinking too much. She was in the right to take off."

"I know how much you two love each other. There're some AA meetings in town. Get yourself straight, and let her know you're serious about it. Give her a chance to come back." Ash willed it to work out for them. He'd never known exactly what went on between his parents, but he chose to believe that his dad had done everything possible to keep their family together. Maybe Lucas and Kara would have a different outcome for their child.

Lucas let out a deep breath, and it swirled in the freezing air. "You're right. I know you're right. And how about you? This... Holly? Are you in love with her?"

Ash knew the answer immediately, though he'd never said it aloud or even to himself. "Yeah, man. I'm pretty sure I am." Suddenly, Ash's brain taunted him with a flash of Holly's green eyes gazing through the trees. He blinked, and only the forest was in front of him. Imitating Lucas, he kicked at the ground.

"Then it sounds like we've both got some work to do," Lucas said as Ash stood. "And I'm sorry about the workshop. I mean it. That was a huge mess up. I can pay for everything that was destroyed."

Ash nodded. "Call me when you get right. I'll be here."

He climbed into his truck, eased down the long driveway, and rolled down the windows to let in the crisp air, attempting to clear out the lingering scent of cinnamon.

Chapter Forty-Eight

As soon as Holly landed in the North Pole, she could tell things had gotten worse. The normally fluffy bed of white snow that blanketed the village year-round had melted much further. The reindeer sniffed at the dirt patches anxiously.

Holly flew down the path toward Merriment Square. The sun was beginning to rise, and nearly all the elves were gathered in the central hub, clustered near the dimly lit North Post.

"Clementine," Holly breathed when she caught sight of the elf mayor moving quickly toward her through the crowd.

Clementine glanced at Holly's wrist, her eyes anxious.

"It didn't work. I couldn't collect any Cheer. I think my watch is broken."

Holly had spoken quietly, but the elves seemed to sense her words. They muttered anxiously, clinging to one another. A few of the younger elves began to cry at the unfamiliar sense of something being not right.

"I'm going to talk to Lumi Kringle."

Clementine brushed a thick blond braid over her shoulder. "She's already waiting for you at your house."

Holly simply nodded and walked past her to her front porch. She avoided running, trying to keep her expression and gait steady to reassure the elves. Walking through her front door, she sensed immediately that the lack of magic was affecting her home as well.

The always-present aroma of cinnamon was gone, and the fireplace, which constantly burned, had been extinguished, leaving the room feeling cold and empty. Shadows she'd never noticed before were cast over her home. Her mind flashed to playing cards with Ash in front of a roaring fire built by her magic, and her stomach twisted again.

Lumi was sitting on a round cushion in the living room. She stood when she saw Holly and drew her into a quick hug before sitting down again, ready to talk business.

"Lumi, I'm so glad to see you. Something is seriously wrong. My Cheer meter won't charge. The North Post has lost some of its light. The snow is melting. The elves are confused and nervous. What do I do? How can I fix this? Can the elves make me a new Cheer meter?" Holly spoke too quickly, desperation creeping into her voice.

Lumi listened patiently then let out a big sigh and clasped her hands in her lap. "I'm afraid you've encountered a North Pole rule of magic that hasn't been needed in a long time."

"A rule? What rule?" Holly asked, her hands shaking. *Am I finally going to get answers to my questions about magic?*

"The North Pole operates on unseen rules. For the most part, there is no need for us to know them. As long as we keep fueling the North Post with Cheer, the rest of the magic sorts itself out and powers everything here."

Holly was bursting with a million questions and wanted to

interrupt, but Lumi, sensing it, simply rested a hand on Holly's and continued speaking.

"In the magic system that powers everything here, there is occasionally a... a variable that comes into play."

"A variable?" Holly repeated, unable to stay silent.

"Yes. Humans might call it... Well, they'd call it love."

Holly's eyes widened, but she stayed quiet as Lumi continued.

"There's more to it than even I know, I'm sure, but the most important part for us today is that when a Claus falls in love, it can cause their Cheer to change. It gets.... more vibrant, I guess you could say. When you returned from Emerald Hollow before and deposited the Cheer, the North Post lit up brighter than we'd become accustomed to. That's because you had experienced love, and it changed your Cheer."

Holly jumped up, too surprised to continue sitting on the plush cushion. "That can't be right. I've soaked up the love emotion many times in my Cheer meter. It didn't change the brightness of my Cheer!" Something she couldn't quite explain was warring in her heart.

Lumi sighed. "You had only gathered other people's love for one another, Holly. You hadn't experienced it yourself. In Emerald Hollow, you found something rare. You gave love, and you received it in return."

With a twist in her stomach, Holly understood what Lumi was saying. Maybe she'd known it all along.

Ash.

He was the reason her Cheer meter had started to go wild the first time he came into the room. Ash was the reason her wrist was constantly warm, and she didn't have to filter for negative emotions. Because of him, she had felt at home in Emerald Hollow. Ash was the reason she had been indescribably happy.

Holly's heart sank even further than she thought possible. She had left Ash behind. Whatever love he'd had for her, if he had indeed loved her, it had to have evaporated as soon as she ran away.

She tried to fight back against the despair. "How come none of this ever came up in my studies?" She fiddled with her watch. It was too still, and the lack of warmth felt like frostbite.

Lumi's features became softer than Holly had ever seen them. "Not every Claus falls in love. For the Clauses who don't or aren't meant to, their Cheer lights the North Post to full brightness the moment they take over from the previous Mr. or Ms. Claus. In those cases, as you know, the next Claus is discovered somewhere in the human world when the time is right. That's why the North Pole has had Clauses with origins from every continent over the centuries."

Holly frowned, her mind brimming with questions. "But wouldn't that mean it's all predetermined? Somehow, the Cheer knew I would eventually fall in love?" She couldn't deny that love was what she felt, but she could certainly hang on to every scrap of information that didn't revolve around Ash, as if delaying the inevitable. "Is there some kind of genetic factor that determines this?"

"We don't know everything about Cheer, Holly. Sometimes, we can ask why all we want, but we don't get an answer. Things just are. Clauses only fall in love once, if they do at all, according to legend. For humans, it could happen multiple times or not at all. Most humans can be happy with a variety of different people, or they can be happy on their own. It often comes down to choice."

Lumi sighed deeply and continued, "It's a different story for you, my dear. You were always destined to fall in love. I've known it ever since your parents left, and your first Cheer mission yielded less powerful Cheer." She reached out to cover Holly's hand. "Don't worry. You did remarkably well all those years. We had plenty of Cheer to keep operations going. I knew you would fall in love when the time was right. Clauses have plenty of time. I'm just glad you found him now."

"But I don't understand. Does this mean I have to... to... what exactly? Keep visiting Ash in Emerald Hollow every Cheer cycle to restock our Cheer? Aren't they going to wonder why I keep going back? And that's assuming Ash is even willing to let me set foot there again after the way I left things." Holly's mind was swirling. She was eager to make things right at the North Pole but not sure how.

"What about my job? My cover story?" She was thinking of Sofia, Enzo, Tyler, and the others she had met in Emerald Hollow —and Ash, always Ash. "Wouldn't that seem strange to all of them?"

"Well, the idea is not that you keep visiting him as friends, Holly. The idea is that the two of you fall in love and build a life together, like your parents did."

Holly's jaw dropped. "This happened to my parents too?" She wondered why that hadn't occurred to her during the conversation yet. "I knew they were in love, but... did my dad's Cheer start off less powerful, like mine did?"

"That's right. It was so long ago that I barely remember it. But after he met your mother on one of his trips to gather Cheer, everything changed."

Holly had dozens of other questions about that, but they all led her back to Ash, and she didn't want to think about him anymore at the moment. She had done the worst thing possible, as Sofia had said, by leaving. She felt like she was going to be sick.

Suddenly, her mind switched gears. "If I've fallen in love, why isn't my Cheer working anymore? Why would it make my Cheer brighter then take it away completely?"

Lumi let out another sigh. "Only you know the answer to that.

Did you leave Emerald Hollow with the intention of never return- ing? Of never seeing Ash again?"

"Yes, but I had to. Ash and I weren't going to work out. It was better for him if I left."

Lumi arched a single one of her pointed ears. "Better for him? Did he tell you that?"

Holly tried not to let the dread that was clinging tightly to her insides like a melted marshmallow on a graham cracker show on her face. "Well, no. I thought I was doing what was best for both of us. And it turns out, I was right, because meeting him has led to disaster for the North Pole! I wish I'd never gone to Emerald Hollow. I never missed a Cheer quota before then. I was fine. Everything was fine."

Holly sank into the cushion again, her shoulders sagging. Even as the words spilled out of her, she knew they weren't true. Her time in Emerald Hollow had been the best in her life. She couldn't imagine a version of her story in which she'd never experienced that.

"Holly," Lumi began gently, "I'm going to have to give it to you straight. Falling in love and tapping into that Cheer doesn't always result in disaster. If neither of you feels real love for the other, you'd be able to continue as you did before. The light of the North Post would have maintained its baseline brightness, and you'd be able to go on capturing Cheer as you did. Now that all this has happened, though"—Lumi waved her hand, indicating the room, which was lit with candles instead of its usual Cheer- powered lanterns, and the empty fireplace, which faced them like a black hole—"I see that it's gone a step farther. You've fallen in love, and I think it's reciprocal. That can't be undone so easily. It's changed your ability to store Cheer."

Holly closed her eyes, shaking her head. "This can't be the

answer, Lumi. We have to find a solution." Holly stared at her with wide, pleading eyes.

"Have you talked to Ash and told him how you feel?" Lumi asked so calmly that it made Holly want to shout.

"I made a mistake, Lumi! I'm sure I hurt him. And I nearly lost the Cheer meter. And then I... I ran away," Holly said, all the fire going out of her voice.

"Oh, child," Lumi said, pulling her in for a hug. "Being in love is scary. It's taking a risk. But you took away Ash's choice, and that's not right. You may be depriving him of his chance to love in return."

"What do you mean? What choice did I take away? To be with me? That could never work. I'm *Ms. Claus*. I'm a fairy tale. Ash is a human. I can't ask him to be with someone who can never tell him the truth. He deserves better than that."

Lumi sighed again, but her eyes were kind. "You could tell him the truth."

Holly thought she must have misheard her. "Sorry?"

"You heard me. Tell him the truth. Give him the choice. If you don't ask, you'll never know the answer."

Holly trembled. "I can't do it, Lumi. I've never told any human who I am, least of all Ash. He would think I was crazy or joking or both. I would lose him forever. And besides, I told you I accidentally took my Cheer meter off when I was there. I didn't even realize it. What if it had gotten lost? I forget all my usual precautions when I'm in Emerald Hollow. That can't be safe for the North Pole."

"The North Pole can take care of itself, Holly, as long as *you* take care of *you*. And as for Ash, if you don't give him the choice, you've already lost him."

Lumi's words seemed to reverberate around the room, and they both sat there for a few moments in a silent standoff.

"I can't," Holly finally breathed, shaking her head.

Lumi met her eyes, and her expression was sterner. "Holly, you have to. This isn't just about your love life anymore, though that was important enough. The entire North Pole is at risk now. Our operations are at risk. *Christmas* is at risk."

Holly gasped. Christmas was the reason they all existed. It was the Clauses' solemn mission to protect Christmas and put Dreams into the world.

If I can't protect Christmas, why do I even exist?

Chapter Forty-Nine

After Lumi left, Holly moved to her back deck and sat quietly under the northern lights, trying to process everything from their conversation. Her father's easy success was due to his love of her mother. He had found his soulmate, which had changed his relationship to Cheer magic, and therefore, the Cheer meter stayed steady, regardless of the Cheer he gathered from humans.

He didn't need to go Cheer collecting as often because the quota he needed to gather was lower than the one Holly had to attain each cycle. Holly had been racing toward an impossible goal. The deck had never been equally stacked.

Until now.

Holly shook her head, barely registering the light show in front of her. Her mind was swirling like a shaken snow globe. Everything she thought she knew about Cheer had gone out the window.

Another thought hit her suddenly. She'd always known her mom had once been a human and had been transformed into a Claus through marrying her father and taking on the magic of the North Pole. *Does Ash's ability to see the reindeer have something to do with that? Is he somehow already being transformed by North Pole magic, just by my developing feelings for him?*

She dropped her face into her hands. *Why did I run away like that, without a backward glance?*

Clementine appeared on the deck just then, pulling her from her thoughts.

At her expression, Holly sat upright. "Clementine, what's going on?" She studied the tight lines of Clementine's usually controlled face. Her ears were pointed almost straight up.

"It happened while you were talking to Lumi."

"What did?" A knot formed in the pit of her stomach. She couldn't stop thinking about Ash and how she had hurt him, and now something else had happened at the North Pole. *Could things get any worse?*

"Ms. Claus, the North Post has gone out."

"*What?*" Holly exclaimed, dread creeping into her veins.

She hurried to the front of her house and nearly sank to her knees. The North Post, which had lit the North Pole and powered its operations for as long as Holly or anyone could remember, was completely dark.

Elves, Keyblers and Kringles alike, were huddled around Merriment Square, murmuring and staring at the North Post in fright. Holly could feel their eyes landing on her. They were desperately relying on her for a solution.

Holly's palms began to sweat, and her heart rate sped up. They were too close to Christmas. "The Dream-making operations?" she asked in a hoarse whisper.

Clementine shook her head, and Holly closed her eyes.

"A few of the elves were working the late shift and said their Dream machines stopped running suddenly."

At that moment, Auryn appeared at her side. Holly could tell that he was struggling to hold it together, ready to help her, even as fear washed through him.

Holly straightened her shoulders. She knew what she needed to do, not just because of Lumi's words but because she knew in her heart that there was only one way to make it right. She had to try. After grabbing a coat, she headed toward the stables.

ASH RETURNED TO THE EMERALD HOUSE, DRAINED OF all energy after the interaction with Lucas.

Sofia's distressed face greeted him just as he stepped through the door. Curls had escaped her ponytail to hang around her face. "What happened? Did you find her?"

Ash shook his head. "I went to see Lucas."

Sofia sucked in a breath.

"It was all a stupid accident. Doesn't do us or the Christmas faire much good, but he seemed truly remorseful. Apparently, some stuff has been going down in his personal life."

Sofia huffed. "So? That doesn't give him the right to trespass and ruin private property! We should call the police."

"No," Ash said quickly. All his anger with Lucas had dissipated. "That's not how I want to handle this."

"All right," Sofia said, taking a deep breath. She was obviously trying to calm herself, but her temper could be fierce. "So what's the plan? The Christmas faire starts tomorrow. Many of the vendors have their own decorations, but without the materials for the Christmas maze, I just don't see how this is going to work. That's the main attraction we advertised to tourists along with the parade. I took a look in the workshop after you left. Most of the float components are destroyed too." She pulled at the hem of her sweater, and a thin piece of fabric sprang free.

Ash stood up and put his hands on her shoulders. "I don't know yet, Sof." For the first time since he could remember, the goings-on of Emerald Hollow were not his top priority. "It'll have to be good enough."

Sofia nearly choked. "Who are you, and what have you done with my friend?"

Ash sighed. "Since we're out of the running for Hallmark now, we'll just have to do our best to make it a good experience. The vendors can still sell their wares to the tourists and locals. The food didn't get ruined, at least. This year will just be much less... magical than all the others. But I guess something is better than nothing."

Concern spread all over Sofia's face, and she took his hand. "Ash, this isn't all on you to figure out. We can call an emergency council meeting. Everyone can pitch in. We'll figure something out, okay?"

Ash simply nodded, and Sofia pulled him in for a hug. He squeezed her back, and his eyes traveled toward the hallway.

It couldn't be the end. She couldn't be gone forever. Maybe he had missed something. When he and Sofia broke apart, he reached behind the front desk and got a key to the suite Holly had been staying in. After speeding down the hall, he entered the room, scanning it anxiously, looking for any clue to where she'd gone. On the bedside table was a backpack.

Her phone was inside, and his heart rate spiked. That she'd left them made his heart sink with worry. *Where did she go without her bag or phone?*

He turned on the phone, which appeared to be prepaid. It was empty. There was no password, no call or text history. It looked like she had never even used it. *What is going on? Is she okay?* He sank onto the bed and thought about all he knew about her.

She was from Canada. That wasn't very helpful. *Why didn't I ever ask her the exact name of her town?*

She worked in marketing for a large company. Again, he couldn't believe how stupid he had been. *Why don't I know the name of the company she works for?*

And her name... he didn't even know her last name. He could have sworn he had asked her, but each time, the question sort of left his mind before he could press further. It was as if Holly had the power to have him focus only on who she was in the present, not all the other details that made up who she was.

He shook his head, angry with himself. There had to be some way to get in touch with her. Humans didn't just disappear into thin air.

But Holly had, just like his mom had.

Sofia's face appeared in the doorway. "She'll be back," she whispered. "I can feel it."

But Ash shook his head. He'd been sure his mom would come back, but she had left and never even seen fit to call. "I don't even know her last name." As the words left his mouth, the invisible weight pressed down firmly on his chest again, as if someone were stepping on him.

Comet pushed into the room and licked his hand.

Holly, with her rosy cheeks, infectious smile, and aura of peace, was gone for good.

Chapter Fifty

Ash woke up early the morning of Christmas Eve. He dressed as usual then prepared to take Comet outside for the morning walk he'd been neglecting recently. That led his mind immediately to Holly, and he tried to shake it away. He forgot to put on his coat, focused only on not thinking about Holly.

With Comet at his heels, he left his room and opened the side door of the Emerald House to a massive berm of snow. His jaw dropped. True, he'd stopped checking the weather forecast every few hours, but the snow had come out of nowhere. Ash was immensely relieved by the distraction it would provide.

Comet looked from Ash to the snow and back, wagging his tail as Ash returned to his room to slip on a coat and gloves. He kept a shovel in the utility closet, and he quickly dug a narrow path to the shed, where the snowblower was stored. Comet trotted after him happily, jumping through the smaller piles of snow like a bunny rabbit bounding through a field. Ash used the snowblower to clear a wider path to his door then got to work clearing areas around the rest of the house.

The distraction didn't work for long. He thought he'd be happy when it finally snowed, but all he wanted to do was see the happiness on Holly's face. Part of him still insisted there had to be a way to contact her.

Maybe her running away was all some misunderstanding, like the workshop disaster had been with Lucas. She blamed herself for that, but there was no one to blame. Lucas shouldn't have been trespassing, and Ash should have had better security, but Holly had nothing to feel bad about at all. She'd been bringing joy to him and everyone else in Emerald Hollow since the day she set foot in town. He wished he'd told her that.

Ash heaved a sigh as he cleared the last sidewalk and pulled out his phone. Without realizing what he was doing, he pressed the contact button labeled Dad.

"Hey, Ash. Everything all right down there? We got dumped on here at my place."

Ash's heart rate slowed at the sound of his dad's voice, which was so familiar and comforting.

"We got dumped on here too." Ash paused then steeled himself and continued, "Dad, I know this is random, but I was just thinking about Mom. I'm sorry if this brings up painful memories but... how did you deal with just never hearing from her again? Did you try to track her down?" Ash cringed, realizing that his questions were coming decades too late. He and his father never talked about his mother, and he was sure his dad would try to change the subject.

To his surprise, though, his dad paused for several moments then sighed deeply, resigned.

"Ash, I wish I had a better answer for you, but I'm afraid I don't. Your mom and I got together at a young age, and things weren't always easy for us. Of course, we got you, and that made us both so happy. But one day, we got into a bad argument. It was the worst we'd ever had. And there was a horrible snowstorm going on, but she just took off in her vehicle. I couldn't stop her."

Ash froze, leaning on the handle of the snowblower. That was the most he had ever heard about the day his mom left. He had a few faint memories of the snowstorm that day, but his dad had never talked about it.

"I didn't know where your mother went. We didn't have cell phones then, and she didn't have any family, or I would have called them. All your mother's friends were here in town, and none of them had seen or heard from her. I had to assume she had an out-of-town friend I didn't know about and that she got there safely. A few car accidents were reported during the storm. Believe me—I checked. But none of them were her.

"I did try to track her down over the years, for your sake, but I never came up with any leads. I figured she just didn't want to be found. I thought I got a postcard from her once. It looked like her handwriting on our address. But I didn't recognize the return name, and there was no address. It just turned out to be junk mail. That got my hopes up more than I realized, and I knew I needed to let her go after that. I wish things had happened differently, but I always hoped she found happiness, wherever she ended up."

Ash's dad was crying softly, and he clung to the snowblower like a life vessel, too surprised and moved to speak.

"I'm so sorry, Ash," his father continued, gathering himself. "I should have told you more about the circumstances of her leaving before. I thought it would be easier for you if you didn't know the details. Her leaving had nothing to do with you. Her dreams were just too big for this town. You were so young when she left that I hoped you would forget that night and be able to enjoy your life. As the years went on, I began to question that strategy, but I didn't have much information for you. I never heard from her again, but I was able to let her go, in a way. I hoped you could too.

"I'm so proud of the person you've become, Ash. And I'm sorry I couldn't give you closure years ago or now. I guess it's something we might never get, so maybe we have to make it for ourselves. Maybe talking to each other about this will help."

Ash took a deep breath, the cold air hitting the back of his throat.

"Ash, are you there?"

The broken sound of his dad's voice brought Ash back from his cascading thoughts. His father had raised him and given him the best life he knew how to without a mom around. Ash couldn't begrudge him that.

"I'm here. Thanks for telling me all that, Dad. That was a lot... for both of us."

His dad grunted, and they both held their phones in silence.

"And I'm glad you told me. I hope we can talk more about Mom in the future."

"Where's this coming from, Ash?"

"There's... a woman," Ash said, relieved to finally be getting it all out in the open.

"Holly," his dad said matter-of-factly.

Ash's jaw dropped. "How'd you know?"

"Son, I don't live so far out of town that I'm not connected to what's going on there anymore. She's all anyone's been talking about recently. I've been waiting for you to tell me about her and maybe bring her out for a visit."

Ash was touched and saddened by his dad's words. "Well, I don't think that will be happening."

"And why not?" His dad's voice had returned to its usual stubborn, no-nonsense cadence.

Just then, Comet took off from Ash's side, wagging his tail and bounding down the path. A strange tingly sensation ran across Ash's skin, and goose bumps popped out on his arms. His eyes followed Comet almost in slow motion, and he was ready to call out, until he saw who Comet was running toward. The words froze in his throat.

Holly, wearing only a thin red sweater and jeans in the freezing weather, was making her way up the path. At least her boots looked fur lined and warm. He could swear she was bathed in sparkling sunshine, like she was reflecting every inch of the brilliant white snow around her. She leaned down to pet Comet when he reached her and let out a soft laugh. The sound sent a thrill through Ash.

"Dad, can I call you back?" Ash removed his hand from the snowblower slowly.

"You just bring her out to meet me when you get the chance. Good luck, son."

Ash hung up, never taking his eyes off Holly. *She's here.*

When she stood, their eyes finally met. She smiled at him, though it seemed a little wary. Snowflakes danced then settled softly in her hair.

He took a step forward.

<h1 style="text-align:center">Chapter Fifty-One</h1>

Ash looked like he'd seen a ghost, and Holly nearly lost her nerve. She was glad to have Comet at her side. At least she knew the dog wasn't mad at her for ditching him. *Dogs. They can forgive you for almost anything.*

She and Ash walked slowly at first, then their feet propelled them forward until they were within inches of each other.

Ash simply stared at her. She started to open her mouth to speak, to explain, but he stepped closer before she could say anything. Holly worried he was angry, as she had the whole trip. She'd done the thing that scared him most, leaving with hardly a goodbye. She wished so badly that she could take it back.

"It's eighteen degrees. Where's your coat?"

She nearly laughed. That was not what she'd been expecting. "Ash," Holly said, breathless. Warmth radiated between them, and her watch came to life again. She didn't realize how much the absence of that feeling had been plaguing her until it was back with such force.

She studied his eyes, which were lined with bags that she'd never seen before. But something else was there as well. *Hope?*

"Ash, I'm so sorry I left. There's... There's more to me than I've told you about. And I got scared you wouldn't accept me. But I was wrong. I should have allowed you to make that decision for yourself."

"You must be freezing. Let's do this inside." He tried to usher her down the path toward the building.

Holly shook her head. "There's something you need to know about me. But first, I need you to hear this. Again, I'm so sorry I left, Ash. I missed Emerald Hollow immediately. I've never felt more at home anywhere else. But it's more than that." She took a deep breath and swallowed. *Time to rip off the bandage.* "It wasn't just Emerald Hollow I missed. It was you." Holly's heart was racing faster than ever. She had so much more to tell, but it was a start. And Ash could end it right then if he chose.

To her immense relief, Ash cracked a grin, and some of the tension in her chest released.

"I missed you too. *We* missed you," Ash said, motioning to Comet, who was still wagging his tail at Holly's side. "This town isn't the same without you."

"There's more. There's so much about me you don't know."

She must have looked as distressed as she felt, because Ash put his arms around her waist then, tugging her close.

"Holly, what are you talking about?" His warm brown eyes were searching.

She desperately wanted to give him answers, but they might never stand so close again, sharing a connection. What she said next could change everything. She wanted to savor the moment.

"I'm not sure if I can tell you. It's going to sound impossible," she said quietly and looked down.

Ash tugged her closer, lifting her chin. "You can tell me anything." His voice was so calm, so quiet, and he tucked a strand of hair behind her ear. The air was getting colder by the minute, the sky beginning to go cloudy.

The snow was falling so quickly that Holly imagined the world in snow globes, and she and Ash were in their own personal one. She was about to shake it, and she hoped it wouldn't break. After taking a deep breath, she dove in.

"Do you remember those reindeer we saw?"

He leaned his head back a bit, peering at her curiously. "Yes. What about them?" The corner of his mouth pulled up a bit.

"Well, they're real," she said, still meeting his gaze even though she was afraid of what she might see.

"What do you mean? Reindeer are a real species. I already knew that." Ash tried for a playful smile, and it made Holly's heart melt.

She had to maintain her courage. "No, they're real, like from Christmas stories. They can fly."

Ash choked out a laugh but swallowed when he saw that her expression was serious. "Okay, so... what does that mean? Why is that a problem for us?"

Holly blinked in surprise. "You believe me?" A glimmer of hope bloomed in her chest. The invisible snow globe was still intact.

"Holly, I know there's more you're trying to tell me. Can you just put it all out there?" He rubbed her arms cautiously.

"Okay..." She thought for a moment then turned toward the forest. "Just follow me." Holly decided she should give him some evidence to back up her claims before jumping in with the most shocking revelation.

Ash took her hand and followed her.

As they strode deeper into the forest, she wished for her reindeer. After coming to a stop, they waited. Within a minute, four reindeer emerged from the trees. Dasher, Gale, Ivy, and Clove had all insisted on being the ones to return with her after they'd had a dose of the reserve magic lichen.

"Go ahead," Holly said. "Show him."

Ivy and Clove both turned to look at Dasher, who nodded. Then, slowly, the four of them rose into the air. Holly chanced a peek at Ash. He was standing perfectly still, his eyes locked on the reindeer. They began to fan their legs in a way that resembled swimming, slowly revolving in a circle above Holly and Ash. He reached over and squeezed Holly's hand a little too tightly. His jaw had dropped.

"What's happening?" he breathed.

"It's just like I said. They're reindeer, and they can fly." Holly squeezed his hand back, hoping she was transferring some kind of calming magic. She didn't know if that existed, but she was putting her faith in lots of unknowns.

"Like in the Christmas stories," Ash said, still unable to take his eyes off the reindeer as they floated softly back to the ground.

"Yes."

He met her eyes then.

"I'd like to show you something else," she said, hoping the reindeer had softened him up enough for it.

"Don't tell me we're going to the North Pole," Ash joked, then his laugh cut off at the expression on her face.

Holly led him down the path to where the golden sleigh was waiting. The reindeer had walked ahead of them and had already harnessed themselves to it.

"This is your sleigh?" Ash asked, incredulous.

Holly nodded, giving a shy smile.

"So what does that make you? Santa Claus?" Ash was still trying to joke, but Holly could see the confusion playing out all over his face.

She reacted to his joke with a loud, startled laugh. "No way.

Santa Claus was my father. I'm Holly Claus. Ms. Claus to the elves." Holly hadn't meant to spill all that at once, but her reaction to his calling her Santa Claus had been automatic.

Ash's eyes grew wide, and he swallowed. "Did you say elves?"

Holly grinned. Since she'd said the worst of it and he hadn't yet dropped the snow globe, she felt a sudden sense of relief and courage. She hadn't told him about her watch or the Cheer meter. But there would be time for that later. She still couldn't believe she'd told him she was a Claus, and that he hadn't run away, fainted, or laughed.

"Do you want to see them? The elves? And the North Pole? I know this is unbelievable, so I'll do whatever I can to prove it to you. Or if you want to return to the Emerald House and pretend this is all a dream, I'll leave you alone." She paused, her voice dropped to a whisper, and she gripped his hand more tightly. "I'd hate to, but I would. If that's what you want."

As much as she wanted him, as much as she knew, even without the Cheer, that she was in love with him, the choice of whether he wanted her would always be his.

She wasn't sure if it was magic or something innate to Ash, but she could feel an unearthly sense of calm settle over him. His expression changed from one of shock to one of wonder. Maybe he really was becoming a Claus. He reached for her hands, and trust and understanding seemed to pass between them. All her anxieties melted away, replaced by a feeling even more powerful. Neither of them pulled back.

He tucked a strand of hair behind her ear again, still holding her other hand. "I want to see it all."

At Ash's words, the Cheer meter on Holly's wrist began to vibrate even harder, the warmth seeping into her skin like water into parched earth.

Chapter Fifty-Two

"I know there are some things you need to take care of now," Holly said, thinking of the Christmas faire. Christmas Eve was upon them, and the town had to be filling with visitors. She glanced down at her watch. Her Cheer meter was completely full and showed no signs of going down. It vibrated, creating warmth on her wrist, just as her blood was pumping warmly through her veins.

Ash had heard her, and he hadn't run away. He'd had a million questions as they sat there in the sleigh, but he hadn't run away. For the first time in a long time, every scale that Holly weighed felt balanced. As much as she wanted to stay and reside in that feeling, she had to give it up for just a little while. She would have to get to the North Pole and discharge the Cheer, or else Christmas would be canceled.

"There's something I have to do also. It won't take long. I promise. I'll be back."

Ash opened his mouth to speak but then closed it again and nodded.

She gave his hand a little squeeze. "I promise."

"Are you going to tell me this involves saving Christmas?" Ash asked, his eyes sparkling, still full of surprise and disbelief.

"It has everything to do with it. I will fill you in as soon as I'm back. Just go get ready for the Christmas faire. How are you feeling about it?"

They climbed out of the sleigh and began walking back toward the Emerald House.

"I think it's going to be okay. We won't have a maze or a parade this year, and we're out of the running for Hallmark, but I know people will still have fun. It's more about coming together than anything. It wouldn't be Emerald Hollow without the Christmas faire, no matter how lowbrow it is."

"Wow, you've gotten way more relaxed about this. Are you sure you're feeling okay?" Holly put a hand to his forehead to check for fever.

Ash laughed. "Almost losing you changed my perspective on what's important. Then there was that whole bombshell you dropped about you being—"

Holly followed his gaze to where Sofia was approaching.

"Did you two kiss and make up yet?" Sofia asked, sounding exasperated. "We've got work to do!"

Holly looked at Ash, and they both smiled sheepishly.

"I'll take that as a yes." Sofia rolled her eyes but was clearly trying to suppress a smile.

"I'll be right there, Sof. Holly has something she has to take care of, but she'll be back tonight. Right?"

She nodded. "Actually, I'd like to talk to Sofia for a moment."

Ash seemed surprised but gave Holly's hand a little squeeze that sent her heart racing. He whistled to Comet and continued along the path. Holly's eyes followed him before she turned to Sofia.

"I messed up, Sof."

Sofia pulled Holly in for a hug. "We all mess up. What matters is that you make it right."

Holly nodded, grateful again for the incredible friend she had made in Emerald Hollow.

"Oh, here. I've got something for you." Sofia reached into her pocket and pulled out a pair of delicate clay earrings. They were shaped like Santa hats but with sparkly bows underneath the white pom-poms. "I was inspired by your ugly-sweater outfit, Mrs. Claus." She placed the earrings in Holly's palm.

Holly beamed. "You had these in your pocket?"

"I had a feeling you'd be back," Sofia's eyes twinkled.

"These are amazing, Sof. Seriously, they're perfect." She slipped the earrings through the small holes that had magically appeared in each ear, and Sofia admired them in satisfaction.

"So, Sof. What do you think about helping me with something? I want to surprise Ash."

Sofia leaned in conspiratorially. "I'm all ears."

Chapter Fifty-Three

Holly's trip to the North Pole was quick and purposeful. The Cheer she had collected in Emerald Hollow filled the North Post instantly, and the elves were able to get the final Dream preparations underway. Holly took a look around then left everything in the capable hands of Clementine. She would have time to celebrate after Christmas.

When she arrived back in Emerald Hollow, she found Sofia first. "Did everything go okay?" she asked, feeling both anxious and excited.

"Are you kidding? Those supplies you brought were dynamite. What did you do? Raid a Macy's?"

Holly laughed. "Something like that. So the maze is set up? And the parade is a go?"

"Yes and yes." Sofia looked proud, and she bounced on her feet.

"And Ash has no idea?"

"Nada. We've kept him busy running the snowplow all around town." Sofia chuckled. "He's going to lose his mind."

"You never know. He might surprise you."

ASH RECEIVED A CALL FROM SOFIA, TELLING HIM TO meet her in the clearing because of a downed tree. Normally, an announcement like that right before the Christmas faire would have sent his anxiety spiking, but for the moment, he felt like he could conquer anything.

He kept looking around anxiously, hoping Holly would arrive soon. *Will she come flying in on her sleigh?* He shook his head. The idea was still preposterous, but somehow, his mind could accept it, like he'd known there was something magical about her all along, and her explanation had fit perfectly with what he'd already observed.

Ash pulled into an open spot at the edge of the woods, narrowly avoiding a large snowbank. He climbed out and walked to the clearing where the Christmas faire was normally held and froze. He thought, after all he'd learned that day, that nothing could surprise him. Yet there he was, unable to believe his eyes. At least thirty people were busy at work.

And in the center of all of them, practically glowing as she watched him approach, was Holly. His chest tightened. She had come back, just as she'd said she would. He stepped toward her and she toward him.

"You're back," he breathed, unable to drag his eyes from hers, even to look around at what appeared to be half the town and some kind of miracle. He supposed he shouldn't have been surprised she'd pulled it off. She was Ms. Claus, after all. A part of him thought he had only imagined her being there earlier, telling him who she really was. But seeing her again, he knew it had all been real.

"I told you I would be." Her forest-green eyes were shimmering with excitement. "And I wanted to surprise you." She beamed and flung her hand around the clearing, reminiscent of when she'd shown him her decorations for the harvest fair, her expression aglow as she watched him.

Ash finally stopped to take it all in. The maze was a work of art. It had been constructed seemingly out of nowhere, with materials he had never seen before. It looked like something straight from a movie set or a Macy's.

Human-height miniature houses, trees, and lampposts lined the streets of the maze. Sparkling lights covered the clearing, and the vendors who had been working there all week seemed rejuvenated by the addition. They had all rolled their carts to the edges of the clearing, surrounding the maze. The tantalizing scent of warm chocolate chip cookies drifted in the air. The trees around the clearing were adorned with lights and ornaments. The place looked like an enchanted Christmas village, more magical than it ever had.

"I would ask where all this came from, but I think I have a pretty good idea." Ash finally took his eyes off the magical sight to look around at the members of the town, his friends, coming together to set up the maze and decorate the clearing.

"Sofia called everyone she knew, letting them know the town could use their help in the clearing. People jumped at the opportunity to help, Ash." Her voice sounded like music to his ears.

"I thought it was just going to be the vendors this year, though I hoped people would still enjoy getting together. But now we have all this, and it's beyond anything I could have imagined."

"I know what you mean." A look that he couldn't quite interpret flashed across Holly's face. "But you have people who love this town and who love you, and they all wanted to help. They wanted to give you back a piece of the magic you give them all year long this Christmas."

Ash took a deep breath, thinking about what she and his friends had pulled off. Then his eyes widened. "Holly, it's

Christmas Eve!" He tried to picture what she had do that night, and it filled him with wonder.

"Don't worry. I still have time for that. I love this town too. And I love you."

The words hit him like the heat from a fireplace during a blizzard. He stepped closer, gently taking her arms in his hands.

Before he could speak, Holly touched a finger to his lips. "There's one more thing." She took his hand and walked toward the edge of the clearing. The reindeer were waiting there, golden sleigh in tow.

"I've been thinking. The reindeer could help us with the problem of the damaged sleigh. This one is perfectly functioning." She waved in the direction of the sleigh then nodded toward the reindeer. "No one will know the difference. I've already tested it out, and the townspeople can see them. My magic must want them to be part of this parade. People can think I brought them here from Canada or something. Or that the vendor you mentioned before came through. I'll have to have Dasher remind Ivy not to start floating out of excitement, but otherwise, they'll be perfect angels."

Holly's face was alight, and Ash felt like he could not possibly be happier.

"That just leaves one question, then," Ash said, grinning.

Holly raised her eyebrows. "Only one?" she asked, picking a snowflake off his jacket.

"I've played Santa in the parade the last few years. I'd love for Ms. Claus to ride with me. What do you say?"

"I think that could be arranged. I *do* know a thing or two about being Ms. Claus, you know."

"Of course you do," Ash said, his voice full of amazement. He pulled her in for a tight hug, never wanting to let her go.

Chapter Fifty-Four

The people of Emerald Hollow readied themselves for the parade like film stars preparing for a shoot. The finishing touches were put on the clearing, the repaired floats were lined up behind the movie theater, and the volunteers had all headed to their various floats or lined the sidewalks of Main Street to watch the parade. The sidewalks were bursting with locals and visitors alike.

Just as Holly and Ash were about to climb into the sleigh, Sofia came running up to them, grinning. "Guess who's here and ready to watch the parade," she said breathlessly, her cheeks flushed.

"Who?" Ash and Holly asked simultaneously.

"The Hallmark rep! And you'll never guess how he got here."

Holly and Ash looked at each other then back at Sofia.

"How?" Ash asked. He had told Sofia to call and cancel with Hallmark, but apparently, she and Holly had done more scheming than he'd realized.

"Me" came a voice from behind them.

Ash turned to see Lucas coming around the corner. His jaw dropped, but he recovered quickly and smiled tentatively.

"I can't apologize enough for the damage I caused with the warehouse," Lucas said. "But when I heard through the grapevine that the Hallmark rep was stuck at chain control, I got in my truck and went to pick him up. It doesn't make everything right, but I want you to know I'm rooting for the Emerald House and for you."

Ash climbed out of the sleigh, stepped forward, and stuck out his hand. They embraced with their other arms as they shook hands.

"It means a lot," Ash said.

Lucas nodded.

"All right, it's time to get this show on the road!" Sofia called.

Ash returned to the sleigh, climbing aboard with Holly, who had pulled out some costumes for them. She'd told him it wasn't what she normally wore while riding in her sleigh, but it matched the American vision of Mrs. Claus.

"Ready?" Holly asked.

Ash smiled easily in return, like climbing into a sleigh with the real Ms. Claus was the most normal thing in the world. Comet, who had been busy licking the snow, jumped into the seat with them. Holly reached into a crevice of the sleigh and pulled up some fabric reindeer antlers and placed them on Comet's head.

The sleigh rounded the corner onto Main Street, joining the other floats, and Ash saw that, like the clearing, Main Street had been completely transformed. The remaining decorations had been hung all over by members of the town. The garlands and baubles adorned the lampposts and small businesses that lined the parade route.

The crowd gasped when Holly and Ash approached in the sleigh. Snow was still falling but softer, with instrumental

Christmas music coming from a nearby speaker. The two larger reindeer, whom Holly had called Dasher and Gale, led them right to the front, while the smaller ones, Ivy and Clove, strutted behind them like proud peacocks.

The parade officially got started, and the residents of Emerald Hollow packed the sidewalks with the tourists and cheered as the sleigh passed by, Santa and Ms. Claus waving to the crowd. Ash's heart swelled seeing them all there. The turnout had been incredible in spite of the massive snowstorm.

As they rounded the corner at the end of the parade, momentarily out of sight of all others, the reindeer led the sleigh under an arch decked with a sprig of mistletoe. Ash grinned and slipped his arm around Holly's shoulders.

He leaned in close, taking a strand of her silky hair in his hand. "I'm pretty sure a part of me has wanted to do this since the moment I first saw you drinking my hot chocolate."

Holly's eyes sparkled with delight, her beautiful eyelashes softly closed, and he leaned in the rest of the way for a kiss more magical than anything she had shared with him before.

Chapter Fifty-Five

Following the parade and a joyful hour spent with the people of Emerald Hollow, Holly knew it was time to go. Though it wasn't late yet, she needed to give the elves time to load the Dreams into the sleigh, and she would need a full team of reindeer.

Holly studied Ash's face as he talked to a small group of townspeople. He was completely relaxed, smiling broadly and laughing with his friends. Finally, he seemed to be completely in the moment, not running around, trying to fix everything. Still, in spite of being surrounded by all his favorite people, he couldn't seem to let go of her hand.

He pulled her in close whenever they turned away from a conversation, gently brushing her hair from her face and making her skin tingle with a tender kiss. Part of her wanted him to be able to stay there and enjoy the rest of the night in his town, but another, stronger part of her felt compelled to pull him aside and ask one more question.

"Hey, Holly. Today has been amazing. Thank you again." He

kissed her softly on the forehead, and her heart melted like whipped cream on warm gingerbread.

"Of course. But now I have to ask you something." She twirled her watch, which was pleasantly warm on her wrist, feeling suddenly shy. "Would you... would you want to come with me? Tonight, I mean."

Ash's eyes widened as realization dawned, then he grinned. "That's a possibility?"

"There aren't any rules against it. You've been able to see the reindeer for a while now, so I think Christmas magic is already becoming part of you."

Ash barely stopped to think about it. Within seconds, he lifted Holly into his arms and spun her around. Snowflakes danced in the air. *Our perfect snow globe,* Holly thought.

"I'm in."

"WHERE ARE YOU TWO OFF TO?" SOFIA CALLED TO ASH and Holly as they passed her jewelry booth.

Ash did a quick inventory of her stall, which was busy, and she looked like she was doing well. "Don't worry about it," he said smoothly, taking Holly's hand.

Sofia raised her eyebrows but was obviously happy for them. "Don't do anything I wouldn't do."

Holly stifled a laugh.

"If only she knew," he whispered.

They left the clearing and trod through the deep snow, Comet scampering between them, until they reached the sleigh. The reindeer were already waiting. He'd ridden in the sleigh in the parade, but that had been different. He was going to be experiencing the real thing. Excitement and nerves rippled through his veins.

"Is this a bad time to tell you I get motion sickness?" Ash asked.

Holly's jaw dropped until she saw the roguish grin on his face. She slapped his arm.

They climbed inside and got Comet settled between them.

"You ready?" she asked, taking the reins.

He nodded.

She raised the delicate-looking ropes, and the sleigh began to rise gently into the air. In spite of his jest, he thought his stomach might react to the motion, but it felt as natural as taking a stroll through the woods.

"This is the fun part," Holly said. She grabbed his hand, and the sleigh took off.

Ash let out a shout of startled laughter as they whisked toward the quickly setting sun.

THE SLEIGH LANDED SOFTLY ON A THICK BED OF SNOW. Ash's eyes immediately went to the northern lights, which Holly was so fond of. They were swirling above them like dancing waves of technicolor. He sat still, watching in awe. Comet jumped out of the sleigh, excitedly sniffing the new environment.

"Hey!" Holly called.

He turned to see who she was talking to. No matter what Holly had told him on the way to the North Pole, nothing could have prepared him. A beautiful woman about five feet tall, with ears as sharp as knives and tightly braided blond hair, greeted Holly. Her golden eyes cruised over to him, rested for a moment, then slid coolly back to Holly. He sucked in a breath. *Golden eyes.* She must be one of the Kringle elves. Then he saw the clipboard in her hands. *Clementine.*

"Ash, come join us," Holly said.

When he approached, Holly slipped an arm around him.

He stuck out his hand. "Clementine, I'm Ash." He put on his most disarming smile, the one he used when he was really trying to impress a customer.

"I know," Clementine said. She looked at his hand in confusion, and he dropped it. Her voice was slightly chilly, but he thought he could sense a bit of amusement underneath it. He would win her over soon enough.

Clementine brushed a jeweled ring on her finger and spoke into it. "Auryn, they're back. Tell the elves to start loading the sleigh." She looked at Ash one last time with those disarming golden eyes and began to walk down a path with lighted arches.

"This is Merriment Square," Holly explained when they exited the path.

In the center of the square was a giant lamppost casting its light for what must be miles. Beneath it was an ice-skating rink and a lighted gazebo that looked much like the one at the Emerald House. Surrounding the square were a bunch of wood buildings, each elaborately carved and decorated. And standing outside those buildings were dozens of elves, all helping carefully load some globular liquid spheres into large carts.

"What are those?" He had a million things he wanted to ask her about and explore, but by the way the elves were handling those globes with such reverence, he knew they were extremely special.

Clementine's ears rose slowly at his question, but Holly spoke.

"Oh yeah, we didn't get a chance to talk about those. I know human folklore says that Clauses bring toys, but we actually bring Dreams."

Ash gulped, eying the globes more closely. He thought he saw tiny, movie-like images floating around inside them. "Dreams?"

"Yep. Everyone gets a Dream, no matter their age. What they do with it is up to them, but we try to give them the best start possible. A lot of care goes into creating each Dream." Holly's face practically glowed as she spoke.

He suddenly remembered waking up one day as a teenager, having big plans for the future of the Emerald House. *Did a Claus bring me a Dream?* The thought was oddly comforting.

"All right, we'd better get ready. The elves will have the Dreams loaded up in no time. Do you need anything before we go? Some food? Something to drink?" Holly studied him closely, clearly making sure it wasn't all too much for him.

He was studying himself for the same thing and kept being surprised to find that, while he was completely in awe, he wasn't in disbelief. Since it was the place that had made Holly who she was, he felt right at home.

"I could go for some hot chocolate. I heard from a tourist that this was the best they'd ever had."

"All right, then. Challenge accepted."

He followed her to a large, cabin-like building on the other side of the square. Holly pushed open the door, and he stepped into a cozy room with a blazing fire and the faint smell of cinnamon. It made his skin tingle. That smell had become so familiar to him. Holly walked to the kitchen and came back a moment later with two matching mugs. They were painted with four reindeer and a golden sleigh gliding through the sky.

"Moment of truth," he said then took a swig. His eyes widened even as he was drinking. "You weren't kidding! This tastes exactly like the hot cocoa we serve at the Emerald House."

"Told you. Maybe that's what made me fall in love with the place," Holly teased then inhaled deeply and took a sip of hers.

"Well, then, I'll be grateful to my family's recipe forever." He put the mug down and gazed at Holly, completely content to be there with her. She started to step into his arms, but all of a sudden, her eyebrows shot up.

"What is it?"

"The hot chocolate," she whispered.

"Yes, we just established that we are tied for best hot chocolate makers on the planet."

Holly shook her head. "I'll be right back. I need to talk to one of the elves."

He didn't know what path her mind had gone down, but he knew better than to question Ms. Claus on Christmas Eve.

"I'll be right here."

"Thanks. I'll send Auryn in to entertain you. I'll be fast. I promise."

"No rush. As long as Auryn can keep the hot chocolate coming. Though is there any coffee around here?"

Holly rolled her eyes at him then dashed out of the building, leaving him alone in the home of the Clauses, waiting for an elf.

Chapter Fifty-Six

Holly stepped into Lumi's tree house. The eldest elf had opened her door before Holly even had a chance to knock.

"Is everything all right with the Dreams?"

"Lumi, that poster for the fall festival in Emerald Hollow that was in your café in Finland—did you put it there?"

Lumi paused and appeared to choose her words carefully. "I didn't. But magic works in mysterious ways. I don't think that poster being there was a coincidence."

"So you do think magic was involved? Why?" Holly hadn't taken a seat, even though Lumi had signaled her to a cushion. She was once again too full of questions.

"All I know is that certain magic use leaves traces. Something tells me there were traces of magic in Emerald Hollow before you ever touched down there in your sleigh."

That caught Holly by surprise. "But how? Did my parents ever travel there, outside of Christmas Eve?"

"Not that I know of, though I didn't know all their movements. But it's not just Clauses who can leave traces of magic."

Holly's eyes widened as realization dawned. "A Kringle elf! But not you?"

Lumi shook her head slowly. "Not me. I've never been to Emerald Hollow. And there aren't many of us left who know how to snow tunnel. But the magic could have been there for many years. It fades over time but takes decades to fully disappear."

Decades. An elf had visited Emerald Hollow years ago, and somehow, magic left behind had led her to Emerald Hollow, where she'd met Ash, and her Cheer had been changed forever.

Lumi's eyes softened. "As I said, magic works in mysterious ways."

"But why do you think the hot cocoa in Emerald Hollow tastes exactly like the hot cocoa here? Why could Ash see Ivy in the woods when she was supposed to be invisible? Do those traces of magic account for that too?"

"They might," Lumi said, her face tightening. "There was a time when snow tunneling got... a little out of hand. We might never know why, exactly, but I can accept that things happen for a reason. If those traces hadn't been left behind, you likely would never have explored the town so thoroughly to begin with." She didn't have to say the rest. Holly never would have met Ash, and she would have spent the rest of her days chasing Cheer, never putting down roots or connecting with others. The thought made her shiver.

"I guess you're right. I just wish I knew more." Something else was bothering Holly's subconscious, but she couldn't put her finger on what it was.

"Maybe one day, you will. But right now, I think you have somewhere else to be."

Holly thought of the sleigh, which was probably nearly loaded with Dreams.

"It's the best night of the year."

Lumi reached out to squeeze her hand. "Safe travels, Holly. Go show Ash what he's been missing."

Holly grinned, and they embraced for a moment longer before Holly left the tree house. She didn't have all the answers about magic, and maybe she never would. But it was Christmas Eve, and she no longer had to spend every day chasing Cheer. Maybe she would have time to find more answers after all. Or maybe whatever was bothering her would work itself out, and the questions wouldn't matter anymore. She wondered what Ash and Auryn were doing back at her house.

Oh, she had so much to show him.

"ARE YOU READY TO DO THIS?" HOLLY ASKED.

Ash nodded and took her hand. She guided him back through Merriment Square and up the path they had come down when they first landed. The entire path was lined with elves, all waving and cheering as they walked by.

"I feel like a celebrity," he said.

Holly laughed. "Don't worry. This only happens on Christmas Eve. The dispatch of Dreams is what we all live for here."

They approached the sleigh, which had eight reindeer attached to it. A large sack sat in the second row, somehow magically holding all the tiny globes that had filled dozens of carts. Auryn had transferred their hot cocoas to thermoses, and he handed them to Holly and Ash after they climbed into the sleigh.

"Sorry there's no coffee here, Mr. Ash. We'll make sure to get some for you before you get back."

Ash thanked him, and the young elf stepped back to join the others.

"Do you want to do the honors?" Holly asked, handing Ash the reins.

He gripped them carefully then gently raised them into the air. The reindeer rose off the ground. Comet wagged his tail excitedly. Below them, the elves cheered even louder. Holly waved at them then turned her gaze back to lock eyes with Ash. The northern lights danced behind her, and her eyes glittered as she smiled at him. He had never seen anything so beautiful. She nodded, and he gave another firm tug of the reins.

"Merry Christmas to all, and to all a good night!" Holly called out as the sleigh sped off into the dark.

Epilogue

Christmas Eve was a full-fledged celebration for the elves. For the first time in history, there almost hadn't been a Christmas delivery, and the relief that came with being successful had them all in fits of joyful hysterics. When Ms. Claus had visited with Lumi Kringle, Ash had taught Auryn how to play rummy. He'd taught his sister, and a full card tournament was occurring in Jingle Bell Hall.

Auryn poured himself a steamed salted toffee and watched the festivities as he waited for his turn to reenter the tournament. The Advent season had been more stressful than ever before, and elves weren't built for stress. Maybe it was time for him to take a little vacation during the Evergreen season. Elves typically vacationed at the ski park or local lakes and forests, but Auryn thought something different was in order.

He'd been in Ms. Claus's house, doing some food prep, when he overheard a conversation between Lumi Kringle and Ms. Claus about snow tunneling. They seemed to be talking through a mirror in Ms. Claus's living room. That had come as quite the shock.

Auryn didn't think he could convince Lumi Kringle to teach him how to activate his magic enough to snow tunnel. It seemed like a well-guarded secret. He hadn't even known about it, and he was sure none of the younger elves did either. But there had to be some way to find out. He would have to do a little digging on his own.

Just then, his friend Roser called out his name. "You're back in!"

Auryn took another sip of his drink then set it down heavily on the table. All that research could wait. It was Christmas Eve, and the elves were going to party.

Acknowledgments

I want to extend a huge and heartfelt thank you to everyone who had a hand in getting this book out into the world!

Mom, for reading nearly every draft and always wanting more.
Zach, for always encouraging me to get in my office and write.
Katie, for reading that messy first draft.
Bethanie, for all your encouragement.
And to all the family and friends who ask how my writing is coming along, thank you for the motivation!

To my cover designer, Kylie Sek, thank you for making my vision come to life.
To the editors and proofreaders at Red Adept Publishing, thank you for getting this book over the finish line.

To everyone who reads my books, your support means more than you know.

About the Author

Heather Schneider is an author of young adult and women's fiction novels.

Heather lives with her husband and their Chiweenie, Toby. When she's not writing, you can find her reading, listening to podcasts, traveling, or spending time with family.

As an indie author, Heather would love to hear your feedback on *Chasing Cheer*!

Please connect with her on Instagram or Facebook @heatherschneiderauthor and leave a review wherever you review books.

You can visit her website and subscribe to her newsletter at heatherschneiderauthor.com.